GOD LOVES GANGS

GOD LOVES GANGS

How The Gangs Responded To God's Love

OUIDA D SAULS

Xulon Press

Xulon Press
555 Winderley Pl, Suite 225
Maitland, FL 32751
407.339.4217
www.xulonpress.com

© 2024 by OUIDA D SAULS

All rights reserved solely by the author. The author guarantees all contents are original and do not infringe upon the legal rights of any other person or work. No part of this book may be reproduced in any form without the permission of the author.

Due to the changing nature of the Internet, if there are any web addresses, links, or URLs included in this manuscript, these may have been altered and may no longer be accessible. The views and opinions shared in this book belong solely to the author and do not necessarily reflect those of the publisher. The publisher therefore disclaims responsibility for the views or opinions expressed within the work.

Unless otherwise indicated, SScripture quotations taken from the New King James Version (NKJV). Copyright © 1982 by Thomas Nelson, Inc. Used by permission. All rights reserved.)

Paperback ISBN-13: 978-1-66289-032-1
Ebook ISBN-13: 978-1-66289-033-8

Table of Contents

Mary Moved to New York 1
Randall, A Drug Dealer,
Loses His Briefcase 7
Mary Discovers She Has
The Wrong Briefcase 15
Sam Goes To The Mansion............................. 21
Randall Is Devoted To Mary 35
There May Be Trouble With Clyde 39
Clyde Fears His Mother Is Dying 47
God Shows His Love For The Gang 61
The Gang Helps
Three Sisters In Trouble 69
God's Gang Goes To Prison 81
Rob Accepts Christ,
And Laura Is Found..................................... 89
God Answers Laura's Prayers 99
Linda Has Very Good News For Mary................. 107
Jim Finds Out Where The Gang Lives 115
Randall Proposes To Mary 121
Randall Meets His Twin Brother 125
Clyde's Gang Meets Their Rivals...................... 129
Laura Faces Rejection At Work 145
With God, Enemies Become Friends................... 163
Mary And Linda Met A New Friend 167
Kate And Kitty Reached Out To Troubled Friends 173

Mary And Linda Met A New Friend	179
Jack Reacts To Jane's Death	185
Janet Joins God's Gang	205
CHAPTER TWENTY-FOUR	211
Ellen Seeks Mary's Help	225
Kevin And Ellen Get Together	229
Tom Finds Love	233
God Fulfilled His Promise To Mary	239

CHAPTER ONE

Mary Moved to New York

M<small>ARY WAS TEN</small> years old when her parents died in an airplane crash. They were missionaries in South Africa. But their legacy lives on here, for they taught her the love of God and all about His loving promises. Mary came to the United States to live with her grandmother, Stellar Robinson, a strong Christian woman who was happy to have Mary live with her.

Mary finished high school and started dating Joseph. He was a Christian studying to be a minister. They fell in love and married when Mary was nineteen and Joseph was twenty-two. Joseph graduated with a seminary degree that same year. Mary had finished two years at the

The University of New York before they moved to Saint Louis, where Joseph became the co-pastor of a church with Rev. Dan Paul. Mary completed her degree in marketing at Saint Louis University.

She was happy living in St. Louis and attending Rev. Paul's church. She made many friends and went to everything at the church. Soon, Mary and Joseph started a family. Lisa was born, and eighteen months later, Lear arrived.

Mary's husband, Joseph, died in an automobile accident. It devastated Mary. She was now a single mother with two children. Rev. Paul, his wife, Angel, and church members helped

Mary with expenses. She started working at the church as a secretary and volunteered to do anything needed, including teaching Sunday school.

Hope Church invited Rev. Paul to pastor a new church in Dallas, Texas. Although it was an excellent opportunity for him and his family, he initially declined the offer because he felt his congregation needed him. However, the church members assured him that they would be fine. They didn't want him to miss this opportunity. He reluctantly agreed to take the position in Dallas.

Before leaving, Rev. Paul spoke with Mary, saying, "I've enjoyed working with you, Mary. You've inspired all of us. You have been through so much, yet your faith has kept you strong. My wife and I will pray that God will continue to bless you and your daughters."

"Thank you, Reverend; I'll keep you and your wife in my prayers too."

Unfortunately, working for Rev. Fox, the new pastor, was not as easy as working for Rev. Paul. Mary worked hard to please him, but he became increasingly critical of everything she did. She often left his office in tears. One day, Rev. Fox told Mary he wanted to see her in his office.

"I'm sorry, Mary, but you must find employment elsewhere. We need to cut down on expenses, so my wife will be taking over your job here."

She was disappointed. As a single mom, she would have to find a job and someone to care for her girls while working. Her children went to daycare at the church for free, making life much easier. How would she support her girls and herself? She thought of looking for another job but needed someone to look after her girls while at work. She thought of living with her grandmother, but her grandmother worked and couldn't look after her girls. "I'll call Aunt Ruth in New York, she thought. No, I'll surprise her."

As Mary got ready for the trip to New York, Helen, Rev. Fox's wife, came to see her privately.

"I'm so sorry, Mary. I tried to get my husband to change his mind and keep you as the church's secretary, but he became furious. He told me that running the church was not my business and scolded me for suggesting he should change his mind. Is there anything I can do for you? How can I help Mary?"

"It's all right, Helen. I know that God is going to bless us, but thanks anyway. I'm so sorry Rev. Fox was angry with you for trying to help me."

"You're already in my prayers. Ask God to show you how to deal with this and love your husband, Helen. God is still answering prayers, and He will soften your husband's heart."

"Thank you, Mary. You have always encouraged me and made me feel better. I'm going to miss you."

When the members discovered what had happened with Mary, they were distraught with Rev. Fox. Some of them even quit the church. Several of those remaining members met with him to try to change his mind. They told him they would find ways to raise money so Mary could stay on as secretary, but Rev. Fox became angry. He reminded them that he was responsible for running the church and that no one had a right to interfere. A few more members left the church after that.

Even God's leaders sometimes forget what their role is in the church. When Mary learned what her friends had tried to do, she asked them not to leave the church but to pray for Rev. Fox and see what God would do. The members all loved her and knew that leaving the church would hurt her, so they assured Mary they would not leave the church. They even got the members who had fled to return. The members gathered at their homes or restaurants to pray twice weekly for Rev. Fox and the church. They were not going to let the devil win.

"God can do anything, and we will believe He will bless our church."

Mary told the members she was going to New York to stay with her aunt and look for work there.

"My aunt can watch my girls while I work. That will make it easier for me and for my girls."

"Mary, if you stay here, I'll watch your daughters for free," one of the ladies told her.

"That's very kind of you, but I believe God is in my decision to go to New York. I'm going to miss all of you tremendously, though. You've all been such good friends. I promise to keep in touch and return to visit soon. God bless you all."

The church members knew Mary was already having financial trouble, so they worked together to raise money for her trip to New York. At the train station, they presented her with travel checks, a beautiful family Bible, and a briefcase. The Bible was the kind of thing people used to document their family tree. It was so big that it barely fit in the briefcase. Mary managed to squeeze a small notebook in with the Bible.

Helen, who had come without her husband, gave Mary a book of coupons for McDonald's breakfasts and lunches. Helen knew how much the girls loved McDonald's. Then, they all prayed together before Mary had to board the train.

"God bless you," Mary said as she hugged each person. "I promise to write and be sure to keep in touch."

After she and the girls quickly made their way to their seats, they continued waving to their friends from the train window until they were out of sight. Then Mary and the girls settled in for the trip. Soon, the girls became hung; thankfully, the church ladies provided them with a packed lunch for their long journey. After eating, Mary got pillows and blankets for her girls, covered them, and kissed them on the forehead. Then Mary took out the Bible she kept in her purse and read it.

As she sat there, Mary thought about the dream she and her husband had about helping drug addicts and runaway teenagers. She didn't know fulfilling that dream would be possible after the death of her husband, but she prayed every day constantly that God would help her to do it, anyway. Then she started thinking about Aunt Ruth and her brother, Uncle David. When Mary's parents were alive, Mary often left Africa to visit Aunt Ruth, Uncle David and his wife Sarah, and Aunt Ruth's husband, Uncle Kevin. Everybody went fishing often except for Aunt Sarah. She never went fishing because she didn't like the outdoors. Aunt Sarah didn't enjoy the fun with Aunt Ruth and Mary when they baked cookies and made candy. Nor did she ever take part in any games they played.

While Sarah read a book, her husband, Uncle David, Uncle Kevin, Aunt Ruth, and Mary played games and watched cartoons. Mary thought Uncle Kevin, Aunt Ruth, and Uncle David enjoyed those cartoons as much as I did. That was years ago. Now Uncle David was on drugs. His wife had run off with his best friend a few years ago, and Uncle David had not been the same since.

Mary's thoughts were on her friend Linda in St. Louis. Linda's teenage daughter, Laura, had run away from home six weeks ago because her mother wouldn't let her go to a party one night; Laura had not heard from her since that night. Linda cried constantly, it seemed, trying to understand why. She and Mary had prayed many times for the return of her daughter.

"I truly believe that God is going to return her to me, Mary, but it still hurts," Linda would cry. And soon Mary would be crying too.

Exhaustion from preparing for the trip and a full stomach from the fabulous lunch made Mary sleepy. She placed her Bible back in her purse, moved the briefcase from the seat, placed it on the floor beside her, and let the gentle rocking of the train lull her to sleep.

Exhaustion from preparing for the trip and a full stomach from the fabulous lunch made Mary sleepy. She placed her Bible back in her purse, moved the briefcase from the seat, placed it on the floor beside her, and let the gentle rocking of the train lull her to sleep.

CHAPTER TWO

Randall, A Drug Dealer, Loses His Briefcase

RANDALL, ANOTHER PASSENGER on the train, put a briefcase identical to Mary's on the rack above his seat, which was directly across from Mary. Sitting down, he noticed the woman and two kids across from him sleeping. Randall didn't notice that he had an identical briefcase beside him. A few minutes later, he rose urgently from his seat and headed toward the restroom. While he was in the bathroom, the train lurched suddenly, and because of the lurching, his briefcase fell from the rack onto the floor and nudged Mary's briefcase further down the aisle.

Mary awoke when she heard the thud of the briefcase as it hit the floor. "That was some jolt," she said as she saw a briefcase in the middle of the aisle. She picked it up, put it between the seats, and went back to sleep.

When Randall returned, he glanced at the rack and didn't see his briefcase. He panicked and glanced around, noticing several items had shifted or fallen to the floor. He then noticed a suitcase in the middle of the aisle a couple of seats down from him. Sighing with relief, he picked it up and, gripping it tightly, carried it to the dining car.

Randall is a member of The Great Ones, a very violent gang in New York City. His briefcase contained seven million dollars.

The money gang members made by doing business with drug dealers from Cuba. For the remainder of the trip, the briefcase went everywhere with Randall.

When he returned to the gang's headquarters, they referred to their mansion several miles from New York. The gang buddies, Clyde, John, Tom, and Mike, greeted Randall enthusiastically when he entered the house.

"This calls for a celebration. We'll divide the money after celebrating with champagne and good food!" Clyde, the gang leader, said as he took the briefcase from Randall and placed it on an end table in the living room.

Clyde asked Tom to order food, "Tom, call Chez Nous and order the most delicious and expensive things on the menu for five. And make sure they send a few bottles of their best champagne!"

John, the youngest and newest gang member, had decided he didn't want this life. He thought, "I wish they would divide the money now so I can get my share and take off. I won't be coming back here. I hate this gang and all the mean things they do."

John's parents were divorced when he was twelve years old, and although they loved him, he was always a depressed boy and felt that it was his fault that his parents divorced. He ran around with a troubled bunch of boys who were into taking and selling drugs. He never took drugs himself, but he sold them. When he was eighteen, Clyde recruited him into his gang.

"Hey guys, I'll eat and get my share of the money later. My friend just called, and we're going to a football game," John told Clyde.

"Okay, if that's what you want, but you've got to be crazy not to want to celebrate with us and get your share of the money now," Clyde responded.

The gang's euphoria at scoring such a huge payoff mounted as the guys listened to music and discussed what they would buy when the stores opened. When the food arrived, they gorged themselves. They all listened to music and lounged around as they ate food that was a feast fit for a king. John left the mansion while the others ate to attend a football game with his Christian friend, Sam. John wanted to wait for his share of the money but was glad to escape them.

"John, we have time to go to my church for about thirty or forty minutes if it's okay with you," Sam suggested.

"Yes, that's fine." Sam had asked him to go to church with him at other times, but John had continually declined. This time, he was glad to avoid the atmosphere looming over the gang.

That evening, God allowed the minister to preach what John needed to hear. He was already fed up with the gang life and wanted out. The minister told John that real peace and freedom were only possible through Jesus Christ. Touched by the minister's message of hope and salvation, John accepted Jesus as his Lord and Savior that night. Sam was ecstatic. He had prayed for John continually but didn't think he was getting through. He didn't even know that John had decided to leave the gang. Sam and John walked down the church steps, both happier than they had been in a long time.

A drive-by-shooter shot John. Before he died, he looked up toward Heaven and thanked Jesus for receiving him into His kingdom; then, he thanked Sam for taking him to church that night. Sam cried as he rocked John in his arms. Sam looked up and saw angels lifting John and taking him to Heaven. Then he looked at John's body and said, "To be absent from the body and present with Jesus is great. Goodbye for now, my friend; I will join you someday."

After eating and drinking, the gang opened the briefcase, and to their horror, they found a big Bible and a notebook. Clyde went into a rage, "What happened?" he shouted. "Did you let the briefcase out of your sight? Did you see them put the money in the briefcase? I told you not to let the briefcase out of your sight."

"I had to go to the restroom, so I left it for a few minutes," said Randall.

Clyde shoved Randall out of the way, even though he could tell Randall was in shock, too.

"We'll get that money back no matter how rough we have to get Randall, who was on the train next to you?" Ask Clyde.

"No one was sitting next to me, Clyde. There was a woman and her two kids across the aisle from me. But they were all sleeping when I went to the restroom and still asleep when I returned."

"Well, what did this woman look like?" Clyde was furious, "Were the kids boys or girls? How many kids were with the woman? How old did the kids look to be? We have to find them, Randall," Clyde continued to shout in Randall's face as he leaned back as far as he could without moving away.

"I told you it was a woman with kids, but I don't know if the kids were boys or girls. I do know that it was only two kids. I couldn't see them well enough to tell how old they were because they were covered."

"Clyde, we've got another problem," Mike interrupted as Clyde glared at Randall. Slowly, Clyde shifted his gaze to Mike.

"What?" Clyde said.

"The instructions. They're not here, and only John knows the instructions," said Mike.

In the briefcase are instructions concerning the money and where it should be laundered for safe spending.

"Where is John anyways?" Mike asked. At that, the three of them looked around, hoping someone knew where John might have gone.

"Oh, I remember," said Clyde, "He's at a football game."

Although John was naïve and the youngest of the gang, they all trusted him. He was the only one who never did drugs. They figured John was too stupid and scared to be crooked, so they had chosen him to get the money in the first place, but Clyde had decided to send Randall instead. They needed to find John because he knew the instructions in the briefcase. He also knew where the money was to go for laundering. Without the instructions or John, the gang felt that getting the money back would be a big problem. They also thought whoever had the money must have known it was drug money. Chances are, they would have the money laundered but would not follow the instructions in the briefcase. It's too bad they hadn't followed their original plan and sent John for the money. They thought of taking a chance on spending the money without having it laundered. It doesn't matter now if they were not to have the money laundered.

"We've got to find John, and then we can figure out how to get our money back," Clyde finally said, "Let's all look for John at the football game."

Mike turned the television on just before they started to leave.

"Turn that off. We're about to leave," Clyde shouted. As Mike was about to turn the television off, the news caught his attention. "Hey guys, listen," Mike turned up the volume.

"Another drive-by shooting has left another victim dead at the church steps. Earlier this evening, as he walked down the church step, John Triumph was killed around seven o'clock when someone shot him from the back seat of a black sedan. He died in the arms of his friend, Sam Hancock. The police have no suspects at this time."

Mike quickly turned the television off, knowing that Clyde would be outraged. As if being obsessed or possessed, Clyde knocked over a small table, sending the lamp and a couple of glasses flying. He stomped out of the room, kicking anything in his path aside. In the next room, he started throwing chairs to the floor.

"Calm down, Clyde," Randall followed him into the next room.

"We'll find the money," said Randall, "Remember, John told us that to have the money laundered, he was going to a southern state, and even though he didn't tell us which state, we know that whoever has the money might be traveling south. On the other hand, they may use someone else to launder the money, and we don't know what direction they will be traveling, but we can look south first anyway. We can use some of our many contacts to determine if someone is spending or banking a large amount of money in the South."

"Randall, this is New York. How many people will be traveling south? How many will be spending or banking a large amount of money? New York is one of the world's financial capitals, you idiot," Clyde said as Randall shook his head.

So what," Randall answered, "I believe they will be spending the money in a southern state. I'm sure we can find them, though. But someone has to get the passenger information from the train station first. We must find out who was sitting across from you, even if it means sending someone back to St. Louis."

"That should be easy to check out," Mike smiled, "Remember, Randall said the kids he saw were the only ones on that part of the train."

Fortunately for Mary and her children, the computer system at the train station crashed, and all the information about people who had traveled by train that week was lost. The gang was frustrated. Finding the person that the gang thought somehow took the money out of their briefcase and replaced it with a Bible and notebook was baffling.

Each gang member picked a southern state to investigate. Randall chose Mississippi, Clyde, Alabama; Tom, Georgia; and Mike, Florida. With all their connections, the gang thought they would find out who had taken their money. Clyde decided to stay at the mansion for a while before going to Alabama. He contacted some of his trusted buddies and asked them to help find the money.

"You know," Clyde told his buddy, Ben, "I'm glad you will be helping us find our money. You are familiar with everything that goes on in the South. At first, I thought Clayton's gang was responsible, but I didn't tell the other guys because they always complain about me causing problems by jumping to the wrong conclusion. I'm glad I didn't act on my assumptions because most of Clayton's guys just got out of jail. Boy, that would have been disastrous if we had approached them, and they had nothing to do with it."

CHAPTER THREE

Mary Discovers She Has The Wrong Briefcase

When Mary and the girls arrived in New York, they headed straight for Aunt Ruth's house. Uncle Kevin died three years earlier, leaving Aunt Ruth lonely and depressed. Despite being close and keeping in touch, Mary hadn't seen her since her wedding. She knew that it would wonderfully surprise for Aunt Ruth to see them. Mary quieted the girls before she rang the doorbell. A few seconds passed before they heard Aunt Ruth approaching the door. "Surprise!" They yelled as she opened it. Aunt Ruth's mouth opened slightly, and she took only a second before realizing who was standing before her. Screaming joyfully, she hugged Mary and the girls tightly, then stood back, looked at them, and embraced them again.

"I've been praying for you and the girls to visit soon, and you are here. You have no idea how much I wanted to see the girls. They're beautiful! Oh, I wish your Uncle Kevin could be here to see the girls. He would have been so happy to see you and the girls. He said if you had a girl, you would have to give her to us because we would need a replacement after he took you from us. Your grandma missed you so much that she got a job working with kids. Whenever I talk with her, she tells me about another pretty little girl that reminds her of you."

"I missed you both too, Aunt Ruth. Let's call Grandma when she's home from work."

Mary cried, "I lost my job, Aunt Ruth, and had nowhere to go."

"Well, you do now. You can stay with me forever. Dry your tears and come into the kitchen while I fix us something to eat.

" Although it was still morning, she and the girls were exhausted. After they ate, Aunt Ruth took the girls to their room and said, "Take a nap, ladies, and when you wake up, we call visit the park. Then she and Mary had a long talk with Mary's grandmother.

The next day. "I thank God you came to stay with me," said Aunt Ruth, "You don't know how lonely I've been without Kevin. It's going to be nice having you and the girls here."

Mary unpacked a few things to get ready for bed. She was tired but relieved and happy about not worrying about getting a job without having someone to look after her girls while she worked. She kneeled by the bed and prayed, "Dear God, thank You for Your continued blessings. Thank You to my two girls, Lisa and Lear. Thank You for Aunt Ruth and her loving heart and generosity. Please let us be a blessing to her as she is to us. Lord, I'm placing my trust in You. Help me to know what You would have me do to serve You, Lord, in Jesus' Name. Although tired, Mary wasn't sleepy, so getting her briefcase and reading the Bible always comforts her and brings peace.

"I can't wait to read my new Bible! Oh, dear God! Oh my God! It must be thousands of dollars in my briefcase." In the briefcase was a note:

THIS IS FROM GOD.
You must take this money to a place
where it will be safe to spend.
Go to the post office in Louise, Mississippi.
A man there will wear a hat with a red

feather. He will take care of everything.
Tell him that God sent you. Keep this
private. Take only the money
you need for a round-trip ticket
and a little extra for expenses."

God uses people who don't know Him to fulfill His plan. Mary knows nothing about how crooks run their businesses. So, she needs to understand why she is doing any of this. And she doesn't know that the man with the red feather in his hat is a crook.

Mary stared at the note, a bit bewildered. "Thank You, Dear Heavenly Father, for the money for me to serve You, but where did You put my Bible? I like that big Bible."

Mary's prayer thanking God and being concerned about her big Bible was like a child truly trusting her father. She has a rare kind of faith. She heard a quiet voice within her reply, "You will get your Bible back."

She looked up toward Heaven and began to praise God. Then she closed the briefcase, put it under the bed, and asked God, "What should I do?"

An angel appeared to her at that moment, "Follow the instructions on the note in the briefcase, Mary. God has a plan for your dream."

Mary's praises to God grew so loud that her aunt and daughters came running into the room to see what was happening. "What are you so happy about, Mary?" Aunt Ruth asked.

"Mom. What is it?" Her daughters knew by how she praised God that it was something good.

"An angel of God just spoke to me and told me that God has a plan for my dream."

"What dream?" They all seemed to shout in unison.

"To help people like Uncle David, Aunt Ruth's brother, who is on drugs, and people like my friend Linda, whose daughter ran away from home. I want to help as many people like them as I can. People with problems that only God can resolve when they are pointed to Him and accept His Son as their Lord and Savior. God will provide everything I'll need to make my dream come true.

I will need temporary housing for people who need a place to stay until they can be on their own. I want a place big enough for rooms for training people to get jobs, classrooms with computers and whatever else we need. That will be a great way to introduce them to Jesus. That will be so exciting! Just think, what a captive audience I'll have. I have to figure out everything that I'll need. And even though this is all new to me, I'm counting on God to teach me."

Before breakfast, Mary transferred the money from the briefcase to another bag the following day. The girls were busy helping Aunt Ruth when Mary walked into the kitchen.

"Good morning. I hope you all slept as well as I did," Mary said, still excited.

"Good morning, Mary. I'm glad you slept well," Aunt Ruth smiled. Mary helped with breakfast while talking with her aunt while the girls set the table.

"Aunt Ruth, would you mind keeping the girls for about a week while I take care of some business out of town?"

"I'd be happy to, but you just got here. Do you have to leave so soon?"

"Yes, I can't put this off."

"Well, let me give you some money for your trip," Aunt Ruth offered.

"Thank you, but I have enough."

When they ate at the table, Mary told Lisa and Lear about her childhood visits to Aunt Ruth for holidays and summers.

"Uncle David and Uncle Kevin would take me fishing. Aunt Ruth went with us most of the time. When we brought the fish home, I helped cook them. I also helped Aunt Ruth make cookies; sometimes, we even made homemade candy."

"Can we do that, Aunt Ruth?" Lisa asked as Lear giggled and nodded her head in agreement.

"Yes, of course. While your mother is away, we're going to make candy and cook your favorite foods, and we're going to do many other fun things," Aunt Ruth said. Then she approached the table and kissed each girl on the forehead.

CHAPTER FOUR

Sam Goes To The Mansion

Sam went to the mansion where he had picked up John many times. John was always waiting for him outside, so Sam had never been inside the mansion. He wanted to comfort John's family by telling them that John had given his life to Jesus before he died. Sam knocked on the door and waited. A few seconds later, Clyde came to the door carrying a shotgun.

"Hi, are you going hunting?" Sam asked.

"Yes, for humans. Are you human?"

Sam laughed. "I think so. John didn't tell me anything about his family. Are you, his father?"

Clyde realized Sam knew nothing about The Great Ones and put the gun down. "I was just getting the gun down to clean it when I heard you knock. I'm not John's father. John's family doesn't live here. I've known him for a short time. He, I, and some other guys went in together to get this place at a cheap price. Come on in. We were getting to know John. His death was a real shock to us. Maybe you could tell me more about him?" Clyde ushered Sam into the living room as he placed the gun in a cabinet.

"John and I were friends," Sam told Clyde, "And although I don't know much about him, he was a nice guy but seemed lonely and unhappy. We talked about sports most of the time.

John also talked about how he would like to marry someday and have many kids."

"Yeah," said Clyde, "That sounds like John, all right. Do you have any idea of who killed him? Not being family, we haven't been able to get much information."

"I don't think anyone knows. Some people are crazy and kill people they don't know for no reason; only God knows who they are."

John and I were going to a football game after church when we walked halfway down the church steps, and a drive-by-shooter shot John. We hadn't planned to go to church that night, but since I came early, I asked him to attend church before the game. I was so glad when he agreed to go. I'd offered many times before, but John had always refused. Praise God! He went this time. John gave his heart to Jesus that night."

Sam paused because he could tell Clyde was unsure what he was talking about.

"Would you like to come to church with me on Sunday? The minister can help you understand the joy and peace John received before he died," Sam explained.

"Seems like your church might be an unlucky place to go to or to leave, but I'll think about it and let you know."

Clyde took Sam's name and phone number to see if it would help them locate their money. Clyde was obsessed with finding their cash.

"It was nice meeting you, Clyde. Call me if you decide to join me at church." Sam shook Clyde's hand and left.

Later, Clyde called Randall to find out how his trip to Mississippi was going. When he didn't get an answer, he left a message. Then Clyde called Tom in Georgia and got the same results. He got through to Mike in Florida, but they needed more information about their money.

As Mary settled in her window seat, she looked forward to her flight to Mississippi. As she took her Bible from her handbag, a tall, handsome man stood before her, "Do you mind if I sit here?" He asked. "No," Mary smiled and began to read her Bible.

"I'm Randall," the man looked at her, captivated by her beauty and pleasant smile.

"Hi, I'm Mary."

Randall looked at her intently, "You are lovely. I bet your husband doesn't like you traveling alone."

"My husband died two years ago, and my girls and I miss him very much."

"I'm sorry to hear that; where are you going?"

"Louise, Mississippi."

"Hey, that's where I'm going," Randall smiled. Mary smiled and turned back to her Bible.

Randall continued to look at Mary from the corner of his eye. He hadn't intended to go to Louise, just to Mississippi and maybe bigger cities in Mississippi like Jackson or Vicksburg to start his investigation to determine what had happened to their money. But Mary's warm smile and beauty made him think, Louise is in Mississippi, so that's where I'll go first. Mary blessed her food when lunch was served and ate just a little. After a moment, Randall asked, "Are you finished eating already?"

"Yes," said Mary.

"Do you mind if I eat your hamburger?" Asked Randall.

"No, help yourself. I don't like to waste food, but I'm not hungry," said Mary.

As Randall continued to eat, Mary told him about her dream of building a place for teenagers on drugs who had either run away or had parents who put them out.

"Some parents in our church are so heartbroken because they don't know where their children are. Some of them know where their children are but don't know how to get them off drugs and how to get them to come back home."

Her voice filled with passion, "These teenagers need help, and I want to help them. Some of them have been abused and think that no one cares. I want to point them to Jesus. I want to let them know that God cares, I care, and other people care. God can restore them, and He will restore them."

Mary sat quietly for a second or two and then said, "Well, Randall, "What's your dream?"

Randall still tried to process what Mary said about her dream and God. He'd never met anyone quite like her before.

"Huh, I don't know," he finally responded, "Your dream is nice. I can tell that you are an extraordinary person."

"Even though run-away teenagers and drug addicts have made bad choices and probably hurt many people, God still loves them."

Randall looked at Mary, confused, "How do you know that?"

"It's in the Bible. God loves everyone, even murderers, robbers, and drug pushers, regardless of their actions. Remember, God's love is unconditional, but our blessings are on the condition that we obey His Word. He wants us in His kingdom, and if we accept His Son, Jesus, and repent of the bad things we have done, God will forgive us and shower us with His love. He will give us peace and a new reason for living. People around us will see positive change, and many will come to Christ."

"What do you mean by repent and the rest of what you said?"

"Well, Randall, repent means to change from doing bad things. To help you transform from doing bad things, ask God to forgive your sins and receive Jesus Christ, God's Son, as your Lord and Savior. God will bless you, and you will have peace, joy, and success. Accepting Jesus as your Lord and Savior is the wisest decision anyone can make. You will also have the assurance that when your body dies, your spirit will not die but will live forever with Jesus in Heaven. Your body will one day come alive, and you will be young again if you die old. If you had missing limbs, they wouldn't be missing when Jesus comes to get you and take you with Him to Heaven. Heaven is an incredible place. Read about it in the Bible."

Randall was quiet for a while, thinking about what Mary said. Randall knew nothing about God or even if there was a God. As he was thinking over her comments, he felt her touch the back of his hand lightly and turned to face her.

"They're showing a movie about God on this flight, 'The Passion of Christ.' Would you like to watch it?"

"Yes," said Randall, not wanting to watch the movie but didn't want to say no to Mary.

When the movie was over, Randall tried to hide how upset watching the film had made him.

They landed in Kentucky in time but discovered that their connecting flight to Louise, Mississippi, was delayed for two days due to turbulent weather. The small commuter airlines only sometimes had flights to all locations daily, which was another problem.

Randall was quiet as he helped Mary with her suitcases and several other passengers. Then they checked into a hotel near the airport, getting rooms across the hall from each other.

Six-thirty that evening, Randall knocked on Mary's door.

"Would you like to go to dinner?" he asked when she opened the door to her hotel room.

"I've heard that this hotel's food is always good."

"Yes, I'm hungry. I can tell the movie upset you," Mary began as they left for the restaurant in the hotel.

"Would you like to talk about it?" Mary asked.

"Many will go to hell, even though Jesus died for us. I don't understand," said Randall.

"Well, we have all sinned and are all doomed to hell if we don't accept Jesus Christ as our Savior. Would you like to know more about Jesus, Randall?"

"This sounds a bit scary, but I think I would," Randall answered.

"The more you learn about the Bible, the more fear becomes a thing of the past. Let's meet tomorrow morning in the lobby for a Bible study. You can have my Bible." Mary took the Bible from her purse and gave it to Randall, "Start reading the book of John in the New Testament, and we can talk about it tomorrow morning."

The following day, after breakfast, they met for a Bible study. Mary explained to Randall all about salvation and that Jesus is the only way to eternal life.

"Many people think they will give up the so-called good life and fun when they accept Jesus as their Lord and Savior. But as some people believe, this good life leads to drug addiction, alcoholism, sickness, death, murder, heartbreak, depression, and destruction. If you accept Jesus as your Lord and Savior, read the Bible, and obey the instructions given in the Bible, you will have peace along with success in life. God can change your desires of being greedy and selfish to being generous and unselfish and your countenance from sad to happy. I remember seeing a minister on television once who told about a man who asked this question:

"Why would a good God allow so much pain and suffering in the world?"

The minister answered him this way: "God gave us instructions in the Ten Commandments. The Ten Commandments are guidelines from God for us to follow."

Mary wanted Randall to understand that it's not God that causes most people's problems but their lack of understanding and disobedience to the Word of God. Mary explains, "God's

Word even says that; 'My people perish for lack of knowledge. Some of our leaders cause us

problems by attempting to turn our nation from the things of God. Our government has taken the Ten Commandments out of our schools and every public place they can. When you think about it, I wonder why anyone would want the Ten Commandments out of public places. If they followed the Ten Commandments, our country would be safer. You respect other people, keep traffic laws, do not drink while driving, do not take your neighbor's things, and do not murder someone.

Would you blame the government if you hit a car because you ran through a red light? Would you blame God? The Ten Commandments are great for people to live by. Think about what this world would be like if people followed the Ten Commandments. They would obey laws that protected them and others. They wouldn't take the Lord's Name in vain. Parents would be happy to have obedient, honest children who follow the Ten Commandments."

Mary was happy to see Randall so interested in what she explained about the Bible.

"Our leaders who want to eliminate the Ten Commandments wouldn't want to be murdered. I don't think they would be happy about someone having an affair with their husband or wife or stealing their things. If people didn't lie about others, it would stop much pain. Our laws are from the Ten Commandments, which God gave because He loves us and wants us to do well."

Randall was still absorbed in Mary's teaching.

"God gives us free will. We can allow the Holy Spirit to guide us or not. Satan will control you if you don't rely on God and His Word. For example, once hooked on drugs or other bad habits, people lose their free will and many times can't stop without God's help or a person with the gift from God to deliver a person from these problems. If you want peace and a better life, turn to

God. He will not let you down. Then, fill your mind and heart with the Word of God. You don't have a choice with the devil. If you walk with him, you'll follow his evil plan without realizing it. One fundamental fact: If you don't choose God, you automatically select the enemy.

There will be hard times and good times, but with God, you can get through the hard times with unbelievable peace. You will not fear death because you will know that when you die, your spirit will be instantly in the presence of the Lord. Some religions teach that if you work hard in that religion and follow what they teach, you can work your way into Heaven. Some church teachers say you must work to go to Heaven, but the Bible says the way to Heaven is through Jesus and Him alone. Working hard to be good is not what saves a person. However, once you have received Jesus, you will want to do things that please Jesus. You will want to help people in need; you will want to help bring the lost to God; you will want to follow the law, etc. Severing Jesus will be a pleasure."

Randall pulled closer to Mary to ensure he didn't miss anything.

"When you receive Jesus as your Lord and Savior, God will reveal the importance of reading His Word. You will become a new person in Christ. God will speak to you through His Word, or you will hear His voice within you, or He may speak audibly, and you will know that it is God speaking. If you continue to seek the living God, He will make it clear that you are a child of His, and Heaven will be your home someday. Remember, salvation is a gift. Jesus died for all of us, and He rose again, and so will we. You don't have to work for salvation; however, when you receive Jesus, you will find joy in working for God and obeying His Word. Helping others to know Him will bring more than joy and blessings. It's straightforward, Randall; all you have to do is accept Jesus as your Lord and Savior and ask

Him to forgive you for your sins. If you'd like, I'll lead you in a prayer of salvation."

"I have been thinking about the things you've been teaching, and I'm not sure I understand enough yet, but I like the Bible studies."

"Don't take too long to decide. Remember, God loves you and wants you to commit your life to Him. 'Delight in the Lord and seek Him with your whole heart; He will give you the desires of your heart.' That's what the Bible says!"

The following day, Randall knocked on Mary's door at eight and asked if she would like to have breakfast with him.

"I have heard that breakfast is the most important meal of the day, but I'm not a breakfast person. I'm not even a morning person. Said Mary"

"Well, how about toast and coffee then?" Randall insisted.

"Okay. Give me a few minutes. I need to call Aunt Ruth and let her know what's going on and why it is taking me longer than I thought."

At breakfast, Randall talked about his childhood. He had grown up in New York City. His father died when Randall was thirteen, and his mother died a year later of a broken heart. Randall knew that his parents loved him, and he loved them. The death of both of his parents made Randall bitter and angry. Before his parents died, they had often prayed for him. They also tried to help him understand the importance of becoming a Christian and the meaning of salvation.

He went to live with his grandparents when his parents died. They continued taking him to church, but he was always rebellious and disobedient. He didn't feel like he was good enough for anything or anyone.

Mary had been listening intently and wanted to encourage him and help him understand the reality of God, "Randall, you don't have to prove anything to God. He already knows who you are, and He still loves you.

"Well, I don't know, Mary. I've got a lot going on, but I'm still thinking about what you've been teaching," Randall started laughing.

"What's so funny?" Mary asked.

"I dreamed that you were on a cliff teaching, and I was afraid you were too close to the edge, but I couldn't get up to pull you back. You said it's okay, Randall, sit there. God will protect me. And I said, "Ask Him to help me get up."

"That was funny, Randall," Mary said, laughing, "I bet God thought it was funny too. Remember, whenever you're ready to give your life to Christ, I'll lead you in a prayer of salvation."

That night in bed, Randall thought, "Mary talked about Jesus as though she knew Him personally, and they were terrific friends. She said God knows me and loves me. How can that be after I've done so many terrible things? She said that He loves me anyway. If that's true, that's cool."

Finally, Randall and Mary boarded the airplane for Mississippi. They sat together during the short flight, discussing their time in Kentucky. After checking into the hotel in Louise, they settled into rooms on separate floors because there weren't two vacant rooms on the same floor. After dinner, they met in the lobby for a short Bible study. As usual, Randall listened with great interest.

In Randall's hotel room, he could only think about Mary, her interest in God, and how he began to feel about her.

The maid came in to clean the room while Randall was talking to himself, "Oh Mary, I love you. I don't know how long I can go without telling you how I feel."

"Just tell her," the maid surprised him. Randall didn't hear her knock.

He turned around and said, "Oh, uh. Uh. I'm practicing for a play I'm in."

"Yeah, sure you are," the maid said under her breath.

"What did you say?" asked Randall.

"Oh, nothing. Carry on with your huh, acting. Huh, your play."

The next day, Randall walked with Mary to her room after dinner. Before she could open the door, he turned her gently to face him and leaned down to kiss her. But Mary put her hand on his chest to stop him.

"Randall, you are such a nice person, and I like you a lot, but my faith doesn't allow kissing or dating a person who's not a Christian. The Bible calls it unequally yoked, especially if a believer marries an unbeliever. I'm sorry, but I must focus on my dream and commitment to God."

"Does this mean that I can't see you anymore?" Randall was upset.

"Oh, no. I just can't become involved romantically with you."

"Okay," Randall said with relief, "I'll settle for just being your friend."

Mary got up early the next day and went to the post office. Standing near the post office boxes was the man wearing a red feather in his hat. She slowly walked over to him, gripping the bag with the money tightly.

"I have a message from God," she said quietly.

These crooks use God's name as their code message.

The man looked at her, a bit surprised. The last message the man in the red got was from John, so he was expecting a man.

"I thought a man would bring the money, but these things require the unexpected." The man in the red hat said. Then he took the bag she was handing him.

Well, then, let's see what God's message is," he smirked,

"Follow me." The man with the red feather may snicker at the 'statement that these crooks decided to use as their code,

God Loves Gangs

but someday, he may call on God. God may remind him of his code message.

Behind the post office, "Okay. Now, where am I supposed to put this?"

Mary gave him papers with the account numbers, phone numbers, names, and addresses of the banks in New York where she had opened accounts before leaving for Mississippi.

"I'll meet you back here in an hour," the man said, "Be sure to be here when I return."

Then he walked quickly down the alley, turning right at the end to return to the main street. Mary just stood there a few seconds, thinking how strange it all seemed. The man had taken seven million dollars to put into her bank accounts in New York. She had never counted the money, so she had no idea how much money was in the briefcase. She trusted God to take care of it. She thought that if God gave her all that money to do work for Him, she didn't have to worry about counting it. She silently prayed, asking God to keep her safe and allow her to serve Him with the money He had provided. Then she went around the corner to a little coffee shop to wait for the man's return.

An hour later, she waited in the alley behind the post office. The man with the red feather walked briskly toward her, reached inside his coat, and dre out ten deposit slips, "I thought a man was going to bring the money, but dealing with something like this, you have to do the unexpected." He said again, hoping to get an answer from her about why they sent her. Mary looked puzzled and said, "I guess so."

"Anyway, I took the usual cut and deposited the rest of the money equally in the accounts you gave me and a list of the banks or in the envelope," the man said, still wondering why they sent a woman.

"Thank you, and God bless you, Sir," Mary said as she took the envelope.

"Yeah, sure," he said as he walked away and resumed his quick walk out of the alley.

Mary went back into the post office. When she looked at the deposit slips, she was shocked. She closed her eyes and took a deep breath.

"Oh my God, I thought thousands of dollars, not millions. No wonder the briefcase was so heavy. I thought either the briefcase was gaining weight or I was gaining weight. Mary mailed everything the man had given her to Aunt Ruth and a letter telling her aunt to put it in a safe place.

The gang was looking for their money in a southern state. They had yet to learn that Mary was the one with the money and was on her way to a northern state, New York City.

As Mary was leaving the post office, she ran into Randall, "Hey, what are you doing up so early?" he asked, grinning at her.

Randall has yet to learn that the money was in the same place where he was and is now on the way to New York City, their hometown.

"I had to take care of some business and thought I would do it early."

"Let's grab a bite to eat and then go for a boat ride," Randall suggested.

"I don't know, Randall. I'm a little afraid of boats and a mass of water."

"I'll protect you."

As they walked down the street, Mary asked, "Did you think about our Bible study?"

"Yes, but I need more time."

"Okay, I won't pressure you."

They ate at a little restaurant near the dock.

"About that boat ride," Randall insisted.

"I've never been on a boat ride. I've never been on a boat."

The sun was warm as they walked to the dock. Randall rented one of the boats and helped Mary aboard. She held her breath, looking hesitantly around her before taking her seat. Mary braced herself as the boat left the dock. But once they were out on the water, she relaxed. The scenery was beautiful. The water was blue, and green trees lined the walkway and flowers of every color along the banks.

"This is really nice and so relaxing," she said as she leaned back on the seat in the boat, "And so peaceful. God's beautiful work is everywhere."

Mary didn't realize that going to dinner with Randall and boat riding was like a date. But God knows Mary's heart and righteous thinking, and He has a plan for her and Randall.

As Randall looked at Mary, he realized he had fallen in love with her.

Mary noticed that Randall looked a little sad. She touched his knee, "What's wrong, Randall." That slight touch caused him to jump. "Oh, huh, nothing, nothing," he sputtered, "I was just thinking about what you said."

"What did I say?"

"Uh, uh, I don't remember."

Mary laughed, "How can you be thinking about what I said and not remember what I said? You must have been in another world from the look on your face."

Then she turned her attention back to the beautiful scenery zipping past them. She never noticed Randall watching her while he drove the boat. He was always sure to look the other way when she turned to look at him. They were enjoying their excursion, talking and laughing as if they had known each other for years instead of days.

CHAPTER FIVE

Randall Is Devoted To Mary

Surprises Mary

Randall's mind was on Mary and not on driving the boat, and he didn't notice the boat was about to hit a log in the water as it crashed. The crash caused Mary to be thrown overboard into the water; Randall cut the engine and jumped into the water after her, diving back under repeatedly until he finally found her near the bottom of the lake. She seemed lifeless. He brought her to the surface and swam back to shore with her. He knew nothing about cardiopulmonary resuscitation. He looked around frantically.

"Help! Somebody, help!" he shouted, but no one responded, and he saw no one nearby. Desperate, Randall looked toward Heaven and cried, "Mary's God." He pleaded, "Please, Dear God of Mary, help her. She said that You would answer us if we asked. Please, God, bring Mary back to life. I love her. Please, God, help. Mary said You would, and I believe You are her God." Randall held Mary close to him as he pleaded with God for help. Suddenly, she coughed and opened her eyes. Randall held her even closer. "Thank You, God! You are real!"

"What happened?" asked Mary.

"I'm not sure. We hit something, and the next thing I knew, you were flying over the railing into the water. You must have hit your head because I never saw you swimming. You can swim, can't you? I dove in after I finally found you and brought you to shore. I couldn't stand the thought of losing you. I'm so glad you're back, Mary."

"I'm tired. No. I don't know how to swim. Remember when I told you I feared a big mass of water? I should have learned to swim when I was a kid. If I had learned to swim, I might have eliminated my fear of a mass of water. "We're all wet, and it's getting late. Let's go back to the hotel."

They started the short walk back to the dock. Randall reported the incident so the rental company manager could call a cab and retrieve the boat. Mary seemed to be doing fine. Still, Randall insisted on walking her to her door.

As she unlocked the door, Randall asked again, "Are you sure you're all right?"

"Yes. I feel a little strange, but I'm sure," said Mary

"I still think we should take you to the hospital to be sure you're alright." Randy was concerned.

"No, really, Randall. I'm okay. I need to sleep. Good night."

But as she entered her room, Randall watched her closely and followed behind her because she didn't seem too steady. He caught her as she fainted.

At the hospital, after the doctor had examined Mary, Randall entered her room.

"Hi, Randall. I'm okay. The doctor wants me to stay overnight for observation to be safe."

That's a wise decision. I'll stay here with you."

"You don't have to do that. I'll be all right."

"Please, Mary. Let me stay here with you."

"Okay, okay, but find somewhere to be while I nap. I'm so tired and sleepy."

"I'll get you some clothes from your hotel room, so you'll have clean clothes tomorrow when you leave the hospital if you'd like," Randall offered.

"Yes, thank you. My hotel key is on the dresser. Get out of your wet clothes before you catch a cold. It's cold in here," Mary whispered, drifting off to sleep a few moments later.

When Randall returned to the hospital, he was clean and dry. A nurse was in the room with Mary, who was still sleeping. "Is she alright?" he asked.

"Oh, yes, Sir. Sleeping a little more isn't unusual for someone who's been through her ordeal. It's the body's way of dealing with such stress. Your wife seems to be resilient. She'll be fine."

Wife? It occurred to him at that moment that he hadn't clarified his relationship with Mary with anyone at the hospital when he brought her in. But instead of telling the nurse that Mary was not his wife and they were just good friends, Randall said, "Here are some clean clothes for her. Is this everything she needs?"

The nurse opened the bag Randall gave her and took out a dress, slip, and dry shoes. "I don't see any underwear."

"Oh, no! I didn't think of underwear," he said, looking at the nurse wide-eyed.

"I'll go back to the hotel and get underwear."

"Don't bother," said the nurse, "Just rinse out what she was wearing today. Her underwear is in the closet. I'll check in on her again later."

After the nurse left the room, Randall went to the closet, got her underwear, and began washing them in the sink in the bathroom.

"Oh, Mary, I love you," he said softly. "If you were my wife, I would do anything for you, even wash your clothes."

The rest of the evening, Randall checked on Mary every few minutes to be sure she was all right. Watching his caring attention, the nurse thought he was a loving husband. She finally suggested that he stay in the room with her. Randall pulled a chair close to her bed and held her hand. Once he was satisfied that she was sleeping soundly and in no danger, he called Clyde.

CHAPTER SIX

There May Be Trouble With Clyde

CLYDE HAD BEEN trying to reach Randall for the last few days, wondering whether he had found the money and left the country. He had no way of knowing that Randall had his phone turned off to enjoy his time with Mary. When Clyde's phone rang, caller ID showed it was Randall. He clenched the phone tightly in his hand. He waited a couple of rings before answering, giving him time to get his anger under control.

"It's about time," Clyde yelled.

"I met a lady, Clyde! She's beautiful, and I'm in love with her!" Randall cut in. The apparent excitement in Randall's voice left Clyde cold.

"Have you found out anything? I've been trying to reach you for days. Where have you been? Why didn't you call? Why didn't you answer your phone? I thought you'd taken the money and left the country."

Clyde yelled so loud Randall had to move his phone away from his ear.

"Wow, he's angry!" Randall thought, not realizing that Clyde was angry because he thought Randall had the money. Randall took a deep breath and began again.

"I met this lady on the airplane in New York and discovered she was going to Mississippi. Our plane landed in Kentucky, and we had a two-day wait because of bad weather. Few commuter companies fly every day. Clyde, I've fallen deeply in love with her, but I haven't been able to tell her. Could you come here and meet her? Can you make it soon? Please don't tell her what we do. She's a Christian. I've always wanted to marry and have a family, but I never thought I'd meet someone like Mary."

One thing about many gangs is that they consider each other their real and only family. Randall wants to share his good news with a member of his family. At this time, Clyde is not interested in anything but the money.

Clyde listened to what Randall had to say, although he almost hung up on him because he was so angry. Randall just kept talking and didn't listen to anything Clyde said, which made Clyde extremely angry.

"Are you crazy?" Yelled Clyde.

Randall then held the phone away from him for a few seconds as if that would bring Clyde to his senses.

"You've only known her a few days," yelled Clyde.

Still ignoring Clyde's comments, Randall said, "Just come here and meet her, will you, Clyde? Will you please? We can look for whoever has our money and check out things that may help us find out something when you get here."

Randall doesn't realize he won't have a chance with Mary when she finds out who he is and what kind of work he's involved in. He must have also forgotten that she said Christians are not to marry unbelievers. He was so captivated by Mary that he only thought of his love for her and how much he wanted to make her his wife.

"I think you're nuts, and you need to get your mind on helping us find our money. But I'll be there as soon as I can," Clyde hung up.

"Something's not right, Randall, my boy," Clyde said as he talked to himself. "What have you done with the money?"

Clyde considered going to Mississippi the next day and playing along until Randall led him to the drug money. Then he'd kill him. The other members needed to know what was going on. Clyde thought he would need the other gang members to help with his plan to care for Randall. His first call was to Tom in Georgia.

"What?" Tom laughed. "You know that idiot may be in love. He's always talking about how he wishes to meet someone who cares about him. Anyway, Clyde, don't do anything crazy. We don't want cops hounding us for murder."

"Yeah, right, Tom. Meet me at the hotel in Louise," said Clyde.

Then Clyde talked with Mike in Florida and explained what he had told Tom about Randall.

"If Randall had the money, Clyde, why would he call you and ask you to meet a woman he has fallen in love with? His mind is probably not even on the money," said Mike.

"Just get to Louise, Mike," Clyde's voice tense in that way Mike recognized as his; you don't want to mess with me today.

"Right, Clyde. I'll see you tomorrow in Louise," Mike assured Clyde.

At the hospital at seven the following day, the doctor entered Mary's room to examine her. He found Randall asleep in a chair next to her bed. The doctor shook Randall's shoulder to awaken him.

"Good morning. If you wait outside, I'll examine your wife, and assuming I find no problems, you can take her home."

Randall glanced over at Mary, glad she was asleep and hadn't heard the doctor refer her as his wife. "Great, thanks, Doctor."

Randall quickly left the room; however, he worried that Mary would hear from the doctors or one of the nurses that he had let them all think she was his wife. He felt he didn't know much about women, but he knew that lying was not a way to start a relationship. I'm so afraid of how she will respond if she feels like I told them she was my wife.

A little later, Randall returned to Mary's room to find her dressed and nearly ready to be released. She smiled at him as he walked over to her.

"Mary, I have to tell you something. Last night, when I brought you to the hospital, the doctors and nurses thought I was your husband, and I let them believe it because I wanted them to see you as quickly as possible. Then, I didn't know how to tell them the truth after not saying anything immediately. Will you forgive me?"

Mary laughed and said, "That's okay. I forgive you," then she playfully choked him.

As Randall and Mary left the hospital, the nurse said, "You are such a darling couple. Mary, your husband has been so loving and devoted to you. You must love him very much. He loves you very much."

Mary smiled, "Oh, yes, I love him very much. I couldn't ask for a better husband." Then she rolled her eyes at Randall, and they quickly walked outside. Then, they laughed out loud once they were outside the room.

On their way back to the hotel, Randall's phone rang.

"Randall?" The voice on the phone seemed muffled at first. Then

Randall recognized Clyde's voice.

"I won't be coming to Mississippi. I was in Oklahoma when I got a call to come to the hospital in New York right away. My Mom is dying, Randall." Randall could hear Clyde crying.

"I'm sorry, Clyde. Is there anything I can do?" Asked Randall.

"She's the only person who ever really loved me. I just saw her a few minutes ago, and even though she's very ill, she was concerned about me. She's a Christian, and although I made fun of

Christians, I promised her many times that I would accept Jesus as my Savior and start going to church and reading the Bible."

Strangely, Clyde seems to need his family now, although earlier, he thought of killing the one who wanted to share his news of loving a woman. The one Clyde was considering killing wants to help him through his suffering.

"I understand, Clyde. Let me know what I can do to help."

Randall told Mary about Clyde's phone call: "You know more about praying than any of us. Would you mind going to New York to help Clyde through this?"

"Oh, I will be happy to do whatever I can, Randall. New York is where I live with my aunt. I'll call her and let her know what's going on."

Mary called her aunt and told her what was happening with her and her new friends, reassuring her that she was okay.

"I know I called you earlier to let you know that my trip took longer than I thought, but I don't know how long it will take to help my friend's friend. He is in New York, so I'll be able to see you because I will stay in a hotel near the hospital for a few days to be close to Randall and his friend Clyde. Going back and forth to the hospital from home daily would be inconvenient. I'll still be close if you need me."

"Of course, Dear. We're just fine. You take whatever time you need to minister to your friend and his Mom."

"Man, Clyde thinks you took off with the money," Tom said before Randall could say anything.

"Randall, I didn't; I think you did, but you better have a perfect reason to turn off your phone and not call anybody."

"Is this Tom?" Randall asked.

"Yes, why didn't you call? Why did you turn your phone off?"

Randall covers the phone with one hand, "Hold on. Mary, I've got to take this. It's business. I'll be right back."

Randall didn't want Mary to hear him talking to Tom on the phone, so he went into the hallway to speak.

"Okay, Tom, now we can talk. About the phone, well, I wasn't thinking. I met a wonderful woman on the flight to Mississippi. I got so wrapped up in her that I didn't consider contacting anybody. Even the money didn't seem important to me anymore."

"Wow, man, you've got it bad. What is your lady friend like?"

"I don't know how to tell you. You'll have to meet Mary and find out for yourself. I can tell you this: she is kind, caring, and lovely!"

Tom changed the subject. "What is the problem with Clyde? Asked Tom

"Yes, this morning he was crying when he called.," said Randall. His mother is dying, and he won't be coming to Mississippi. Mary and I are going to New York to be with him. He was upset about his mother," said Randall.

"Man, I'm sorry to hear that. Clyde loves his mother very much. I think she's the only person he has ever really cared about." Tom said sadly.

"Yeah," said Randall, "We all knew how much he loved his mother."

"Hey, don't go anywhere, Randall. I'm on my way to Louise. I'll meet you in the hotel lobby in about an hour," said Mike.

"Mike," said Tom, our plans have changed; we will go to New York instead of Louise. We'll tell you what is going on when you get here.

When Tom arrived at the hotel, he bumped into Mary as he looked around the lobby for Randall, "I'm sorry."

"Oh, that's okay. I wasn't looking where I was going."

"Well, if I hadn't been looking for a friend of mine, I would have seen you. I'm looking for a guy named Randall Nelson," said Tom.

Mary smiled, "A Randall and I just finished dinner. He's meeting me here in a minute or two. Why don't you join me and we'll wait together. We can see if it's the same, Randall.

"My name is Mary."

"Oh," said Tom, "You're the beautiful lady Randall mentioned when I talked with him. I'm Tom."

"Nice to meet you, Tom."

As they walked to a quieter corner of the lobby, Randall appeared carrying a bouquet and a Bible.

"Hey, Tom. You got here quickly. I see you've met Mary," Randall said, grinning.

"Yes, and you're right, Tom. Randall's lady friend is beautiful."

"Mary and I are going to have a Bible study. Would you like to join us, Tom? I've learned a lot about God from our Bible studies. It's fascinating," Randall said as he handed the flowers to Mary.

"No, I'm too tired and hungry for any kind of study, maybe another time." Tom went to the desk to check in and then walked over and sat at a table in the restaurant.

Mary and Randall had chosen a table near a window overlooking the lake where they had been having their Bible studies since being in Louise. Randall hung on to every word Mary taught from the Scriptures as always. Suddenly, he opened his eyes wide as if he understood everything and interrupted Mary.

"I'm ready! Pray with me!"

Mary took his hands in hers, and he repeated the sinner's prayer after her. When he finished reciting the prayer, Randall jumped out of his seat, grabbed Mary out of her seat, and began swirling her around, "Hallelujah! Jesus has saved me! Thank you, Jesus!" Randall yelled out, praising God. There must have been other Christians in the restaurant because many people began applauding instead of looking at them like they were strange or weird.

Tom told Mary the next day, "I didn't believe all that Bible stuff." Mary told him she understood his point because she remembered when she, too, found it hard to believe some things in the Bible.

"Tom, I remember someone telling me we should believe things that are not as they are. I didn't think that was even in the Bible; if it was, it didn't make sense. What's worse, I called myself a Christian. But just because I didn't believe what that person said didn't make it untrue. I found the same verse in the Bible myself one day. I tried hard to understand some things in the Bible. It was frustrating until I found this in the Bible: Proverbs 3:5-6 NKJV Trust in the Lord with all your heart, and lean not on your understanding; 6 In all your ways acknowledge Him, and He shall direct your paths.

When I read this in the Bible, I felt free and relaxed because I didn't feel I had to understand everything. I needed to trust God and found that God would clarify things I didn't understand as I prayed and read His Word. Somehow, God made these things clear to me through His Word as I began to read it every chance I got. The more I read, the better I began to understand also what God wanted from me. The fact that God's Word says to believe things that are not as though they are was faith-building and so comforting to me. As I stayed in the Bible and maintained a close relationship with God, my life changed, and the Bible became my lifeline."

One night, God spoke to my heart and told me He loved me. It was a kind of love that I'd never experienced. I was overwhelmed with joy. And now I have even more peace because I believe His promises, which are numerous and unbelievably wonderful."

CHAPTER SEVEN

Clyde Fears His Mother Is Dying

CLYDE CALLED TOM in tears, "My mom is in a coma. She lies there. I don't know what to do."

"Hold on, man, we're on the way there. It will take a little while because of the commuter service here, but we'll be there as soon as possible."

Tom hung up and told Randall what Clyde said.

"We should leave now to get to the airport on time," Mary informed them.

Just as they got into the cab, Tom remembered Mike, who had arrived late the night before: "He's still sleeping. I'll call him and get him moving."

While Tom explained the urgency to Mike, Mary called her aunt again. Her aunt put Mary on speakerphone so the girls could hear her.

"I'll be in New York late tomorrow night, Aunt Ruth. We'll be leaving Kentucky soon, and once we get to New York, we're going straight to the hospital. I'm not sure how long I'll be staying there. Girls, I love you. Keep minding Aunt Ruth, and go to bed at your regular time. I'll see you guys as soon as I can. I love you!" The girls yelled back. "We love you too, Mom!"

Mike was the last person to board the plane. The three men and Mary were all seated near each other. Mary explained,

"God's Word says that if we believe, He will do whatever we ask. Let's pray," Mary commanded.

Mike rolled his eyes at Tom. Here we go with that religious mambo jumbo, he thought. But Tom began to cry.

"Are you all right, Tom?" Mary asked as she took his hand in hers. It's all right, Tom. It's okay to cry. God loves you."

"God can't love me," he sobbed. "I've done too many bad things."

"Let me tell you about a guy who did a real bad thing," said Mary, "He had an affair with another man's wife, and when she became pregnant, the man tried to get her husband to have relations with her so her husband would think he was the baby's father. When the man refused to go to bed with his wife, her lover had her husband killed. This man had always loved God, so he was upset when he faced what he had done. He was truly sorry, repented, and sought God's forgiveness. In other words, he turned away from his sin. And God not only loved him and forgave him but also called him the apple of His eye. That man's name was David, the famous king of Israel. David loved God and always wanted to please Him. God knew David's heart and blessed him."

The guys listened as Mary continued, "We have all sinned and come short of the glory of God, Tom. If you invite Jesus into your life and ask Him to forgive your sins, He will. Tell him that you are sorry for the bad things that you have done. Then stop doing things that you know are bad and start serving God. God will forgive you and won't even remember any of your bad deeds ever again, according to the Book that has no mistakes in it, the God-inspired Book, the Bible. You will have peace and Joy that even you don't understand."

Mary started to pray again: "Dear God, we agree that You will honor Your Word. Heavenly Father, as Your Word says in

Matthew 18:20-NKJV For where two or three are gathered in My Name, I am there in the midst of them."

Mary continues: Jesus is here in the midst of us, and we can ask anything, and He will grant it. Dear God, bless Clyde and heal his mother. Give them a good report and peace in Jesus' Name. We thank You, Dear God. We thank You and give You the honor and praise for answering our prayer."

Later, Tom talked silently to God, "Please let what Mary said be true; I mean about You forgiving people no matter how bad they've been."

After speaking briefly to God, Tom began to feel very peaceful and soon fell asleep. As he slept, he dreamed that Jesus looked down from Heaven and said, "My son, you are forgiven."

When they finally arrived in New York, Tom grabbed Mary's arm.

"I have to talk with you right away, Mary."

"Okay, let's all go to dinner and talk then."

After the waiter cleared the table, Tom began.

"Last night, after this dream, I couldn't go back to sleep, Mary! A voice spoke to me and said, 'My son, you are forgiven.' I felt so peaceful and excited. I know it was Jesus! I just knew it was Jesus! What do I do now?"

"Let me lead you in the prayer of salvation, Tom." After the prayer, Tom began to cry tears of Joy.

Mike sat there, listening to everything, "I think I'm the only sane person here," he said as he looked around the table.

"I don't know," said Randall, "I think you're the only insane person here, especially if you're not ready to gain eternal life."

"Randall," Mary asked, "Did you call Clyde to tell him we'll be at the hospital soon?"

"I called earlier but got no answer. I'll try again." Randall got up from the table to have some privacy and keep from interrupting the others. He returned a couple of minutes later with a sorrowful look on his face. "What's wrong, man?" Mike asked.

"I've never known Clyde to react this way. He is in such a bad way. We need to go to the hospital now."

As they took their eyes off Randall, Tom paid the check while Mike hailed a cab. Mary patted Randall's hand, "It will be all right, Randall. God's in control."

Mike was the first to reach the information desk inside the hospital lobby, "Room 7707," he told them. They took the elevator to the seventh floor and followed the signs to find the room. They found Clyde sitting on his mother's bed, holding her hand, and crying. His mother was in a coma, yet she seemed only sleeping peacefully. As they walked over to the bed, Clyde stood up.

"Thanks for coming, guys," he said, trying not to show that he was about to lose control.

"This is Mary, Randall's friend," said Tom.

"It's nice meeting you, Clyde. Randall was looking forward to my meeting you," Mary said as she extended her hand, "May I pray for your mother?"

Clyde blinked back tears and cleared his throat, "Yes. My mom always believed in prayer."

"That's good," said Mary, "God does answer our prayers. Let's all hold hands."

They quickly formed a circle, with Mary next to Clyde's mother, gently touching her forehead, and Clyde on the other side, holding his mother's hand.

"Dear Heavenly Father, Jesus gave us the right to go straight to the throne with our request when He died on the cross for us. We know Jesus rose again and intercedes for us. I request that you heal Clyde's mother, put life back into her body, and make her body function normally. We believe You and thank You for answering our prayer in Jesus' Name. Amen."

"Everything's going to be fine, Clyde," Mary comforts him, "You need to know that Jesus loves you very much, no matter what you've done. However, He does want y27ou to accept Him as your Lord and Savior."

Clyde was so heartbroken over his mother's condition that he didn't hear what Mary said. (God was listing.) Clyde squeezed his mother's hand, placed it gently on the bed, and walked over to the window. He stared into the darkness for several minutes as the others stood around the bed silently. Then he turned to look at his mother, "Did you see that?" He shouted and rushed to her side, "She moved her hand."

Everybody looked at Clyde and wondered why there was sudden excitement. "Mom. Mom," he said, "I love you. I'll do whatever you tell me; don't leave me."

Clyde's mother opened her eyes and smiled at Clyde, "Hi, honey," she said, "Will you get me a glass of water."

"Yes, Mom, I'll get it right away." Clyde rushed to the nurse's desk, "May I have a glass of water for my mom?"

"Dear," the nurse said, "Your mom can't drink anything."

"But," said Clyde, she asked for a glass of water."

"Your mom can't drink anything," the nurse said again, putting her hand gently on Clyde's shoulder.

There was a time when Clyde would curse the nurse and demand that she get the water immediately. Instead, he said, "Please come and see for yourself." The Holy Spirit was already working on Clyde.

The nurse followed Clyde to his mother's room. Clyde asked his mother, "Didn't you ask me to get you some water, Mom?"

"Yes, Honey, what's taking so long?" The nurse opened her mouth, "I'll get your mother a glass of water immediately. Mrs. Anderson, would you like something to eat too?"

"Yes, I would like scrambled eggs and coffee if you don't mind."

The nurse rushed out of Mrs. Anderson's room and called for the kitchen to bring scrambled eggs and coffee for Mrs. Anderson. Then she called for the doctor.

"I saw Jesus talking to you, Clyde Anderson," said Mrs. Anderson, "What do you have to say about that?"

"I don't think Jesus would say anything to me because I've done too many bad things."

Mary said, "Did you know that Jesus died for the world's sins, including you, Clyde? He forgives the sins of everyone who asks for forgiveness and accepts Him as their Savior. He also rewards them with eternal life. That means you, too, Clyde. How about it? Do you want to receive Jesus now?"

"Yes," said Clyde, smiling, "I think I'm ready."

"I saw you with Jesus in my dream," said Mrs. Anderson, "Jesus said, 'I have heard your cry for your son. Jesus also said He loves Clyde and has forgiven him; then He said to tell Clyde to forgive himself and others.

Clyde began to cry as the bitterness, anger, and self-hatred left him. He began to love everyone regardless of religion, race, or origin Clyde was never racist, but he was judgmental and often turned people off. He judged people because he didn't understand them, which is the same as prejudiced. The dictionary put it this way: influenced by prejudice, having a preconceived opinion or feeling, especially an unreasoning or unfavorable one.

Hearing his mother say she heard from Jesus made his heart skip a beat, and Joy filled his whole being.

"I heard a voice say the same thing to me," Tom said with excitement,

"God is so real, Clyde. You're in for the Joy of your life," said Tom as the others prayed silently. Mary led Clyde to Jesus.

Clyde waited with his friends outside the room as the doctor checked his mother and confirmed that she had received a miracle. Clyde wanted to spend a few more minutes with his mother before leaving the hospital and asked everybody to wait for him in the lobby. When the doctor left his mother's room, Clyde returned and stood by her bed, holding her hand, "I did it, Mom! I accepted Jesus as my Savior!" Clyde whispered in her ear as he kissed her forehead.

She smiled and squeezed his hand. "I'll see you in the morning, Mom. I love you."

In the lobby, Clyde joined Mary and the guys, hugging each one. Joining hands, they prayed, thanking God for blessing them, for Tom and Clyde's salvation, and for God healing Clyde's mother. Then, they headed toward Clyde's car and walked across the parking lot. Clyde said, "I feel so light, guys, like I'm floating on a cloud. It's so strange how I made fun of Christians, and now I'm one of them. Clyde laughed with everyone.

Then he danced the rest of the way to his car. Clyde thanked Mary for being there for him as he drove her home.

Weel later, when Clyde opened the door to the mansion, the phone was ringing.

"Jesus loves me," Clyde answered the phone. But as he listened, everyone who had come in behind him saw his face turn white.

"What's wrong?" Mike asked.

"You won't believe this," said Clyde, "That was the police. The drive-by-shooter that shot John had turned himself into the police. The police said his name was Andrew Brown. The police also said that Andrew has accepted Jesus as his Lord and Savior and has started a Bible study at the prison. Andrew told the police he would go by the church where he shot John and cried for no reason. One day, he drove to the church and parked in the parking lot. Suddenly, he felt compelled to go in. He confessed everything to the minister, and he led him to Jesus. Andrew got the church to help him find John's phone number and asked the police to call John's people and tell them that he is very sorry about what he did and that he hopes John's family forgives him."

Clyde paused momentarily, looking at the others standing in the room, "Man, this has been a wild and wonderful day!"

"I can't tell you how peaceful my life has been the last few weeks," Clyde told Tom and Mike as they were sitting in their living room one day, "We have to figure out what we're going to do now that we won't be doing the drug and money scene. It feels good not to be worrying about that briefcase of money."

"Yeah, it sure would have been nice, though," said Mike. Even though Mike has not given his life to Jesus, he has changed much for the better. The spirit of the guys must be rubbing off on him. He said the money would be nice, but he didn't seem too bothered about not having it.

"The money," said Clyde, "Isn't important anymore, and strangely, I'm happier now without it than I was when Randall walked in with it. Well, what we thought was it." They all laughed at that.

"Yeah. One thing for sure, it's nice not having to worry about the police coming after us," Mike said as Tom smiled and high-fived him.

"We need to find an honest way of making a living," Clyde said as they all looked at one another blankly. It had been some time since they had had to work to support themselves.

You could consider what we used to do as a form of work or some job. The guys laughed at Clyde's reasoning.

Finally, Clyde said, smiling, "We can all get jobs at a construction company. Randall, Mike, and I used to be pretty good at construction work, and we can teach Tom."

When the guys first got saved, they volunteered to help the police with several of their charity organizations. They did so much for the police and saw them so much that they became good friends with the police.

One day, the police chief told Clyde, "I don't know what kind of jobs you guys have, but I know this community is much better off because of you. The Great Ones had been cautious about ever involving the police for years. Everyone knew them but the police. People were once afraid to tell the police anything about them. Although many years ago, Clyde's gang did have a few problems with the police. The police didn't know them then. The people who were fearful of them at one time knew that they had changed, and now they are friends with Clyde's gang, although they don't look upon them as a gang. Clyde took the guys to meet with Ben, a construction manager he knew. Clyde asked him about hiring them to work with his company. The guys were all hired after the interview with the company's owner.

"You won't regret hiring us," Clyde told the owner, "We're hard workers, and Tom's a fast learner."

Their first day of work was grueling. The men returned to the mansion dirty and exhausted, almost too tired to eat. After cleaning up and having dinner, they sat in the living room to watch a game on television. After a few minutes, they were all asleep on couches and chairs.

One week later, as Clyde talked with the guys, "Guys, I've been thinking, we need to serve God with the money we make now. Helping others seems to be the right thing to do. Working with the police is just not enough."

The others nodded in agreement. They all had substantial bank accounts, but they no longer desired the lifestyle they used to live. They were trying to please God. They had gotten jobs, and now they wanted to share with others. Randall walked in and overheard Clyde's comments to Tom and Mike.

"I know how we can get started if you're serious about this." He then told them how they could help Mary with her dream, which would also be working for God.

"Perfect," said Clyde, "She was certainly there helping me when she didn't even know me. Helping with her dream will be a perfect way to help the community."

After work, Randall called Mary, "We want to help with the dream you've talked about." Randall was so excited at the thought of seeing Mary. He liked being around her and listening to her talk about the Scriptures.

"Boy, I never felt this way before about anyone." He thought. "How can I ever tell her how I feel about her?"

"That sounds great; I'll see you tomorrow," said Mary.

When she arrived, the men escorted her into the living room.

"Mary, we have changed so much since you came into our lives,"

Clyde was happy to do anything that pleased God, so he and Randall got together with Mary and planned to work on Mary's dream.

Clyde tells Mary, "We want to use our money and time to help others. Randall told us about your plans for a shelter for runaway teenagers, people with drug problems, homeless people, and others needing help. We want to help your dream become a reality."

"That's wonderful, Clyde. It's an answer to my prayers. Thank you so much. Let's ask God to guide us in this."

She hugged Clyde and the other guys. Then, they talked about plans for getting started on Mary's dream.

When Mary returned to Aunt Ruth's, she told her about the gang's generous offer to help her with her dream, "We're staying in New York, Aunt Ruth. I hadn't been sure, but I believe this is part of God's plan for all of us."

"I was hoping you'd stay. I don't want to think about what I would do if you all left. You've made me so happy since you've been here. Having the girls here reminds me that the Lord still has a purpose."

Mary and her daughter had filled a void in Aunt Ruth's life and ended her depression and loneliness.

Randall invited Mary and her daughters to dinner at the mansion two weeks later, "I've missed you, Mary. It will be nice to see you again, even if it's with the guys. Everyone is so excited about working with you and your dream project. We can't wait to get started."

The guys all knew that Randall was in love with Mary. It's unbelievable that Mary doesn't notice because he's so devoted to her. Although he tries not to let her see him looking at her so much, she must catch him sometimes looking at her like a man looks at a woman when he's in love. Mary is so naive she probably wouldn't notice anyway.

"We'd love to come to dinner, Randall. The girls and I are going skating today. But any other day will be fine."

"How about tomorrow then?"

"That's fine. We'll see you then."

When Mary and her daughters arrived for dinner the next day, the guys pretended they were at one of the finest restaurants in New York City; Clyde wore an oversized white chef's hat and white jacket. Randall acted as the doorman, dressed in a black suit. Tom and Mike were waiters dressed in black with white dishtowels draped over their arms. They served the ladies a wonderful catered meal since they only ate frozen dinners or something in a can if they didn't go out to eat. They didn't like to go out for breakfast, so they knew how to fry eggs and make toast.

After eating, they adjourned to the living room. There were lots of boy toys on the coffee table.

"Come on, girls. Let's play with the toys we bought for you," Randall responded as he led the way into the den. The guys grabbed the toys off the coffee table to show the girls how they worked. The girls watched the guys sitting on the floor playing with their toys. After about two hours, Mary walked out of the living room where she had been watching television and into the den. She began to laugh when she saw her girls sitting there quietly, watching the guys play tirelessly with the toys that they bought for the girls.

"Do the girls get to take those toys home, or do they leave them here for you boys to play with?" she laughed.

"I think we bought the wrong kind of toys. We'll get girl toys next time," Mike promised; we'd never been to a toy store before, and we just got the toys that seemed like the most fun, and we had fun buying them."

"The boy toys seem to be the only toys that would be fun to play with, but we will check with the girls the next time we buy them," said Tom.

The girls were left in the den to play by themselves.

Later, "I've got more ideas about our home for runaway girls. Could we talk about it tonight?" Clyde asked.

"It's getting late, and the girls need to get home to get to bed. If you need to talk now, I'll have Aunt Ruth pick the girls up and take them home."

"Yes, we want to get started with our project, uh, your dream project, as soon as possible."

When no one answered the phone, Mary remembered that Aunt Ruth was at her Bible study, "I forgot it's Aunt Ruth's Bible study night—sorry guys. I'll come over tomorrow when you get home from work. Will five o'clock be okay?"

"Sure, but we need to talk as soon as possible. We'll see you tomorrow," Clyde said.

He was disappointed that Mary had to leave before they got a chance to tell her about their plans for the project. The guys followed Mary into the den to get the girls, who were enthusiastically playing with the toys and were having a wild war.

When Mary and the guys entered the den, they couldn't believe what they saw.

"How did you learn how to work those toys?" Mary asked.

"It was easy, Mom. We watched the guys," said Lear.

"I certainly couldn't have learned that fast even if I had watched the guys play with the toys," Mary responded.

The guys made an exciting and funny evening for Mary and her girls. After walking Mary and the girls to Mary's car, the men happily danced back inside.

"Wow!" shouted Tom, "I feel the way Clyde did when we left the hospital weeks ago that night like I'm floating on a cloud. There are so many things that come with receiving Jesus. Can you imagine finding Joy in giving your money and time to others? You need to experience the Joy you will know when you do what you know, please God.

CHAPTER EIGHT

God Shows His Love For The Gang

For days, Mike had listened to Randall, Clyde, and Tom rejoice over Jesus and the peace He brought them.

"Mary," Mike screamed as she walked through the front door. "I want what the guys have. Will you lead me to Jesus?"

"I will be happy too." She went with him into the den to explain the plan of salvation, which he had already known after hearing it many times. The guys liked hearing about God's plan of salvation and were happy to follow her as she explained everything to Mike. They all joined hands and prayed for Mike to be strong in the Lord and to receive the Holy Spirit, which he did.

Later that day, "I have some ideas about our home for runaway teenagers," Clyde explained. "We must get started as soon as possible."

Before Clyde said another word, a man wearing a stocking cap burst into the den, grabbed Mary, and held a gun to her head.

"Where's the money?" he demanded. "I know you have it. Give it to me, or Mary is dead." He was holding the gun almost close enough to touch Mary's head.

"Let her go. She knows nothing about the money." Clyde was Concerned about Mary's safety, "Randall lost the money on a train. We never got it."

"I don't believe you, so give me the money. Get me the money now," the gunman yelled.

Tell us what to do, Precious God. Randall prayed silently. As he watched, the gun pointed at Mary's head. Then he heard a voice within him say,

"Rob's gun won't fire; Rob's gun has no bullets in it."

Randall knew it was the voice of God. He relaxed and strolled toward the gunman.

"Don't come any closer, or I'll blow her away," the gunman yelled. But Randall kept coming. When Randall was close enough to touch the gunman, he grabbed the gunman's gun and pulled Mary out of his grasp as the other men grabbed him and tied his hands behind him. Then Clyde took the stocking cap off his head and asked, "Rob?" Clyde stared at Rob, his mouth open in disbelief.

"What do you think you're doing?"

"You guys double-crossed me. I set you up, and then I got nothing. I want my share."

"What's he talking about, Clyde?" Mary asked. The others, not even Randall, could look at her.

"Who is this man? Randall?"

"He's someone we used to do business with," Randall finally answered.

"What kind of business? What did he mean by setting you up? Do you all owe him money?" Mary continued to question Randall, who was so upset as he looked helplessly at Mary.

In desperation, Clyde responded, "Mary, we were The Great Ones, one of the worst gangs in New York, until we came to know Jesus through you. We haven't lived that life, but we used to sell drugs. Rob helped us locate people with an addiction who would buy drugs from us. He also helped us with drug dealers. When Randall met you, we had just lost a huge amount of money that was a payment from the Cubans for drugs and other deals we made with them. That's how you met Randall. He was going to Mississippi to look for our money."

Randall interrupted, "Mary! We often prayed and talked about telling you about what we did in the past, but we never got up enough nerve to say anything. Can you please forgive us, Mary? We are very sorry for not telling you to trust us. We have talked and prayed about it many times.

We want to do what is right, Mary, but let us pray first. If we call the police, They will discover our past, and the fact that Rob attempted to kill Mary will not go well for us.

The police are our friends now, but they might have to arrest us or be responsible for not following the law."

Mary stood looking at them in disbelief. How could she have not known? Still, they had accepted Christ and were different people now. She looked at each of them again, breathed deeply, exhaled, and turned to Randall.

"We've been studying the Word of God for some time, Randall. What do you think we should do first?"

"Pray!" he shouted, happy that Mary didn't just walk out on them right then and there.

"Then let's pray," Mary prayed first and then asked each one to pray out loud.

With everyone upset, Mary knew they had to wait for the Lord to answer their prayers. She also knew that, somehow, she had to let the group know that God was in control and that we had to rely on His guidance. After silence, Mary turned to the men, "I bet everybody is hungry. I'll fix dinner if somebody will show me where you keep the food and pots and pans."

After spending a few minutes in the kitchen and waiting for someone to show her where the food, pot, and pans were, she returned to the den, "Your kitchen is beautiful but a bit strange. I finally found the pots and pans, which were not for cooking the foods I usually cook, but there's no food in your kitchen anyway."

Clyde was looking for Mary to come out of the kitchen, complaining about either no food or the kinds of pots and pans in the kitchen. "Yeah, about that, we usually order out. What kind of cuisine are you interested in?" Clyde walked over to the desk, opened a drawer, and pulled out a stack of take-out menus at least three inches thick. When Mary saw them, her soft laughter filled the room. When their food finally arrived, they entered the dining room where Mary had set the table.

Randall escorted Rob to the table, his hands still tied behind his back.

"How is he supposed to eat?" Mary asked.

"We can't untie him," said Randall, "He tried to kill you."

"I'll feed him then." Randall had Rob sit in the chair next to Mary.

They discussed how exciting helping Mary with her project would be and detailed their plans.

"We are going to enjoy helping runaway teenagers, people on drugs, and others in need," said Clyde.

Mary was quiet all this time, listening to the guys talk, feeding Rob, and watching his reaction to the comments the guys were making. She wondered what he thought about these guys talking about helping people who were on drugs when they made a living selling them drugs. When she brought another bite to his lips, Rob turned his head away slightly as tears rolled down his cheeks. Mary put down the fork and wiped his tears with her napkin as he continued to cry. The others talked while Mary ministered to him.

Mary put her arms around Rob and held him gently. "It's all right, Rob. Jesus loves you no matter what you've done," she explained that everyone has sinned and that Jesus died for everyone.

"Jesus is the answer for everything," Mary tried to assure him, "You can receive Jesus right now. I'll pray for you and lead you in a prayer to Jesus." Rob still needs to respond.

"It's okay, Rob; just know that Jesus loves you and wants you to have peace. Also, know this: He'll forgive you for everything you did wrong. But you have to be sincere and repent of your sins. That means to stop doing the wrong thing that you did before. It won't be easy at first, but reading the Bible and getting to know God will become easier. You will be surprised at how looking to Jesus and following his teachings will help you. You won't even want to do the things you used to do. It may take some time, but it will happen if you stay with Jesus and His teachings."

Mary continued talking to Rob, "I asked God to give me a burden for the lost. One person that I love and respect is Oprah Winfrey. She is a compassionate person, loved by so many people. She has, in my opinion, a delightful, generous spirit. She has helped so many people here and in other countries. She has many Christians on her television show, people of other religions, and people of no religion. I have listened to ministers talk about her with such love and admiration, even though some debate whether she's a Christian. Christians like to rejoice in the knowledge that people they love and admire will receive Jesus and that they will see them in Heaven someday."

Things were written about Oprah before her position on Christianity was clear. The people who loved her still love her but disagree with her belief that there are many ways to get to Heaven. Many Christians still pray that God blesses Oprah with learning the truth.

Mary told Rob about a lovely woman on Oprah's show who told Oprah that she believed in the same God that Oprah believed in. She said that she even believed in Jesus but didn't think that Jesus was the Son of God. She also said that Jesus was a prophet but not the Son of God.

"Rob, people who don't believe Jesus is the Son of God but believe he was only a prophet and a good man are not listening to what they're saying. Jesus said that He's the Son of God. Would a good man lie? I don't think so." Rob appeared to be listening.

"Many people also believe that there is more than one way to Heaven. Jesus said that He is the only way to the Father and that we have to go through Him to get to the Father, and that's the only way to Heaven, according to the Bible. I believe in the Bible.

Scripture says that Jesus is God's begotten Son and that God created us. God didn't call anyone his begotten Son except for Jesus. I think these statements alone make Him the Son of God. You could say he has the same material or substance as God. My daughter has the same body material as me; she has my blood and flesh. If Jesus is begotten of God, He would be like God in every way.

If you understand the difference between 'begotten' and 'created,' you know that Jesus couldn't be God's only begotten Son and His created Son."

Rob listened intently and quietly as Mary spoke. Feeling that he needed time to process all she said, Mary smiled, "I know that's a lot to think about. Why don't we finish eating, and then you can ask questions, or we can pray or whatever you would like to do.'

Rob nodded and slowly chewed the bite of food Mary gave him. A little later, Rob looked at Tom, "I need to go to the restroom. Can you help me?" Nodding toward his back, his hands remained tied behind him.

"Now what?" Tom asked Clyde. Mary intervened, "Untie him. He doesn't have a gun or anything. What could he do?"

Clyde looked at Mary and then at Rob and slowly nodded toward Tom. Tom placed his napkin on the table and untied Rob's hands. Rob rubbed his wrists to restore circulation. "Where's the restroom?"

Twenty minutes later, "You'd better check on Rob, Tom. It's been long enough," Clyde commanded.

Tom turned the doorknob of the bathroom door and found it locked, "Rob. Rob, open the door," he yelled, pounding on the door, "Hey, do we have a key to this door?" he shouted to Clyde.

"Just take it down," Clyde shouted as he left the table and headed toward the bathroom door. Tom brought his foot up toward the door and kicked it in. Rob had escaped through the bathroom window.

"We need to pray for him, guys," Mary said, knowing they were angry at his escape. "He's God's problem, not ours. God has taken care of us and will continue to do so."

Later that afternoon, Clyde told Mary, "We want to discuss sharing our mansion for your project. Is that a great idea? Your mansion is a big building and more than enough room for many people, and when we get runaway teens, they will need a woman here to help them.

"Clyde, I don't know what to say! Are you sure? I mean, this is your home!"

"We're all sure. We want to give back so you can get started. Even if we have to add a few rooms later, we can start helping people almost immediately. Today."

"Yes. Thank you. I'll need to get someone to help me teach and counsel people as we rehabilitate them. I can come over every morning and go home in the evenings while Aunt Ruth looks after my girls."

"I don't mean for you to come over every day; I mean for you to move in," said Clyde.

Clyde, I know this place has a lot of room, but how much space do you have?"

"There are thirty-five rooms, not counting bathrooms, plus a large swimming pool outside and a theater and workout room downstairs. We can use the living room, dining room, and kitchen as is. All three of those rooms are big. We can turn the den into the office and the family room into a counseling center and library. All of us have rooms on the third floor. There are plenty of bedrooms on the first and second floor, most with bathrooms. The others can use the common bathrooms on each floor, but we could do some renovation later to meet the needs of our project. There is more than enough room for some people who need temporary housing while they get back on their feet."

"You seem to have thought of everything." Mary smiled.

"We have. We've even devised a new name, God's Gang."

CHAPTER NINE

The Gang Helps Three Sisters In Trouble

AFTER PRAYING AND asking God to guide them, Mary got her license for counseling to practice in the state of New York. Zoning and a permit for the mansion were easy to attain because the mansion was a few miles from the city. Everyone felt God wanted the guys to start by rescuing girls who worked in the Red Zone area, known for teenage prostitution. Girls in the Red Zone were like prisoners. They worked for a man named Jim, who allowed no independence. If any girls tried to leave, the men who worked there beat them. Sometimes, the men would kill them. The owner of the Red Zone, Jim, and his men thought no one cared about the girls there. Men at the Red Zone felt that keeping the girls would not cause problems because no one had reported them missing.

Randall, Mike, and Tom devised a plan to get girls out of the Red Zone and into God's Gang. When Clyde wasn't working, he usually stayed at the mansion to help Mary with challenging assignments, and he also managed things when Mary was not there. To carry their tools, they purchased a new van shortly after being saved and entering the construction business. They could use the van to cruise the Red Zone, free the girls, and bring them to God's Gang. The windows on the van were dark to shield the girls from view whenever we took them from there.

God's Gang left the mansion around nine o'clock the first night they put their rescue operation into effect. It wasn't long before they spotted three young girls standing on a street near the Red Zone. Mike pulled to a stop beside them, and Randall got out of the front passenger seat.

"Hey, ladies, how about going for a ride?"

One girl answered, "We'd love to, but we can only see people here in our building."

"Are your friends interested too?" Randall asked, "We're Christians and want to help you. You can't possibly want to live this kind of life in a building that looks like it's falling apart. From here, it doesn't even look safe. We have a safe place where you can stay until you get on your feet. Come with us, and no one will harm you."

The girls were afraid and didn't know what to do. Randall looked at them more closely and saw that they all resembled each other. "Are you sisters?"

"Yes, we're sisters," the oldest girl said, moving a bit in front of the other two as she desperately needed to protest her sisters.

"Girls, we just want to help the girls here have a better life," Randall tried to reassure them.

"I don't know. The treatment here is horrible, but getting into a van with three strange men doesn't seem like the brightest thing to do," Anna said with concern for their safety.

Kathy, the youngest girl, tugged on the sleeve of her oldest sister.

"I'm cold and hungry. Can we get in the van to get warm for a while? And maybe they will buy us something to eat."

"You know Jim wouldn't stand for that. We have to take the men back into our building or else." Sue looked sad as she put her arm around Kathy's shoulder to comfort her.

"Kathy," said Randall, "We'll open the side door, you all jump in, and Mike will get us out of here before anyone can chase us. Then you can decide what you want to do."

Kathy turned to her sisters. "I think any place is better than this place. Let's go with them, and we will be free to find a safe shelter."

Tom opened the side door for each girl to get in the van. Randall closed the door and barely returned to his seat before Mike pulled away from the curb. He made a U-turn to get them out of the Red Zone quickly.

"Are you sure about this, Kathy?" Anna, the middle sister, questioned,

"We don't know anything about these guys. At least Jim was predictable. When he finds us gone, you know he'll come looking for us and kill us."

Anna was becoming horrified. She became so frightened that she was not reasoning. Sitting next to the side door, her hand gripping the handle, she said, "I think we should go back. Stop the van!" she shouted to Mike. "I want out."

As the van pulled up to a red light, Anna opened the door and ran into one of the six buildings owned by Jim. Tom reached for her, but she was outside the van before he could stop her. Sue screamed from the back of the van, "Stop her!" But Anna disappeared into the darkness.

"It's all right, Sue. We'll come back for Anna."

Randall tapped Mike on the shoulder to keep driving as the light changed.

"You don't understand," Sue screamed. "Jim had a girl killed in that building. Anna didn't know that, and neither did Kathy. I learned from one of our friends before she escaped the Red Zone."

"Oh no! No!" Kathy began to cry. Mike drove the van to the curb as Tom leaped from the back seat and started running to the building that Anna had entered. Anna hadn't had time to think about what she would do next. Anna thought she needed to return to their building before Jim found out and beat her to death. She was worried about her sisters.

"I'll tell Jim," Anna talked to herself, "That some guys kidnapped my sisters, but I got away. And that's why I ran into a building."

This building was similar to the one they lived in, but it had no light in the halls, and trash was littered everywhere. Anna tried to find her way to the back of the building, but the maze of hallways slowed her down, as did the lack of light except a bit of light coming in from a streetlight. She was stumbling over broken furniture, glass, and other things that were so frightening. She gasped when two strong arms grabbed her.

"What are you doing here?" Anna knew that voice. She'd heard it a thousand times; she knew the anger that boiled over just below the surface and the violence it covered. Jim was holding Anna tightly as her face turned to him. He stared into her face, his fingers digging into her arms; the stench of his breath made her hold her breath until she turned her head away from him.

"Why aren't you in your building or working on the street?"

Before she could answer, she heard someone crashing through the debris, coming toward her. Jim tightened his grip as Anna barely made out Tom's face.

"Hey, you caught her. Why did you run, sweetheart?" Tom asked, trying to judge the situation and silently praying for knowledge to do the right thing and not get Anna hurt.

"Who are you?" Jim demanded.

"Hey, I just wanted to take the little lady for a bite to eat before we had fun?" Tom smiled, hoping to settle Jim.

"That's right, Jim, but I knew you would be mad. That's why I ran. I was trying to get back to our place. Honest," Anna tried to keep her voice calm and sweet, denying the turmoil and pain she was feeling. But Randall and Mike came crashing through the hallway before Jim said anything. Jim had a gun, pulled the slide to load it, and pointed it straight at Tom's chest.

"You've got two choices. Get lost or get dead." The icy sound of his voice was all the guys needed to hear to know Jim was not bluffing.

"Look, man, we just…" Mike was interrupted. The door to the apartment from the back room opened, and Rob stood surprised that someone was there.

"What's going on?" Rob asked as he noticed Jim pointing a gun at Tom. Rob remembered the kind treatment Tom and his friends had shown him.

"These clowns say they want to take Anna out to eat, but I don't think that's the case. I'm taking Anna back to her building. Take care of these clowns. If you have a problem with them, you know what to do. Joe picks up the trash tomorrow morning."

"Yeah, sure, Jim, I'll. I'll take care of them." Jim started to walk, still holding Anna and dragging her with him. Rob quickly rushed over and knocked Jim's gun out of his hand, and it went flying across the room. Tom lunged toward Jim as Anna bit down on his arm. He screamed in pain, letting Anna go in the process. Tom moved her out of the way as the three guys wrestled Jim to the floor. Mike, with Jim's gun, was pointing it at him.

"Okay, guys, Jim won't bother Anna anymore," said Tom. "Anna, go with Randall and Mike. Rob, it would be safe for you to come with us, too. Jim, you're staying here till we're long gone. Make sure you stay away from us. We don't want any problems, neither do you, but if you cause problems, we'll see that the police cause you bigger problems."

Waiting in the van, Sue and Kathy were so happy to see Anna and the guys return to the truck and take them away from the Red Zone. Rob sat in the van crying as the girls watched him, no longer afraid of him. God's Gang planned to help the police close the Red Zone immediately. They wanted to ensure that no one hurt the girls as they worked on a plan to shut down the Red Zone.

Almost every room in Jim's buildings locks from the outside. The police have had problems with these crooks and have been trying to close them down, but Jim's guys are dangerous and known for getting away with murder. The police found out that the girls would be hurt or tortured whenever the police showed up, so they had to be very careful. Jim's guys also threatened to burn the girls building with them in the building if they managed to call the police.

By the time Mike drove into the driveway of God's Gang, the girls had calmed down. The sisters felt they could trust the guys who had taken them from the Red Zone. After all, they had risked their lives to get them out of the Red Zone.

"No one had ever done anything like that for us before. We are safe because of the guys who rescued us," Anna thought as she looked out the window at the vast residence.

"Who lives here?" Anna asked.

"That's where you're going to live," Randall answered, "do you think you'll like it here?"

"Wow!" I like it even before I see the inside!"

"I do agree!" said Sue as Anna, still shaky, looked on in amazement.

Randall walked in with them, really excited.

"Our first rescue mission," he grinned as Mary greeted them.

"Hi, I'm Mary. Welcome to God's Gang."

"Mary, this is Kathy, Anna, and . . ." Randall was trying to think of Sue's name.

"Sue," said Sue, "I'm the oldest sister."

"It's nice to meet you, girls. Would you like a grand tour?"

Mary showed the girls around, and the guys invited Rob, who had finally stopped crying, into the kitchen. Tom made him a sandwich and gave him a glass of milk. Rob reassured the Gang, "Please believe me, I won't try anything. I'm sorry about everything. I can't stay here."

"Why not? Where will you go?" asked Mike.

"I don't know. I'll find a place."

"Do you have a job?" Tom asked.

"No, it's hard for a guy like me to get a job, but I know I'll be able to find something."

God's Word does not return Void. When Mary ministered to Rob when he was tied up and crying, he was blessed by hearing God's Word through Mary.

"You don't have a place to stay, and you don't have a job," Tom was concerned about Rob. "You can stay here if you let us lock you in the basement." The expressions on Tom's face let Rob know that he was kidding.

"Rob, you helped us back there, keeping Jim from shooting us, and you showed remorse for attempting to hurt Mary. Besides, you know Jim will be looking for you, so you need to be in a safe place," said Tom.

"We have a nice room in the basement," Randall explained, "And you can help us out here until you get on your feet. But before you decide to live here with us, you must know that everyone must attend church with us every Sunday and Bible study every Wednesday night."

Randall stood there smiling at Rob before taking a drink of his milk.

"I'll be happy to stay, but do you think Mary will mind? One thing, guys, you don't know. I never intended to hurt Mary. My gun had no bullets in it?"

"She won't mind. It's us you have to worry about," Mike laughed, "And we found out that your gun had no bullets in it, so we know that you were not planning to hurt Mary."

"Tom, could I have another sandwich?"

"Okay, another sandwich coming up!"

Mary could see Kathy, Anna, and Sue were pretty tired.

"We can finish the tour tomorrow, girls. Come and choose your rooms. I decorated most of them myself."

One room they came to first that Mary had decorated was a beautiful pale pink with beautiful furniture.

"I love it," squealed Sue as she ran in and jumped on one bed. "We don't need to look at another room; this one is fine. This bed is so comfortable, Kathy. Try the other bed."

All the sisters agreed it was a beautiful room and perfect for them, except it had only two beds.

"It only has two beds, and we want to stay together, Mary. Could we have another bed in here?"

"Sure, Kathy, it's a big room, and the guys can get another bed, dresser, and desk in here so everyone has their own."

Mary got the guys to move another bed, dresser, and desk into the room.

After the girls settled in their room, Mary joined the guys in the kitchen. She poured a glass of milk for herself before she sat down.

"The girls are all settled."

"It's good you are going to be here; the girls need a woman to help look after them," said Clyde.

"That's right. I hadn't expected to have anyone so soon to help," said Mary.

The girls will feel comfortable with a woman they can talk with, and we want to do everything just right. Having a woman chaperone would be in keeping with the laws of our project here.

"Well, I could stay next week?" said Mary.

"You need to stay tonight, Mary. We didn't make any plans for our girls tonight. The woman Mrs. Willis, we hired to work here, won't start for two weeks."

"You're right. I'll ask Aunt Ruth and my girls if they want to stay here for a while. They love this place. It will be like a vacation for them. In the meantime, let's get ready to eat. I know the girls are hungry."

"Mary, could you move in permanently?" Randall asked, "It would be so much easier for everybody. Clyde thinks we could run this place more smoothly if you moved in."

"Yeah," said Clyde. "You won't have to travel so far to cook." They all laughed.

After spending the night at God's Gang, Mary took the sisters to Aunt Ruth's to meet her and her daughters. The sisters played with Lisa and Lear while Mary talked with her aunt. "I'll pack more things when I move in permanently. I didn't want to move in permanently at first, but it will be easier to live there instead of going back and forth, and it's big enough for all of us. I could also use some help. Would you be interested in coming with us? That way, we could still live together as a family and be doing God's work," Mary explained.

"Oh, my, I love being with you and the girls, and I'm just as excited about God's Gang as you are, but what would I do?"

"Aunt Ruth, first of all, you would be a great role model for all the girls. You've given me love and kindness and good advice. Besides, I've got my hands full cooking for everyone, and we'll need your skills to help run the place as we get more girls to live with us. There will be more work than I can manage, even with the girls helping, and the woman we hired doesn't start for two weeks."

"I do love that place, Mary. I'll need to either rent or sell my house if I move," before Mary could respond, she added, "But we can think about that later. Let's tell the girls."

Lisa and Lear screamed for joy when Mary told them they would live at the mansion. They had visited many times and were always intrigued by the number of rooms and places they could play in the mansion. The sisters hugged the girls, Mary, Aunt Ruth, and each other. They were so excited. At last, they were going to be part of a great family. The sisters' parents had died when they were very young, and their grandparents had cared for them.

Laughing, the girls ran up the stairs with Mary and Aunt Ruth as they finished packing what they would need for a few days.

After returning to the mansion that afternoon, Mary and Kathy were the first to see the enormous banner the guys had hung over the archway between the living room and dining room:

WELCOME TO YOUR NEW HOME, PRINCESSES!

"Come see," Mary called to the rest of the girls. As they all looked at the banner, giggling and hugging each other. The guys came up from behind them.

"Surprise," the guys yelled. Sue was so overwhelmed with joy and excitement that she began to cry. Mike walked over to her and put his arms around her. "These are tears of joy, right?"

Sue answered, "We love you guys. Thanks for getting us out of that horrible place. We will always be grateful. I hope we can show you how much we appreciate what you did for us."

"You can show us by being happy. We love you, too. It was truly our pleasure to get you out of there. You don't know how overjoyed we were that our first rescue mission was three beautiful sisters."

After dinner, Mary gathered everyone into the living room to talk about the dream that God had given her.

"I know many of you have heard this before, but I want Kathy, Anna, and Sue to understand what God's Gang means to us. Thank God for allowing my dream to become a reality and blessing us with you, sisters. I hope you find Jesus as your Lord and Savior, as we all have. Only through Him can you overcome things like what you have been through. Our guys were all lost not long ago. They were gang members, living lives not in God's will. But as we got to know each other, they realized that without Jesus, something was missing in their lives. Now, they are all on fire for God. God's Gang is a result of God's love and power. We're praying for you and ask that God bless you and us in our endeavors to help you and other teenage girls like you." Mary then hugged each girl and the guys.

Mary awoke the following day to the sounds of a lawn mower. She looked out the kitchen window and saw Rob pushing the lawn mower. Randall was already in the kitchen and had started coffee.

"I love that boy!" Mary exclaimed as she looked out the kitchen window at Rob.

"What about me?" Randall asked.

Mary turned around to see him smiling at her. "I love you too," she

said, taking the cup of coffee he offered.

Randall finds it hard to be around Mary and cannot tell her how he feels about her. If I work on something with her, it will help me get used to being around her.

"Mary, I know you don't have much to do, so I have something for you to help me with," said Randall, joking about all the empty time she had to fill.

Mary laughed and said, "What is it?"

"Mary sipped her coffee, her eyes focused on Randall, waiting for him to explain what he needed.

CHAPTER TEN

God's Gang Goes To Prison

Randall told Mary about Jake, who was in prison. He also told her about writing to him about God's Gang and how their gangs had changed since they knew Jesus. Randall's friend Jake had also become a Christian.

"Jake has a Bible study at the prison and wants to help the other prisoners know God's love and the importance of receiving Jesus. I thought you could help him and the prisoners there."

"I have often thought about going to prison to minister," she replied. "We can get our whole team to come along. Let me see what I can set up."

Later that day and several times throughout the month, Mary tried to contact the warden at Arthur Kill Correctional Facility. Unfortunately, he was not a Christian and didn't like Christians. The warden was determined to keep Christians out of the prison. So he never took Mary's calls or returned them when she left messages. Because something related neither Mary nor the guys to any of the prisoners, the warden didn't have to let them in to see anyone. Even if he had let them in, that would not have been any help to the other prisoners because he would not let them talk to them. Jake wanted a meeting that would bless all the prisoners.

Mary wasn't going to give up. She knew someone more powerful than the warden. So she prayed.

In a letter, Randall informed Jake that God's Gang, with Mary, was trying to get into the prison to minister to the prisoners. In the letter, he told Jake that the warden had refused to communicate with them. Still, he said not to worry because they would keep trying to get into the prison to minister to everyone there. Jake held onto that letter and Mary's phone number.

One month later, Jake was in prison for armed robbery. One chaplain in the prison led Jake to Jesus while he was awaiting trial.

Jake called Mary. Jake hadn't been a Christian for very long but had significantly grown in the Lord. After he was convicted and sentenced, Jake decided to find ways to honor God while serving his time. Getting Mary to come and minister to the others serving there was just the opportunity he had been praying for, so when he had his next chance to place a call to someone outside the prison, he called Mary.

"Hello, Mary. I know you from Randall's letters. My name is Jake, and I'm at the prisoners at Arthur Hill. I heard about you trying to talk with the warden about bringing Christians here to minister to us. I'm a Christian, and that is what we need here."

"I'm so glad you called, Jake. We have talked with your warden, but surely you know the warden won't let me or my team in now."

" That's why I'm calling the warden you tried to talk with earlier is ill and on leave. The warden who replaced him is a Christian. Please try again. We're excited about having Christian ministers to meet with us."

When the new warden agreed to Mary's request, she called the pastor of her church. He had extensive experience working with prison populations and was happy to work with her in this capacity. Rev. Smith, all the guys, and Mary spent two weeks praying and fasting before their first scheduled visit, asking the Holy Spirit to use them to reach the prisoners. On the appointed day, the group drove to Arthur Hill. They underwent the same procedures all visitors had to experience. Still, they had to meet with the warden before being allowed access to any prisoners. Being a compassionate Christian, the warden wanted this meeting with the prisoners to be successful, so he carefully reviewed the ground rules: During the services, the prisoners had to stay seated. They could not touch any member of the group. The warden stationed guards around the room's perimeter to ensure the prisoners kept all the rules.

The warden then escorted the group to where they could hold their service and returned to his office.

It was a large room with windows high above the floor, each covered with wire mesh and security bars. Access to this room was from two doors, one at each end of the room, solid steel doors with electronic locks controlled from the command post. Cameras were placed strategically around the room to allow remote monitoring. The warden was going to watch the service from his office. A podium in the center of the room for the speakers and a row of chairs were ready.

The prisoners arrived and were escorted into the room and seated. Two guards took their place, facing the prisoners at each end of the stage. Mary exchanged looks with Rev. Smith, who began the service when the last prisoner was seated.

"Good afternoon, gentlemen," Rev. Smith said, introducing the prisoners to Mary and the guys. The prisoners eyed him suspiciously as Rev. Smith looked at the three hundred men before him, noting their crossed arms, dead-eyed stares, and vacant expressions. He began with prayer.

"Dear heavenly Father, thank you for the opportunity to minister to these men. Bless them to receive the gospel of Jesus and understand that you love them and their families and want them to receive eternal life. Bless those who need healing and whatever else they may need. Bless them to read your Word so they understand your promises and how to live for You. We praise You and thank You for answering our prayer in Jesus' Name." Rev. Smith explained the plan of salvation and the joy and benefit of receiving a loving God. As he continued to minister, the men began to warm up to him and his message.

Mary listened intently to the minister but heard someone sniffling behind her. She turned around cautiously and spotted one of the younger men, his eyes red, trying hard not to cry. His sad face revealed pain and agony, and this troubled young man was fighting to keep control. Although the prisoners were supposed to stay seated, and Mary was not to touch any of them, she had to try to comfort this young man.

"Dear God, please show me how to minister to this young man," she prayed.

Then she got up, touched the young man on his shoulder, and motioned for him to come with her to the back of the room with unoccupied seats. One guard started toward her to stop them, but the guard in charge knew the young man was one of their best prisoners, never making any trouble. The guard, in order, somehow trusted that this would be all right, so he waved the other officer to let them alone. Seeing what had happened, Mary looked at the officer in charge and mouthed, "Thank you."

"What's your name?" Mary asked.

"William."

As Rev. Smith continued to preach, Mary held the young man's hand, letting him know that someone cared. She whispered, "Do you know Jesus as your Lord and Savior, William?"

"I've heard of Him but don't know much about Him."

"Do you want to know Him?"

"Yes, but I don't think Jesus would accept me. I've done some terrible things."

"If you invite Jesus into your life, ask for forgiveness, and repent you of your sins, he will grant you eternal life. Now, start believing that.

When you read God's Word, He will help you stay on track. Make up your mind to stay with Jesus no matter what comes your way, and you will always come out on top."

Seeing what was occurring, Rev. Smith continued to preach, giving Mary more time to explain more about God to the young man.

"I believe what you say, Miss Mary, and I want to accept Jesus, but I just don't think I'm good enough."

"None of us are good enough. Jesus took on your sins when He died for you on the cross. If you were the only person on earth, Jesus would have died for you."

After Mary explained the love of God and the meaning of salvation, William was ready to receive Jesus. After William received Jesus, his tears were now obviously tears of joy. As William cried, Mary cried; even the guard closest to them, who had heard the entire exchange, began to cry.

That day was spectacular in the Name of the Lord. The guard and several other prisoners listened to Mary minister to William who received Jesus. Others received Jesus after listening to Rev. Smith's sermon.

After the meeting, many prisoners came to God's Gang. They thanked them for sharing their testimonies and for coming to minister to them. The prisoners hugged them, and some of them cried on their shoulders as God's Gang comforted them. The warden came in and clapped his hands to let everyone know he was happy to see what was happening, even though all the rules were not followed.

The prisoners were lined up to return to their cells. Mary smiled at William, "I'll write to you between our visits to the prison, and I'll bring you more books and articles that will be helpful with your walk with Jesus."

"Oh, thank you, Miss Mary. I hope you come back soon," said William.

As everyone was getting ready to leave, Randall heard someone call, "Randall, Randall," Randall turned around and saw Jake.

"Jake," Randall hugged him, "Where were you? I looked for you."

"I was about as busy as Mary was ministering to William. I led two

of my friends to Jesus."

"Wow!" said Randall, "That's great."

"Hi, Jake. That's wonderful," Mary replied, "And it's nice to meet

you in person. I brought you some books for your Bible study and some

Bibles."

"It's nice to meet you too, Miss Mary, and thank you so much for coming and for the books and especially the Bibles."

Mary hugged him and told him that she would keep in touch.

Clyde came over to Mary, "Before we leave, I would like to ask if there's a prisoner here named Andrew Brown."

"Yes," said the warden who was standing with them., "Would you like to speak with him?"

"Yes," Clyde said, so happy to meet and talk with Andrew.

The warden went to the back of the room and returned with Andrew. Mary had walked away to speak with one of the prisoners, and Clyde and Andrew were alone.

"Hi, my name is Clyde. The police called our house and told us that a person had received Jesus and called to say he was sorry for shooting John and hoped his family would forgive him. Andrew, I want you to know that John's family forgives you. John received Jesus about an hour before he died. So you will see him in Heaven one day."

Andrew stood for a moment, unable to speak, then sat down in a chair, leaned forward, covered his face with his hands, and began to cry, "Oh my God, thank you for letting me hear that John is with Jesus. I'll have peace now, and I can sleep at night. I cry to God every night to forgive me and give me peace. I knew God forgave me, but I had no peace because I didn't know if I had sent someone to hell. I'm so excited to know that John is in Heaven. Thank you all for ministering to us and telling me about John."

Clyde put his arms around Andrew and told him they would keep in touch; then God's Gang left the prison as the prisoners cheered and applauded.

On their way back to God's Gang, "I'm so happy," said Clyde, "The way things turned out. I think we were all great witnesses."

CHAPTER ELEVEN

Rob Accepts Christ, And Laura Is Found

TWO MONTHS LATER, Mary, her daughters, Aunt Ruth, the Gang, Rob, and the three sisters sat near each other in church. The minister's sermon was on assurance of salvation. As Rev. Smith preached, Mary noticed Rob hurriedly wiping his eyes with the back of his hand. A few seconds later, she heard him crying and saw that he continued to cry despite all his efforts to stop. She quietly approached him and sat down, putting her arm around his shoulders. Then she whispered to him, "Rob, would you like to receive Jesus as your Lord and Savior?"

The minister began inviting people to receive Jesus as their personal Savior. As people came to the church's front near the altar to receive Jesus, Rob still sat and cried with Mary.

"I don't know."

"I'll go with you," Mary said softly. Rob looked up at her through tear-filled eyes.

"I just don't think I'm ready because I don't know enough."

Rob stood up, and then he fell to his knees, crying. The minister came down from the pulpit, kneeled beside him, and put his hand on his shoulder. "You have nothing to fear, my friend. Jesus is here waiting for you. You don't have to be good enough. All you need to do is receive Him and believe Him. It is easy to ask for forgiveness and receive Him as your Lord and Savior. May I lead you in a prayer of salvation?" Rob nodded and repeated the sinners' prayer after Rev. Smith.

When he finished praying, Rob jumped up, smiling and shouting, "I know God is real, and He loves me! I can feel it! I felt His presence as though He was right there with me. Thank you, Jesus!"

Rob reached for Rev. Smith's hand to shake it, but Rev. Smith hugged him instead of shaking his hand. The whole church stood and applauded.

When it was time to go, Rob took Mary's hand, "Let's go; I can't wait to tell everybody that I'm one of them now."

At dinner, Rob was still high on the Holy Spirit. He talked about how happy he felt after receiving Jesus as his Lord. He told everyone about how different he felt and how peaceful he felt. Anna asked him what Rev. Smith said that made him so happy. Rob was delighted to talk about his encounter with Jesus. All three sisters were mesmerized as they listened to Rob talk about Jesus and how he could feel God's love and presence.

"Rob," Kathy asked, what did you mean when you said I could feel His presence?"

"I don't know how to explain it, but I could feel His love around me. I felt so light like I could walk on air. When Rev. Smith said, 'He's here among us now,' I was overwhelmed with the assurance that He was not only real, He was there! Jesus was there and let me know He approved of me!"

"That is so cool," said Anna, "I can't wait to go back to church."

That night, as Mary walked past the sisters' room, she overheard them talking about a friend they wanted to help. She knocked on their door, already slightly open, "I heard you talking about one of your friends. Do you mind telling me about her? We may be able to help."

"She's with the same people we were with," said Sue D., "And the men at that place are evil. Laura begged them to leave her alone, but they wouldn't stop trying to make her cooperate. She cried all the time. One of Jim's men grabbed her when she walked near the Red Zone, thinking she was one of their prostitutes. They kept her anyway When they realized Laura was not one of their girls. They locked her in a room when the men didn't want anything to do with her, but they forgot she was there. She couldn't stop crying. Their customers and Jim's guys didn't know what to do with her. Before they locked her in a room, I overheard one of them say they were considering getting rid of her. After I heard that, I couldn't sleep for a long time. I never told my sisters; I didn't want to frighten them. We were all locked in separate rooms at night when we weren't out on the streets together.

One night, one of Jim's men didn't realize he'd left my door unlocked. Since the men were not around that night, I thought it was my chance to call for help, but those evil men had the phone turned off at the front desk, so I couldn't call anyone for help. I was locked in the building from the outside, so I couldn't get out of the building either. I sneaked out of my room, got the keys to all the rooms from the front desk, and looked for the room Laura would be in. I had heard the men say they would lock Laura in one of the rooms. We had not seen her on the streets, so I didn't know what the men had done with her, but I was hoping to find the room they put Laura in.

We had only seen Laura walking and crying on the streets once when we worked the streets. I feared what they might have done with her, but I had to look for her. I looked at rooms and found one with Laura Daniels' name on the door. I didn't know Laura's last name, so I thought it must be the room she was in."

Sue D found out that the men gambled on a particular night.

"The mem gambled on this night and returned to the building early the next morning. So, since my door was unlocked and I had some time, I decided to find the kitchen before I entered the room where Laura was. I had a feeling she would need food. There was a big box in the kitchen. I filled it with canned foods, crackers, and other non-perishable foods, a can opener, a knife, a fork, and a spoon. The box was heavy, but I got it to the room's door. I put the box down at the door, ran back to the kitchen, got a case of bottled water, brought it to the room, and then unlocked Laurs's door."

"Wow!" said Mary, "You are remarkable, Sue D."

"I had to find her, Mary. Laura screamed when the door opened. She thought it was Jim or one of his men. Laura was so happy to see me. We hugged and cried. Then we brought the box into the room, and I held Laura and attempted to comfort her. When I told Laura, I didn't know her last was Daniels. She told me that her last name was Madison.

I said, oh! It is!" We laughed at that. That must have been a room for someone named Laura Daniels, who was no longer there, and they forgot that they put Laura in that room. I'm glad I didn't know her last name because I would've kept looking for Laura in other rooms."

"You were courageous to do what you did to help Laura,"
Mary complimented Sue D.

Sue D told Mary how they thought they would escape: "I gave Laura our grandmother's phone number and told her to slip out of the room when she had the chance in case the men forgot to turn off the phone at the front desk. Laura's room was close enough to hear the man talking sometimes. Then I told her to call our grandmother and tell her where we were and that we were locked in a building from the outside and we could not escape. As I said, I tried to call my grandmother, but the phone was turned off. They must turn the phone off when they all leave.

"We're so grateful to you, Mary," said Anna, "For helping us escape those evil men. Laura and the other girls were still there, but I worried more about Laure because she had no food or anything and was alone. I can't wait for her to be out of that horrible place. I told Laura to ensure her grandmother knows what's happening here."

"We will pray for Laura and all the girls at the Red Zone. I believe God will see that all of them are rescued." Mary said.

"Get some sleep, girls. Good night," Mary said, thinking how nice it was to have the girl safe from the Red Zone.

"I dread calling our grandmother," said Kathy. I'm so ashamed of running away just because she wouldn't let us go out partying. Nothing was worse than being kidnapped by Jim's men."

The girl's names were misspelled on the police report, and that's why they were never reported missing. That doesn't make sense to me. It sounds like the police were negligent.

Kathy and her sister talked with their grandmother and told her where they lived and that they would write often. The sisters spoke with her and were so relieved when she forgave them and said to them that she loved them. Their grandmother was overjoyed that they were safe. She told them that she had cried many nights over all of them, and now she could finally sleep peacefully. Mary told their grandmother, Mrs. Paul, that she could spend time there with her granddaughters anytime.

Mary told her they had enough room for her to visit as long as she wanted.

Later that week, Mrs. Paul called and said she was excited to visit them during the Easter weekend.

Laura was happy that the sisters had escaped and was determined to join them. She had to be careful since the men didn't know that she was there and that her room was no longer locked. She'd been trying to contact Kathy's grandmother for several weeks but had no success so far. Someone always managed to be around. She'd almost been discovered the few times she had managed to get to the desk.

One night, after she slipped out of the room, she heard someone coming. So she grabbed a bag with two cheeseburgers, fries, and a carton of milk and rushed to her room. She opened the door just a little and could hear two men talking.

"Frank's food is gone. He hadn't been here to get," one of the men said.

"What happened to it?" The other man said.

The two men looked at each other and headed for the stairs to look for whoever had taken Frank's food. But before they could get to the first landing, the phone rang. They both stopped, and one returned to the desk and answered the phone. A few seconds later, he replaced the receiver and looked at the other man, "Forget the food. Jim wants us to come to the hospital right now. Frank got hit by a car, and he's in the hospital."

"Nice to have cheeseburgers and fries for a change. And, oh yes, milk! Thank you, Lord!"

When Laura heard the main door close, she began eating the burger. She tried several more times later that same night to call the sisters' grandmother, but someone was walking in the hall each time.

The next night, Laura waited until the house was quiet before running to the phone, but just as she was about to pick up the receiver, she heard footsteps and ducked under the desk. It was the janitor doing his version of sweeping. Fortunately, he was a hit-and-miss kind of guy and didn't go behind the desk to sweep. But she couldn't risk him finding her, so she returned to the room when he left the area briefly.

She slept for about an hour and later tried again. Again, the janitor came in to take care of something. Back safely in the room, she thanked God for having a bed and sink and went back to sleep.

When she awoke, the building was quiet except for the phone ringing. That meant the phone was not cut off. She was still determining the time but knew it had to be late. She opened the door a little and listened. All was quiet. Carefully, she slipped out of the room. She waited a few more minutes, ensuring no one had heard her. She carefully lifted the phone from the desk and dialed the sister's grandmother. The clock on the wall read two o'clock. Indeed, Mrs. Paul would be home at this hour as she held her breath, listening to the phone ring.

"Hello?" The voice sounded groggy and a bit uncertain.

"Mrs. Paul, this is Laura. I'm a friend of Kathy's," Laura whispered.

"Hello? I can barely hear you. Can you speak louder?" Laura glanced around nervously and decided to risk speaking a bit louder, "It's Laura. I'm a friend of Kathy. She told me to call you."

"Oh, yes, Laura," Mrs. Paul said, her voice sounding more alert, "Kathy called and said you might call. She gave me a number for you to call. Write this number down." Laura got a pen and a piece of paper from the desk drawer and wrote the number down. She couldn't take a chance on forgetting the number.

"Call Mary as soon as you can. She and her friends were the ones who helped Kathy and her sisters escape, and they plan to help you the same way, but you have to contact them so they can put things in motion. Using the police is too dangerous. God bless you, Laura. Call Mary as soon as you can."

After Mrs. Paul hung up, Laura sat quietly for a few seconds, listening for evidence that someone was up and might discover her, but everything remained silent. Carefully, she dialed Mary's number.

"Hello?" said a sleepy voice, "God's Gang. Can I help you?" Mary's voice became more alert as she listened, knowing it could be Laura.

"This is Laura. I need to speak to Mary."

"Laura, we've been waiting for your call. This is Mary."

Mary has no idea this is her friend Linda's daughter on the phone, and Laura doesn't know she is talking to her mom's friend Mary.

"I can't talk long." Said Laura.

"I understand. We've been praying for your safety and have a plan to get you out of the Red Zone. Can you get out on the street tonight or tomorrow morning? We can have someone in position to pick you up as soon as you show up."

"I don't think so, Mary. I'm supposed to be locked in a room. They have never come for me since I've been here, so I'm sure they have forgotten I'm in this room. If I get back on the street, they will realize that I'm here. Then there's no telling what they will do to me."

"Okay, Laura. God is with us. He'll help us formulate a different plan. Try to call back tonight. We'll pray for your safety and for a revelation."

"Thanks, Mary. I'll call back as soon as I can."

Mary told the sisters and the guys about her conversation with Laura.

"I'm so excited because I know you guys will get Laura out of that hell hole soon?" said Sue D.

"Yes, Sue D, "We must devise a different plan. I'm sure those crooks have forgotten about her. We need to get her away before they discover she's still there."

"They obviously aren't checking on her," Mary concluded, "But she can't get back on the street for us to pick her up the way we did the three of you. Just keep praying. God will give us an answer."

Throughout the day, Mary prayed unceasingly for God's revelation, for wisdom to fashion a plan to free Laura from Jim's clutches. Mary fasted as well and remained awake through the night, praying that Laura would be able to call. Around two o'clock the following day, the phone rang.

"Laura," Mary knew it had to be Laura.

"Hello, Mary. I learned that the men are all attending a party this evening, and the whole house should be empty by nine o'clock.

"Okay, Laura, here's what you need to do."

CHAPTER TWELVE

God Answers Laura's Prayers

MIKE, RANDALL, AND Tom were in their van, parked on the side of some bushes near the entrance to Jim's building. Kathy came with them because the guys had never seen Laura. They lhad watched the men leaving the building since eight o'clock. It was nine-thirty, and the building was dark and quiet aside from a dim light on the first floor. They waited. At ten, Laura prayed that one key from the desk would fit the door leading out of the building, and when it did, she came out from the front door.

"There she is!" Kathy said quietly, pointing to Laura's frame in the doorway. Mike started the engine and drove up the street, stopping just across from the building where Laura was walking on the sidewalk. Randall opened the side door quietly and motioned to Laura. Laura moved quickly down the sidewalk, trying to stay in the shadows until she was close enough to the van to get in without being seen.

"Laura," Kathy called out to her as she ran to the van and jumped in. Randall quickly closed the door as Mike stepped on the gas, causing the tires to squeal as he pulled away from the curb. He looked into the rearview mirror and saw two men running after them.

"Get down; there are two men with guns," Mike said as he swerved from side to side, not allowing the man with the gun to focus on the van if he shot at them. As they crouched down in their seats, they heard a gunshot. Randall raised his head to glance in the side mirror and saw one man fall to the ground. They later learned the bullet had hit something and ricocheted back at the gunman, killing him instantly.

The other man was Jim, who, instead of turning the street into the Wild West, memorized the license plate numbers as the van sped away. The light on the street allowed him to see well enough to get the license plate numbers. He smiled as the truck disappeared into the darkness.

"Well," said Jim, taking a pin and his checkbook from his wallet and writing the license plate number on one of his checks.

"Sometimes it pays to go to a party late. I know just how to find my girls. That was Laura, the girl who cried all the time. Where in the world has she been? That's where my other girls are, I'm sure."

Kathy told Laura how nice living at God Gang was and how wonderful everyone was, especially Mary. When they entered the mansion, Kathy cried, "She's here. Laura's here!"

Sue and Anna came running down the stairs to see her. They were still hugging when Mary joined them in the foyer.

When Mary saw Laura, she was shocked. "Laura!" Mary screamed.

I had no idea I was talking to you." They stood there staring at each other, hugged, stopped, looked at each other, and hugged again.

"I didn't know when I called it was your number, and I didn't recognize your voice," said Laura.

"I can't believe I didn't know it was you, Laura, that I was talking to."

"I didn't know it was you that I was talking to either, Mary."

Mary stood there, looking at Laura. You will be a wonderful surprise for your mother, and I'm so happy to see you, Laura!"

Laura held on to Mary and began to cry. Mary's arms were around her as she consoled her.

"Let's call your mother now; she will be so happy. She can finally stop crying!"

"I'm so sorry, Mary. I never wanted to hurt Mom. I love her. What do I say to her after what I did?"

"You'll find the right words, and I'll support you." Mary took Laura to her room for privacy when she talked to her mother on the phone; then, she dialed Linda's number and waited for her to answer.

"Hello?" Linda answered her phone.

"Hi, Linda. I have someone on the phone who wants to talk to you. Hold on!" Mary winked at Laura, gave her the phone, and left the room.

"Mom, it's Laura."

Mary could hear Linda shouting for joy even though she was leaving the room.

"Where are you? How are you? Are you all right?"

"I'm fine now, Mom. I'm with Mary. She and her friends got me out of a horrible place."

"Oh, I love you, I love you, and I missed you. I'm so glad you're safe," said Laura's mom. "Put Mary on the phone." Laura handed the phone back to Mary.

"Mary, thank you so much. I can never repay you for what you have done."

"Linda, God has answered our prayers. He's the one that has made this all happen."

"I know, Mary, but because of your obedience to God, you have also been a great blessing to us."

"Linda, Laura has been through a lot. Can you come to New York to be with her?"

"Believe me, I want to, but I don't know how I can afford to get there right now."

"That's okay. I'll wire you the money. God has blessed us with more than enough so we can bless others. I'll send the money tomorrow morning. Then call me once you've made travel arrangements so we can pick you up at the airport."

Mary took Laura upstairs to the sister's room. Laura was going to share a room with the sisters for a while. They were all so happy to be in the same room. They will one day want their rooms, but for now, nothing is more important than being together. When Linda comes, Laura may share a room with her mother for a while. Laura needed the reassurance of familiar faces around her for now. Randall and Mike put another bed in the sister's room.

"This is a big room. It's enough room to play touch football in here!" Randall said as he threw a dust cloth at Mary.

"I hope you guys have learned not to play ball in the house. Remember that beautiful lamp you broke playing ball in the living room?" Mary said as she threw the dust cloth back at Randall.

Later that evening, Mary found Laura a nightgown, and when Laura got in bed, she began to cry. Mary held her in her arms and prayed with her. A quick prayer can make a big difference. After that short but powerful prayer, Laura opened up to Mary, and at one point, she laughed about one of Jim's men falling on his way up the stairs to lock her in a room. Laura is a Christian, and she has faith in God's promises. She prayed they would be set free on her way to the room. His falling was like a sign to her that they would all be free soon. That thought often comforted her.

"Oh Mary, I feel so much better; you and your team rescuing us makes you guys miracle workers," Laura said as she lay in bed, excited about seeing her mother soon.

God and our guys deserve most of the credit for rescuing you girls. God has blessed us with a great team."

Mary tucked her in and sat with her until she was asleep.

The following day, Kathy came down for breakfast.

"We tried to get Laura up, but she said okay and went back to sleep. Should we try again?"

"No," Mary's soft voice showed concern for Laura, "Just let her sleep. She needs a long rest."

Laura slept in until dinnertime. Everybody got ready for dinner. When the girls came to the table, and Laura saw Rob at the table, memories of The Red Zone made her very upset. She ran out of the dining room and locked herself in the bathroom.

Rob began to cry. "I never hurt Laura, but I didn't do anything to help her either."

"That's right, you worked at the Red Zone with Jim," Mary remembered. "I'll tell Laura that you are not the same person and are a committed Christian now. She'll understand."

Mary knocked on the bathroom door and pleaded with Laura to come out, but she wouldn't.

"Let me talk to her?" Anna asked. Anna knocked on the bathroom door. "Laura, I know how you feel. I was terrified of Rob. Just think about it: Rob was afraid, too. He was so afraid of Jim and the other men who worked there that he did whatever they told him. That's not the only thing I want you to know about Rob. He saved our lives at the risk of his own. Does that sound like someone you should be afraid of? Jim had a gun, and he was threatening to kill us. Rob came in from a back room and knocked Jim's gun out of his hand while Tom, Mike, and Randall wrestled him to the floor. Rob has given his life to Jesus, and you know better than I how that can change a person, Laura. He's sitting at the table, crying because you're afraid of him. He has become a loveable teddy bear."

After a while, Laura slowly opened the bathroom door and came out. Anna took Laura's hand and returned to the dining room, where Rob was still crying. Laura looked at him, had compassion on him, and said, "Don't cry, Rob. I'm okay now."

After about an hour, Laura and Rob talked and trusted each other. They ate dinner and sang songs. After dinner, Mary, the sisters, and Mary's daughters washed the dishes. They cleaned the kitchen as they talked about how wonderful it would be living together at the mansion.

After dinner, Laura went to the sister's room and went back to sleep.

Mary knew that God's Gang had rescued all four girls from the Red Zone and needed more than a safe place to live. They also required Christian counseling to help them heal from the physical and psychological abuse that they had gone through. Before the girls had come to God's Gang, Mary had contacted various professionals in New York to find the appropriate counselors for girls who needed counseling. This enabled her to prepare information on counselors for Laura and the sisters. Mary noticed Laura seemed more troubled than the other girls, so she decided to see if she could get to the bottom of what was bothering her. After talking with Laura, Mary realized she felt guilty and blamed herself for everything. Laura had been left alone in a room and discovered the men had put her there and had forgotten about her. She also knew that when she was on the street, everyone was always locked in, so she worried about them finding her in that unlocked room. Not knowing what was going to happen to Laura made her very afraid.

"Laura, we have all done something that we regret, blame ourselves, and feel guilty. It's normal to feel that way. But when we ask God to forgive us, there is no need to keep feeling that way. God loves you, and He wants you to be happy. So forgive yourself and be happy."

Mary could tell that Laura was feeling a little better. Laura hadn't gone through nearly as much abuse and trouble as the sister, but she was affected more by what had happened to her. Being alone and knowing that you could be killed at any time is enough to drive someone crazy with fear, even though none of the men at the Red Zone had touched her.

Later, Laura came down from the room, where she had taken another long nap.

"Hi, sleepy head," Mary greeted as she joined them in the den.

"Hi, Mary. I've never slept so much in my life."

"That's good. That's one way the body deals with stress. It will be a little while longer before your mother gets the money and arranges to come to New York. Would you like to talk with her again? I know you two didn't have much time to talk last night."

"Yes," Laura began to cry softly. Mary left the room as Laura dialed, "Hi, Mom."

"Laura? Are you all right? I'm coming to New York as soon as possible, baby."

"Oh, Mom, I'm just so sorry for what I did to you and the mess I got into. Please forgive me. I love you," Laura cried.

"Oh, sweetheart, of course, I forgive you, and what's more, God forgives you too. But you must forgive yourself before you can truly have peace."

"Mary told me that I need to forgive myself, too. Mom, I'm beginning to forgive myself. I'm also beginning to feel peaceful. I knew God was always watching over me, but I was still afraid sometimes. There were so many bad things happening at that place. But I have to tell you that God protected me. None of the men touched me because I couldn't stop crying. Jim was so angry with me that he had one of his men put me in a room, but that stupid guy forgot to lock the door. My crying repulsed the men, and they didn't want anything to do with me. It's funny when you think about it; they put me in a room, forgot to lock the door, and then just forgot I was even there. If they had remembered that I was there, I wouldn't have been able to escape that horrible place."

Laura continued, "Sue D, one of the girls at the Red Zone, heard one of the men say that they had put me in a room. She decided to look for me. Sue D had a feeling that I would not have food or anything. She got the keys from the desk and unlocked my door. Sue D brought a box of food and a case of bottled water that she got from the kitchen to the room that I was in. She had to make several trips for all the stuff she bought. I can't imagine the men not milling some of those things. I don't know what I would have done without that food. Boy, was I glad to get it! I was so hungry. The next night, Sue brought clean clothes she found in one of the closets, a toothbrush, toothpaste, a face towel, and face soap. She is so brave I would have been terrified. One of Jim's monster men discovered Sue D's door unlocked. That was the end of Sue D's partial freedom."

"I can't tell you how happy I am that you are safe," said Linda,

"Mary and I prayed for your safe return every day. I felt in my heart that God would bring you back to me. I learned the power of prayer and how it brings peace when you pray and praise God. Only that would bring me peace when I didn't know where you were."

"Mom, God was always there, and He surely protected me. And it also comforted me to know that you and others were praying for me. It may seem strange, but there were times when I could feel the presence of God because people were praying for me."

CHAPTER THIRTEEN
Linda Has Very Good News For Mary

LAURA SPOTTED HER mother coming down the escalator to the baggage claim area at the airport.

"There she is, Mary," she squealed. The airport is crowded, with people from flights arriving around the world. Laura and Mary made their way to the bottom of the escalator, coming just a second or two before Linda. Linda dropped her carry-on and embraced Laura, forgetting the rush of people behind her.

"I think we better move over a bit, ladies," Mary directed as she picked up Linda's luggage and herded them as she led them out of traffic.

By this time, both Laura and Linda were in tears. Linda looked at Mary and smiled. "Oh, Mary, how can I ever make it up to you for what you have done for us?"

"Just being my friend is enough. Remember the dream Joseph and I had? Well, it's coming true. God has blessed us above all I could ever think of. I want you to meet everyone at God's Gang. Our guys are the real heroes; they are the ones that rescued the girls."

Mary was eager to hear about their church family in St. Louis.

"Have I got good news for you, Mary!" Linda said that after Mary successfully navigated them out of the airport parking lot and headed toward God's Gang in Mary's car, Linda was excited to tell Mary what was going on at St. Louis.

"Rev. Fox called a meeting and asked everyone to forgive him for all the wrong things he had done and how he had been treating the church members. I told him that you had found Laura. I also told him I was going to New York to be with her and we would stay with you; he gave me a hundred dollars for my trip!"

"Really? My, he has changed! I'm so happy to hear that."

"Oh! Oh! Uncle David has given his heart to Jesus and joined our Church and Mary; he's no longer on drugs!" said Linda.

"Oh, thank You, Lord! Thank You, Lord! Aunt Ruth is going to be so happy. I can't wait to tell her. "Hallelujah! God does answer prayers; Aunt Ruth has been praying for her brother David for years."

Linda updated Mary with news about her Church and friends in St. Louis. Mary gave Linda a little background on the work she had been doing and what had happened with Laura, who had fallen asleep in the back seat.

At God's Gang, Mary introduced Linda to everybody waiting in the living room. Then she rushed into the kitchen to find her aunt.

"Aunt Ruth," she said, hugging her, "Uncle David has accepted Jesus as his savior! And he's off drugs! Linda just told me he also joined our Church in St. Louis."

"Oh, thank You, Jesus," said Aunt Ruth. "Where is Linda?"

"She's in the living room," Mary said as they walked into the living room.

"Linda, tell me all about David and what happened," Aunt Ruth asked.

Linda explained, "One guy at David's job invited David to Church. David was not interested in the church services, but he knew that Carol, a woman he admired, went to the Church, so he went. Carol invited him to Bible study. He was not interested in the Bible study either, but he went anyway to see Carol. He and Carol became close friends, and she eventually led him to Jesus.

David was going to surprise you and bring Carol to New York to meet you, but he decided to invite you to his wedding in St. Louis instead.

Aunt Ruth was so excited that she got Mary to inform everyone about David's wedding plans and for them to plan to attend the wedding.

Aunt Ruth explains why she is so happy for her brother. David.

"David rarely wrote, but when he did, his letter was sad. I decided to open the letter when I had time to pray for him," said Mary.

"Where is the letter?" Aunt Ruth asked, "Read it now. Linda said he has met someone he goes to Bible study with, and you have not gotten a letter from David for some time now, so his letters are probably happy now."

Mary got the letter, and she and Runt Ruth were so happy about this letter. David was inviting them to his wedding.

"Linda was right about the letter being happy; so glad we read it now before we prayed, not we can thank God for the Good news.

"I'm so happy for David. He has accepted Jesus as his Lord and Savior and found someone who loves him. Said Aunt Ruth.

Then Aunt Ruth hugged Linda and thanked her for bringing such good news.

After spending several days with Laura and Mary, Linda had to return to St. Louis to settle her affairs so she could return to the mansion and spend more time with Laura.

Welcome back, Linda," Rev. Fox greeted her as she entered the Church, "How's Mary? Did Laura come back with you?"

"Mary is fine, and she sends her love. Laura didn't come with me, but she's doing fine considering everything she's been through. God truly answers our prayers. Even though she was kept against her will by those evil men, God protected her. She could not stop crying, which turned the men off, so no one ever wanted to deal with her, so the men never touched her."

"Praise God. We were so glad to hear that Laura was safe and with Mary, and it's so nice to have you back. We have missed you, Mary, and Laura. Please come back this summer and bring your potluck dish to our picnic," Rev. Fox said, smiling.

"I know Mary would love to come back this summer. We will visit, and it might be before the summer. I'm not going to stay long. I need to get back to Laura. She's seeing a wonderful Christian counselor and making good progress. She said to tell all her friends hello and that she misses them and hopes to see them soon. Mary is involved with a wonderful ministry that has always been her dream."

Linda described God's Gang and its work to Rev. Fox. He and the Church joined her in praying for Mary's ministry and thanking God for Laura's safe return.

Two weeks later, Rev. Fox and his wife drove Linda to the airport. She managed to rent her house, which would give her an income while staying at God's Gang.

"We're going to miss you," Rev. Fox said as they pulled into the curbside check at the airport.

"I promise to keep in touch, Reverend. And we'll visit as soon as we can."

"Whatever you do, don't forget about our annual church picnic and your famous potluck dish!" Rev. Fox reminded her again.

"You can count on us being here, and I'll bring Mary and my potluck dish with me."

"That would be wonderful. Bring everyone from God's Gang. I'd love to meet them and have them share their testimonies. We can find a way to help with their ministry.

"Thank you again, Rev. Fox, for all your help in the last two weeks. I'll be in touch." Linda hugged him and his wife, checked her bags, and entered the terminal, stopping to wave as they drove away.

Home at God's Gang, Linda talked about her trip to St. Louis and how "Rev. Fox wants you and all of God's Gang to come back with me for the annual church picnic this summer."

It was the first week of December, and the weather had turned cold. The skies were an ashen gray, and the promise of snow was coming. Thinking about the picnic, Mary felt warm, summery, and homesick.

"That's great. We sure did love those picnics."

Mary gazed out the window as a few snowflakes drifted down the sidewalk. She shivered slightly and said, "Why don't we go sooner? School will be out for all the girls in about two weeks, and they have ten days off for Christmas. Rob and the guys have a month off from the universities. And the other guys won't work in construction because of the weather. So they will be free to come too."

"I'm sure Rev. Fox would love to have the guys give their testimonies," said Linda. "So, the two ladies began making plans.

Even though they wouldn't be in New York for Christmas, Mary wanted the mansion to reflect the Christmas spirit, so they went Christmas shopping. They needed decorations for the mansion, presents, and a few things for their trip. Everyone loaded into the van, and when they got to the mall.

"The guys don't know what they're missing, not going shopping with us," said Mary.

"They know what they're missing; that's why the guys don't want to go shopping," Linda said as they laughed.

Mary and Linda shopped on different floors from Laura and the sisters and told them to meet at McDonald's in the mall later. Mary had given each girl $150 to spend. They bought gifts for everybody and themselves. They had more fun than they had ever had.

When they returned to God's Gang late that afternoon, Linda entered the den and saw Randall put a present under the tree. When Randall left, she went to the tree, picked up the gift, and looked at the tag. Mary entered the room a minute later.

"What are you up to, Linda?" Mary asked as she bounced into the room, filled with the spirit of Christmas and the thoughts of returning to St. Louis.

"Do you know who put this gift under the Christmas tree?" Linda asked as she showed Mary the gift. "No, I don't."

"Randall put it there, and it has your name on it." Mary looked at Linda blankly, not sure of her attitude.

"You do know that Randall is in love with you, don't you, Mary?"

"Well, I know he likes me, but . . ."

"He more than likes you, Mary. He's in love with you. When you aren't looking, his eyes are always on you. When you ask for something, he can't get it fast enough. When you're late, he's so concerned about you. He called to ask why you were late. He worries about you as a mother, worries about her children. Everybody else knows how he feels about you, but they don't want to embarrass him, so they pretend not to notice. How can you not notice?"

"I do like Randall a lot, but I never thought of him that way," said Mary.

"Why not? He's such a nice, caring man," Linda said, a little annoyed.

"I'm sorry, Linda, I thought ,,,."

Linda interrupted, "Randall is a Christian. Ask God to help you decide what to do. He's such a nice guy, and your girls love him; they even call him Dad."

"I don't know if I'm ready for that relationship. I know it's been years since Joseph died, but I still miss him."

"I know, honey, but Joseph would want you to be happy. Maybe it's time to move on just as you have with the rest of your life by coming here and starting God's Gang. Let's pray about it."

That night, Mary thought about how nice it felt to learn that someone was in love with her. Randall has become a gentle and kind man, and he's so much fun to be around. Mary thought. It sure feels nice to have his strong arms around me when he hugs me for doing him a favor. Mary turned out the light next to her bed and went to sleep.

Mary doesn't know it yet, but she's falling in love with Randall.

A week later, Randall came to Mary's room one night and knocked on her door. "Mary, may I talk with you?"

Sure, Randall, what's wrong?"

"Nothing. I need to talk to you. Will you put on a coat and go for a drive with me? I need to talk to you."

"Okay. Are you sure there's nothing wrong?"

"No, I'm not sure, so will you put on a coat and come with me?"

"First, you say nothing, and then you say I'm not sure. That doesn't make much sense."

Mary put her coat on, and they drove to the park where Randall parked the car.

"What's on your mind, Randall?"

"You're always on my mind, Mary. I love you."

Randall didn't say anything else. He started the car, drove back to God's Gang, and walked Mary back to her room. Neither of them said a word. When Mary put her hand on the doorknob to open her door, Randall stopped her, turned her around to face him, gently put his arms around her waist, kissed her quickly on her forehead, and attempted to leave. Mary grabbed him, stood on her toes, put her arms around his neck, and kissed him on his cheek; then she said, "You're such a sweet guy."

Then she turned and went into her room. Randall went upstairs to his room. He said, "Praise You God. I love you; thank you for everything.

"Oh, my God. I'm in love with Randall." Mary said as she entered her room.

CHAPTER FOURTEEN
Jim Finds Out Where The Gang Lives

AFTER EVERYONE LEFT the following evening, Linda and Mary sat at the kitchen table, drinking coffee and discussing plans for their trip to St. Louis.

"Did you hear something?" Linda asked as she put down her cup.

"No. It's probably just the wind." Mary took a sip of coffee. Then she heard an essential turning in the lock, and the doorknob jiggled.

"Everyone's gone, and no one will be home for hours. I am still determining who that could be. We should call the police, Linda."

When the back porch door opened, Mary had just risen from the table to get the phone, and Jim came in.

"Merry Christmas, ladies," Jim sneered as he pointed a gun at them. "Just thought I'd drop by to collect my stolen property."

He walked closer to Mary and waved Linda out of her seat to join her. Both women backed away from him until they were stopped at the counter's edge.

"Now, where are my girls?" Jim points his gun at them.

Before either woman could respond, Rob came through the front door and froze when he saw Jim. Rob walked in on Jim again, pointing a gun at someone.

"Well, what do you know? Scary Rob has defected. Lucky day for me," Jim said, waving Rob to join the ladies. "I've been looking for you, too. I owe you for what you did to me."

Rob stood there, knowing he had to do something. Jim was waving the gun around, first at Mary and then at him, but Rob was most afraid that he would shoot Mary.

"Get over here, Rob. Join our little party," Jim commanded. His eyes revealed the anger and hatred building in him. You may need a little incentive."

Jim aimed the gun toward Mary, but Rob leaped in front of her before he could pull the trigger. Jim fired, and the bullet entered Rob, throwing him to the floor. Rob didn't even take the time to call on Jesus for help before he acted. God will bless him anyway for his unselfish act.

Linda reached behind her, grabbed the pot of hot coffee, and threw the steaming hot coffee in Jim's face. Jim screamed and dropped the gun, holding his face. Mary hit him on the head with a big iron skillet, knocking him to the floor. Then Linda picked up his gun and pointed it at him while Mary called 911. She quickly began working on Rob, trying to stop the bleeding until the ambulance arrived. By the time the ambulance got there, Rob was unconscious. Observe how God can change a person. Rob held a gun at Mary, trying to make the gang give him money. Although he had no intention of shooting Mary with an unloaded weapon, this time, he risked his life to save her. Earlier, Rob had risked his life to save Anna.

With Jim in prison, the police raided his place, and the other guys who worked there were arrested and taken to jail. Jim thought his threat to blow up the building if the police showed up made him feel safe from the police because the police knew that he had rigged the place to blow up if the police showed up there. Still, he was the only one ready to detonate the bomb. Being handcuffed made him unable to complete his plan.

God's Gangs helped the eleven girls recused from the Red Zone. Counselors are helping them return to everyday life. Mary talked with all of them and assured them that God's Gang would have an excellent place for them to stay as soon as the new rooms were built on the mansion, which would be in about two months. In the meantime, they had temporary places to stay.

Mrs. Willis was so much help with everything. Mary and Linda were free to leave the girls at the mansion anytime because Mrs. Willis was there when Aunt Ruth wasn't there.

Mary and Linda rode in the ambulance with Rob to the hospital. Linda called the gang, and they came to the hospital after hearing about Rob. They waited for the doctors to leave the operating room at the hospital with news of Rob's condition.

The surgeons came out to see God's Gang in the waiting room. He informed them that he had removed the bullet, but they would have to wait to see the outcome concerning Rob's recovery.

Two days later, Rob was still in a coma. The gang took turns sitting with him and reading the Bible to him as they continued to talk to him and pray for his recovery. After three days, Anna wanted to talk to Rob, so she went to his room and held Rob's hand tightly.

"Open your eyes and talk to me, Rob. You're upsetting everybody," she complaiing ed, trying to remain strong. But tears won out as Anna began to cry.

"God is going to heal you. I just know He is. Please, Rob, talk to me." Anna still trying to reach Rob by talking to him. "Remember how sad you were when I saw you sitting at the table when we were getting ready to eat? Laura was so afraid of you? I let her know that you were our hero. Everything worked out. And it will work out again as soon as you wake up. Laura's not afraid of you now. She loves you. We all love you. I love you, Rob." Anna began to pray, "Oh, God, my sisters, and I believed in You. Rob made it easy for us to believe in You. When he said, he felt Your love and presence. Dear Jesus, we all have given our lives to You because of Rob. I praise You and thank You for healing, Rob, in Jesus' Name. Aman."

Anna held Rob's hand and said boldly, "Okay, Rob, God is healing you, so open your eyes and say something."

Rob slowly opened his eyes. "Something," he whispered and smiled. Anna laughed and yelled for Mary. The nurse rushed in to see what was happening, afraid Rob's condition had deteriorated. But as they entered the room, they saw Anna laughing and Rob smiling at her, his eyes open and full of life.

"Praise God," said Mary, "You're back, Rob. How do you feel?"

"I feel happy that you guys are my friends."

The nurse checked the monitors, took his vital signs, and paged for the doctor.

"Rob, "I asked God to heal you," Anna said, and He did!"

"I know. I heard you praying, but I couldn't move at first; then I felt like warm oil was going through my body, and then I could move. Is God great or what?"

The schools were finally out for the holidays. The doctors couldn't believe Rob had recuperated so fast and could not find a reason not to release him from the hospital. So Mary and her daughters, Linda and her daughter, the three sisters, and the five men boarded the plane for St. Louis and Rev. Fox's church. That Sunday at church, Rev. Fox and the church members greeted them warmly. Their friends immediately surrounded Mary, Linda, and Laura, each trying to talk to them simultaneously. After introducing everyone, they felt loved and welcomed. Lisa and Lear ran into the arms of the daycare workers who were in their rooms when they went to the daycare there. The daycare workers hugged Lear and Lisa and gave them gifts.

"Listen, everyone, we will learn about Mary's work and God's Gang. The Lord has truly directed them; they are doing wonderful work for Him. Now let's pray," Rev. Fox spoke firmly but lovingly to his congregation, motioning them into their seats.

After the prayer, he asked Mary to come up front. As she spoke to the congregation, she felt the Holy Spirit was with her and God's Gang.

"Some of you know Joseph and I had a dream of doing God's work with troubled teenagers and others needing help. I'm here today to tell you that God has allowed me to see our great plans come true with God and the help of my friends. You all know how Joseph and I talked about helping people in all kinds of trouble and problems, with our focus on teenage girls. You even prayed for us to accomplish our dream. That makes you part of this beautiful dream that is now a reality. I wish Joseph were here to see what we have achieved. I believe He is praising and thanking God in Heaven for answering our prayers.

I could never have imagined that God has blessed us with people, money, and facilities. Our first rescue operation was the four girls that are here today. Some of our girls are at the mansion with Aunt Ruth and Mrs. Willis, who work there. Laura is one of the evidence of what prayer can do through the power of God. He shielded her from those evil men who had imprisoned her. God blessed her with not having to go through any physical abuse. I know you will enjoy hearing of God's love and how He helped the guys save the girls in the Red Zone, so I'll let God's Gang tell you how they rescued the girls."

All five men gave their testimonies. They first told how they received Jesus, and then Randall told how the guys rescued the three sisters and how they had to have a different plan for saving Laura. Everyone was fascinated by the rescued girls. Even though Randall had explained how they rescued the girls, the young people wanted to ask more questions about how the guys did it. When Randall finished answering questions, the church stood and applauded for a long time.

Rev. Fox congratulated everyone on the success that everyone had made in doing God's work. Then, he asked them if they would plan to return once or twice a year. At that request, the church again stood and applauded.

When Mary returned to the pulpit, she said, "I just love you, people! We plan on returning once a year, and if we can, we will make it twice yearly. I want to thank everybody for everything, and we will keep in touch."

The power of the Holy Spirit was evident in the church. Rev. Fox gave the invitation. "If you are suffering, alone, and wondering if anyone cares, know that Jesus cares, and when you get to know us, you will see that we care, too. Accept Jesus as your Lord and Savior, and ask Him to forgive you of your sins, and He will forgive you. As we have seen with Mary and her friends, Jesus will transform your life. Come now and receive Jesus as your Lord and Savior. Many were saved that day.

Mary and all the members of God's Gang prayed at the altar for Rev. Fox's church members. Many people came forward to share their decision to receive Jesus, and they praised God for their salvation. Others renewed their commitment to live for God and to be the Christians Jesus wanted them to be. Others joined those praying at the altar, seeking God for the salvation of loved ones.

CHAPTER FIFTEEN

Randall Proposes To Mary

Everybody returned to New York. Mary met briefly with Rev. Fox in the church lobby." Rev. Fox, I want you to know how happy Aunt Ruth is because you led her brother David to Jesus. Thank you for not giving up on him."

Rev. Fox looked very serious. "Mary, I want to apologize to you. I'm so sorry for how I treated you when you worked here. The members told me how you stood up for me. I don't know if you realize it, but you are why we even have a church. Even though I was not nice to you, you were a loyal friend. I appreciate your kindness and your loyalty. My wife and I will always be grateful to you, and we love you, Mary. Are you sure you and your friends must return to New York immediately?" Rev. Fox asked: It would be fantastic if you could stay one more week. You and your friends have profoundly affected our young people. They haven't stopped talking about you and your friends."

"I'd love to, Reverend, but the girls must get back to school in New York. But I promise to stay in touch and tell you how work with God's Gang is going. We ask for your continued prayers and will keep you, your family, the members, and your ministry in ours."

"Rev. Fox looked in the refrigerator at church. Linda left you a surprise dish (Rev. Fox's favorite potluck dish) with your name on it," Mary said, smiling as she was leaving.

Everybody could sit close together on the airplane back home to New York. Randall interrupted their conversation as he stood before Linda. Linda and Mary were seated beside each other, talking.

"Linda, I need to talk with Mary for a minute. Would you mind switching seats with me?"

"No, not at all, Randall." Linda smiled as she unfastened her seat belt. She and everyone else in God's Gang knew what Randall was about to do. Only Mary was oblivious. Randall continued to stand in the aisle next to the now-empty seat. A bit puzzled, Mary looked up at him and watched him as he bent down on one knee on the airplane. He gently took her hands, gazed into Mary's eyes, and cleared his throat.

"Mary, will you do me the honor of marrying me?" Then he withdrew his hands, took a small box from his pocket, and opened it. There, encased in black velvet, was a beautiful diamond ring with a stone large enough to be seen from the back of the airplane.

Mary answered yes, and he then put the ring on her finger. Not only was the mansion family shouting and laughing joyfully, but the rest of the passengers were also joining in as news of the marriage proposal swiftly spread throughout the airplane. Mary's daughters were happy because now he would officially be their dad.

One month later, Mary and Randall were married in a beautiful ceremony at their church.

"Mary, let's take the girls on our honeymoon. They would love that."

"That's okay with me. I know the girls will love to go with us."

Randall couldn't wait to tell the girls. He called them to come into the living room. "Do you know what a honeymoon means?"

"No," said Lisa, "What is it?"

"Mary, you explain it to them." Randall thought Mary would be better at explaining. Mary knows he would like to be the first to tell them.

"Honey, you'll do just fine. Just tell them it's like going on a vacation after two people get married."

"Hey, Lisa and Lear, I want to explain the meaning of honeymoon," Randall called the girls back into the living room. "Well, honeymoon means when two people get married, they vacation together. Your mom and I want you to go with us. Would you like to go?"

Lisa and Lear jumped up and ran to Randall. "Yes. Yes." They shouted, and Lias asked. "When do we leave?"

Mary laughed as she went into the kitchen to check on her cooking.

"We leave in a few days," said Randall.

After two days on their honeymoon, Mary became ill. Randall took her to a doctor while they were at Disney. The doctor informed Randall that his wife was pregnant.

Randall was so happy. He went to the gift store in the hospital and bought her a bouquet of roses.

"Thank you, Randall. Did I tell you that yellow was my favorite color?"

"No, the girls told me. How do you feel?"

"I feel a lot better."

"Were you ill when you were pregnant with your daughters?"

"Yes. Why do you ask?"

"The doctor said you are pregnant! Randall said as he hugged Mary, "Are you as happy as I am?"

"Yes, I am, and Lisa and Lear will be happy too. Whenever one of my friends comes over with their baby, Lisa, and Lear have fun playing with them, and they beg me to buy them a baby sister or baby brother."

Randall and Mary laughed and alighted.

One month later Randall answered the phone, "Hello."

"Hello, my name is Harry. May I speak to Randall Nelson?"

"This is Randall Nelson speaking, "How can I help you?

"I'm not sure, but I think we are brothers. Can I meet with you and discuss what I have learned?"

CHAPTER SIXTEEN

Randall Meets His Twin Brother

"**Hey, Harry, where** are you going?"

Randall was at a drugstore when he heard someone call him Harry.

"My name is Randall. Harry must look like me," said Randall.

"I can't believe I have seen two people that look so much alike," said James. Do you have a twin brother? I have a picture of Harry in my wallet." James shows Randall the picture.

Randall is amazed when he looks at the picture. "I don't have a twin brother, but that looks like me. I can understand why you thought I was the person in the picture in your wallet."

James and Randall talk for a few minutes, and they say goodbye.

Later that day,. "Mary, I met a man who thought I was a man named Harry. He showed me a picture of Harry, and he looked just like me."

"Did your parents have other children? Asked Mary.

"I have a brother who died in the hospital when he was only seven days old. I was born months later, and they had no other children." Said Randall.

"Let's find out if there is a reason why you and Harry look so much alike. You could have a relative you don't know about," said Mary.

"I don't know where to even look for Harry. But we could look for James, and he could tell us how to get in touch with Harry." Said Randall.

Randall and Mary went to the drug every day looking for James when he finally showed up.

"Hi James, we have been looking for you. I want to meet Harry and find out if we might be related since we look so much alike." Said Randall.

"Oh, I have been looking for you too," said James when I told Harry about you. He wanted to meet you too," said James.

"Harry is off from work today, and I can take you to his house if you like."

"That would be wonderful." Said Randall.

At Harry's house, "Hi, greeted a 12-year-old boy, "You look just like my dad. He and my mom have been looking forward to meeting you."

Before Mary, Randall, and James came to the door, James's wife, Miriam, and his nine-year-old daughter came to the door."

Everyone on the front porch was staring at Harry and Randall

"Come inside. I have made lunch," said James's wife, Miriam.

At lunch, they all talked and got to know one another.

After a few months, James' children fell in love with Randall and Mary and called them uncle and aunt.

Miriam works for an adoption agency, and she tried to find something that might help them learn if Harry had any blood relatives they didn't know about, but they found nothing. Harry knew that he was adopted, but he thought it wouldn't hurt to look, anyway.

Harry looked for one of his aunts who remembered when his parents had adopted him.

Randall's parents also remember everything he was told about the time his parents were told that their baby had died. Mr. Nelson was in a car, and his wife was having so much trouble after the baby was born that she could not do anything. I don't know anything else except that their baby died in the hospital a few days later. I do know that the Nelsons divorced some years later.

Now we have to talk with Harry's parents and see if they know anything about their relatives that could help.

"We adopted Harry," said Mrs. Wilson, "When he was a few days old, and since I don't know how to find out anything, why don't we get the police to investigate for us?" Asked Mary.

"Will they do that?" asked Miriam.

"I don't know," said James, "But let's try it."

The police invested, and this is what they found:

A couple stole the baby and left it in the hospital lobby for a few minutes and went to their car to get blankets when they were forced into the vehicle and later killed by a gang who stole the money that they had gotten from trafficking babies.

They also find out that Harry was indeed Randall's twin brother.

Randall's family, the Wilson family, the Carter family, and God's Gang celebrated Randall and his twin brother, Harry.

Randall and his brother have become very close. They have so much in common despite being reared in different environments. Harry is so happy that his brother has a personal relationship with Jesus.

CHAPTER SEVENTEEN

Clyde's Gang Meets Their Rivals

WITH LIFE SETTLING into a routine, all the girls, including Lisa and Lear, were enrolled in Christian schools. Rob drove them to school every morning and picked them up every afternoon. Rob's hard work and loyal support of God's Gang had earned him a new car.

Kathy, Anna, Sue, and Laura see a Christian counselor weekly to help them heal from their ordeal at the Red Zone. Rob had enrolled in a university near the mansion to get his degree in electrical engineering. Mike, Tom, Randall, and Clyde continued working at a construction company, tithing their wages and contributing to God's Gang. They also help Mary with things around the mansion and their favorite job—rescue missions.

All the guys attend a university part-time, taking introductory college courses. As they joked, the guys would decide what they wanted to be when they grew up. Mary continues running God's Gang and teaching the other girls introductory courses until they can manage independently. Some have found good jobs and volunteered for a few hours at God's Gang.

Some girls have improved to the point where they have enrolled in regular schools. Some of the girls have returned to their homes and are doing great. Whenever a girl has to move out of their home because of abuse or other problems, God's Gang takes the girl in and works with the whole family. Many times, the entire family becomes whole and can function normally.

Social services often ask God's Gang for help with someone who has been abused or has other problems. Everyone who has been to God's Gang has always kept in touch and felt free to visit anytime.

Mrs. Willis, whom Mary hired a while back, has become a family member. Her husband had died before she came to God's Gang a few years ago, and she had no other family, so Mary asked her if she would like to move into the mansion. She was delighted. All the girls adore her and go to her and Runt Ruth for advice. They both have super knowledge of God's Word, making them perfect for giving advice. Aunt Ruth and Mrs. Willis are the best of friends. They have so much fun together. When Mary needed them on their off day, they told her she could reach them at a friend's house, where they make quilts for our soldiers and their families.

Mary has added more people to the staff of God's Gang. She asked Linda to join the team at God's Gang. She told her it would be nice to have her and Laura live there.

"I'm sure Laura would be happy to move in here, and so would I. I have learned that working with these young girls has been my calling," said Linda.

Linda is a whiz at teaching sewing, computer programs, and other courses, skills the girls at God's Gang can use to help them get back on their feet and become contributing members of society. After Linda's husband died, she struggled to pay his hospital bills. She had a good job, but it was hard for her and Laura.

Months later, Mary yelled from the kitchen, "Will somebody get the door?" Randall opened the door and stood there in shock. There stood Louis, Clayton, and James, members of their rival

Gang. Clayton, the gang leader, held up his hands to let them know they didn't come to make trouble.

"We don't want any trouble, Randall. We heard about your Gang's changes and want to talk. That's all."

"All right. What do you want to talk about?" Randall stood there in the doorway, not inviting them in.

"We've been hearing all over town about you and how you don't do, you know, do the drug stuff anymore. We heard you got jobs and don't have to worry about the police. We also heard that your whole Gang is friendly with the police and that you help the police raise money to help kids and others in your neighborhood who need help. We know that being friends with the police and helping them has to make your life peaceful. We can't imagine being friends with the police. We haven't had a good night's sleep in years," said Clayton.

"Yeah, man," said Louis as James nodded in agreement.

"We're tired of hiding," said James, "From the police. We're always afraid of getting shot by drug users or other drug dealers when we walk down the street. We don't want to live this way anymore. All the money we make from drugs and, you know, other things we do does not make a peaceful living. We decided we'd rather not have the money if we could have peace and be safe walking down the streets. Can you tell us what you did to make such a big change?"

Randall could scarcely believe what he was hearing. These guys had been out to get The Great Ones, as they were called, for years, and now Clayton and his Gang were coming to them for advice.

"Come on in, guys. We were about to have dinner. You can have dinner with us while we talk."

Louis, Clayton, and James followed Randall into the dining room. Clyde, Tom, and Mike immediately rose from the table when they saw the three men, assuming there might be trouble.

"Relax, everybody," Randall said quickly, raising his hand to motion to God's Gang to sit back down.

"They just want to know how we were able to stop doing the drug and other gang stuff."

Mary and Linda heard everything and entered the dining room carrying a bowl and a food platter. They placed them on the table and went to the China cabinet for plates and silverware.

"Let me get more glasses while you guys sit at the table," Mary said as she went to the kitchen for glasses. Randall introduced Mary to Clayton's. She had compassion for them. She could tell that they were sad and troubled. They had overdressed to impress everybody and were uneasy, hungering for something although they knew not what.

James was starting to serve himself when he picked up the platter. Mary said softly, not wanting to embarrass him, "Randall, will you bless the food." James then put the platter down and bowed his head.

After dinner, Mary and Linda invited them into the living room. At the same time, God's Gang sat around them, happy to bring these men, once their enemies, to Jesus. God's Gang shared their testimony with the men. Louis, Clayton, and James listened intently, interrupting occasionally to ask questions.

After nearly two hours, Mary and Linda, who had allowed the guys to dominate the talks, said, "We're going to church Sunday. Would you like to come with us?" The men looked at each other, knowing that going to church would be a very different and new experience for them. Louis and James nodded to Clayton, who accepted the invitation. Randall walked them to the door and shook their hands.

"I'm glad you all came. We'll pray for you and look forward to seeing you Sunday."

The guys thanked them for taking time with them and said goodbye as they reluctantly left. Hearing the door close, Mary joined the guys and placed her hand on Randall's shoulder.

"God is bringing them in," said Mary, "He's a good and loving God." Mary moved her hand from Randall's shoulder and squeezed her arms around him. He laughed and kissed her cheek.

After Clayton, Louis, and James had been attending Mary's church for three months, James ran into George, an old drug buddy.

"Hey, James, how have you been? What are you doing these days?" asked George.

"You're not going to believe this, but I gave my life to Jesus," said James.

"Praise God," said George, "I did too! I'm now a minister. God has blessed me and given me the chance to serve Him. I have a church across the river. We haven't been there long and could use more Christians to help us spread God's Word. Why don't you visit?"

James, Clayton, and Louis went to George's church that Sunday. James had called Mary to tell her so she would know that they were still committed to serving God but were visiting a friend's church. The service was excellent. I can't believe George has learned so much about God. But James could see they needed help with their newly started church. Clayton and his guys could feel the Holy Spirit bringing them peace as they decided to join George's church. They also felt that George's church needed them. They drove to God's Gang and told Mary about their decision.

"Hi, Mary," Clayton greeted her at the door.

"Hi, guys," Mary escorted them into the living room, "Would you like coffee or tea?"

"No thanks. We just needed to tell you this in person," said James, "Mary, we have felt pulled all week to join George's church. We know that God wants to use us in that church, lawe didn't want you to think we had abandoned you after all you have done for us."

"Oh, Clayton," said Mary, "It sounds like God is truly speaking to you. I certainly know about that. Your working with George and his church is wonderful. We've been looking for other ways to help spread the Word of God. Perhaps God is also leading you there to give us another opportunity to serve. We would love to partner with George and his church. We could give them financial support and help them with Bible study so they can become firmly established in their church. Our guys will be happy to hear you will be helping George's church. Let George know that we will be happy to help with anything."

"Thank you, Mary and Linda," said Clayton. I'll tell George, and he can contact you directly."

The guys hugged Mary and Linda and were so happy they had found such good friends.

It had been two weeks since the ladies met with James and the others. Clayton had told George about Mary's offer to help them with financial support and a Bible study once a month. George was happy that Mary wanted to help them with their ministry.

The next day, Clayton contacted her, and they made plans for Mary to work with them.

"Let's call James and see how things are going with their church since we could not make it last month for their Bible study," Mary said as she and Linda sat in the kitchen having their usual cup of coffee.

"Why don't we see if they can come for lunch tomorrow at noon?" Linda suggested. Mary smiled and picked up the phone.

Around noon, the doorbell rang, and Rob was the only man there.

Rob opened the door. There stood James, Clayton, Louis, and six other men.

"I know you didn't expect all these guys, but this is our whole gang, and they were determined to come when we told them about God's Gang," said Clayton.

Rob smiled, happy to see their interest in knowing what God's Gang does.

"Come on in. Welcome to God's Gang, guys. Randall and the other guys are normally here today but were called on an emergency job and won't be here for lunch. I'll get Mary and Linda."

Rob took them into the living room. "Make yourselves comfortable."

Rob returned with Mary and Linda. When Clayton saw them, he immediately stood up.

"You don't need to stand, Clayton," Mary smiled.

James introduced them to the other guys, "You already know Clayton and Louis. Well, going around the room, Jerry, Jones, Larry, Robert, Hunter, and Randy are here."

"We are happy to have all of you in our home," Mary told the others.

"We don't expect you to feed this many guys," said Clayton, "So we would like to order food for everybody. How about McDonald's,' or pizza?" They are both fast, and the one on State Street is close and the only one I know delivers."

"Oh, I love McDonalds. That sounds great," Mary replied.

"We just wanted you to meet the rest of our gang, or rather, they wanted to meet you," James explained. "They have all been going to George's church, and they like it but wanted to talk with you and the guys about how they got saved, how they make a living now, and how they stop doing the drug stuff. Clayton told us about God's, but we wanted to hear from them."

"Well, we are always honored to share the love of God with anyone who wants to listen," Mary smiled and made them feel welcome. She informed them that most of their guys work for a construction company as their source of income. Rob works for God's Gang when he's not in school. She also told them that not working for drugs was a long story and that God had a hand in it. Everyone would learn all about these things as Mary and God's Gang taught them how God works in people's lives when they turn to Him. Getting saved is the easiest thing of all.

"The guys that work in construction found the work very hard when they first started. Clyde, Mike, and Randall had worked in construction years ago but had not worked that hard for some time, so they had to get used to it. The pay was good, and they soon got used to the work. The guys say they sleep well at night after working all day, and it has helped them build strong muscles. The guys will be happy to help you start in the construction business if that's what you want to try. I can also help with resumes, and we can look into various types of jobs. God has given all of us talents, so let's find out what your talents are. You can also take a few classes to further your education, which will help you get better jobs that pay well."

Mary was happy the guys wanted to get legitimate jobs. While waiting for their food, Mary explained that Rob was the only guy there that day.

"We'll be happy to talk with you and answer any questions. You can still return another day when the guys are home to talk with you. Are you all attending George's church?"

"Yes," James answered, "The three of us go there every Sunday and Wednesday night. The rest of the guys go sometimes. That's one of the reasons we came. They need help forming a deep relationship with Jesus and understanding the Scriptures. We love George's church, but they've just started with their church and need help making our members understand the importance of reading the Bible and praying. Although the Holy Spirit clarifies many things, which fascinates us, we would like more help."

"Yeah," Louis said, "But most guys can't get over feeling guilty and unworthy.

Mary and the other guys made things so clear that we hoped you could help the rest of our Gang." Mary's compassion came to light as usual.

"If you had any idea how much God loves you, you would know that even though He's not pleased with what you did, He loves you anyway and will forgive you for whatever you did if you ask Him. The Bible says that He will not only forgive you, but He will also forget your sins. I love that when God forgives you of your sins, He no longer remembers them."

Rob jumped in, "He will forgive you as Mary said, but can you imagine God not remembering your sins? When I feel depressed and guilty about something I did, I remember that God forgave me and forgot about it. I can't tell you the joy that it brings me! Why should I worry about what I did years ago when God forgave me? I had stopped doing those things when God not only forgave me, but He did not even remember the thing I did.

I came here to collect money from Clyde's Gang, grabbed Mary, and held a gun to her head. When Randall started walking toward me, I told him I would shoot her if he came closer. But although I was terrible, I had no intention of hurting Mary. I thought the gun would make them give me money. They didn't know the gun wasn't loaded. Randall told me later that he started to pray and suddenly heard God's voice say; Rob's gun has no bullets. After taking the weapon, they tied me up, and Mary fed me and told me about the love of God. A little later, she convinced them to untie me so I could go to the restroom, and I climbed out the bathroom window and ran away."

"That's all true," Mary interrupted, "But later, Rob risked his life to save our guys and Anna from Jim, who owned the Red Zone. Months later, Rob was shot in an attempt to shield me from Jim, and he was in a coma for three days. Anna came to the hospital and prayed for him, and he came out of the coma and was completely healed."

"I didn't have any peace," said Rob, "Until I surrendered everything to Jesus."

Rob told the whole story about how he received salvation.

"What fascinated me the most about what Rev. Smith said was that it didn't matter what I'd done; Jesus still loved me and wanted to forgive me for my sins. Then he said Jesus is here among us now. I felt God's presence and love surround me when he said that. That's one day I will never forget. I have been so full of joy and peace ever since. We all have ups and downs, but with God, we get through the troubled times with peace. You have to put your trust in God. I'm always happy, even when things are not going my way. God often gives you peace and joy as you go through problems," Rob concluded.

"Remember to read your Bibles every day. Does everyone have a Bible?" Mary asked. Only Louis, James, and Clayton had Bibles.

"Roll get six Bibles from the storage room? We keep extra Bibles for anyone who doesn't have one."

Mary began to pray, "Thank You, Dear God, for bringing peace to our lives through Your Son, Jesus. Thank You for forgiving us and loving us. Thank You for bringing these guys to us today and allowing us to minister to them. Bless them to be strong Christians, in Jesus' Name. Amen."

Linda had gone into the dining room to wait for McDonald's.

"McDonald's is here." Said Rob.

After lunch, the men began asking questions. Mary noticed that one of the men, Larry, had become quite upset.

"I know we've talked about some things that may have upset you, but just remember that God loves you and wants you to be happy and successful."

Larry seemed to relax a little. As the guys left later that afternoon, they hugged Mary and Linda, thanked them for having lunch with them, and helped them understand more about God and the Bible.

"Rob, I liked your testimony, and I hope God blesses me the way He has blessed you," Louis remarked.

"He will, man! Just stay in the Word."

As Larry walked down the driveway, Mary noticed he was crying

and called to him, "What's wrong, Larry?"

"I don't know," he cried. "I don't know. I believe what you said about God is true. And I don't know how to explain it, but I know that Jesus loves me. I know that Jesus is giving me peace. But I'm unsure what to do next and can't stop crying."

Mary walked over to him, gently put her arm around his shoulder, and led him back inside the mansion. In the living room, she explained more about the plan of salvation and led him to Jesus.

Mary, Linda, and Rob told their guys what had happened that afternoon as they ate dinner.

"Can you imagine?" Mary began, "We witnessed six other men of Clayton's Gang today because of our work with James and his friends. We were able to lead one of them to the Lord, and we could see God working in the hearts of the others. They are hungry for God. We need to call Randy, though. I could see that he needs encouragement and reassurance that God and others love him."

Mary has a beautiful gift of discernment. That gift and her compassion allow her to be very helpful to hurting people.

"God is mighty!" Randall added, "We need to keep in touch with the guys and help them in their spiritual walk."

Mary had agreed to teach Bible study on Thursday nights until George could, or the Lord sent someone else to help that little church grow.

"By the way, Mary," Randall was excited, "Tom helped three of Clayton's Gangs get jobs across the river at a large construction company.

Tom had taken the guys to the construction site, and Mr. Bird, the owner, a Christian who had known Tom for many years, was delighted that he had become a Christian. Tom said that Mr. Bird was not surprised that he had become a Christian because Mr. Bird had been praying for him for years to accept Jesus as his Savior. Mr. Bird also said he'd heard about God's Gang and the work the guys were doing and was very impressed."

"That's wonderful, Randall; Linda has been helping Larry with computer programming. He's going to be very good on the computer. He loves it! I have never seen anybody learn anything so fast. I'm so excited about Clayton's Gang. They will all be working soon. I was concerned about Randy. He changed completely after receiving Jesus as his Lord and Savior. He is happy and has an unbelievable sense of humor. He should be on television. He is amusing, and we can use more Christian humor!"

Randy eventually worked as a Christian comedian and was exceedingly good at it.

Weeks later, "Mary, is something wrong?" Clyde asked.

"Oh, no, Clyde. I wondered how we still use the word gang to describe Clayton's guys. I don't want to change that because we have changed what 'gang' can mean. I love that our guys and the mansion are known as God's Gang."

"Hello," Linda answered on the phone in the kitchen.

"Of course, James. We'd love to see you and your family. Why don't you bring them to dinner tomorrow evening?"

As soon as she hung up, she went to Mary's office.

"Who was on the phone?" Mary asked as Linda walked through the doorway.

"James. He needs to see us and wants us to meet his family, so I invited them for dinner tomorrow."

"That's great. I didn't know James was married. Did you?"

"No, but we haven't had a chance to learn much about Clayton's gangs.

"That's okay to call them gangs. Gangs everywhere can know that gangs can mean good people helping people and working for a loving God."

James ran into Jerry. "Hey, James."

"Hey, Jerry. How are you doing, man?"

"I would be fine if I could get my daughters to stop hanging out with their girlfriends. Those girls are bad news."

"I'm taking my wife and two sons to see Mary and the guys."

James told Jerry, "They need to hear what she and their guys have to say about God and salvation. My wife and I are new at this Christian stuff, and I want my sons to hear from somebody who knows the Bible much better than we do."

"Would they mind if I brought my family too?" Jerry asked, "We need to learn more about God too."

"I'm sure it would be okay, Jerry. Why don't you call Mary and ask her if it's all right for you to bring your family too?"

Mary answered the phone in her office, "Oh, hello, Jerry. How are you doing?"

"Fine. Thank you. James and his family are coming to your place for dinner tomorrow evening to talk with you about God and salvation. And I would like to know if I can come with my family. My daughters, Kate, sixteen, and Kitty, seventeen, run with an evil group of girls. They won't listen to their mother or me. Could you help us with them? But I want to be a manageable amount of a bother so that we will buy dinner for everyone. That way, I won't feel imposing so much."

"Jerry, it's no imposition, but if you'd like to provide dinner, that would be great. We enjoy sharing the Word of God and helping our friends find Jesus as their Savior."

"How does pizza sound?" said Jerry.

"Wonderful, I don't know anyone who does not like pizza. We'll see you tomorrow evening."

Mary smiled as she replaced the receiver and then said a silent prayer of thanks for the opportunity to share Jesus with more people.

The next evening, all the members of God's Gang—James, Jerry's family, and Rev. Smith—gathered in the living room and dining room areas to share pizza and the Word of God. James introduced his two boys, who were twelve and sixteen. "I want them to have a more secure and safer life than I have had, and I would like them to know God," he told the group. "I've already led my wife to the Lord!"

"That's wonderful, James," said Mary. I'm so happy for you and your family."

Then Jerry introduced his daughters, Kate and Kitty. Mary let them know how happy she was to have them, too.

Rev. Smith taught about salvation as the whole group listened attentively. Then Clyde, Rob, and Randall gave their testimonies.

Mike replied, "I don't have much of a testimony. My testimony was watching Randall, Clyde, and Tom walk around the house so happy. They were so at peace, and nothing ever bothered them, even when things were not going their way. They were driving me crazy, being so joyful all the time. Mary laughed when I told her to help me get what the guys had. I was serious and ready for Jesus! The rest is history."

Rev. Smith had led everyone in prayer before he taught about salvation.

By the end of the evening, Jerry's whole family had accepted Jesus as their Lord and Savior, and James's boys later received Jesus as their Lord and Savior. They have also led some of their friends to the Lord. Mary is training them to teach Sunday school students attending grade school. One by one, all the members of Clayton's Gang eventually became Christians and then led their families to Christ.

The girls at God's Gang became friends with Jerry's daughters over the next three months. Soon, all the girls were working together in their neighborhoods, sharing the love of Christ and leading the young people to Christ. Mary continued to speak at George's church once a month and taught Bible study twice a month. Because of God's love and everyone's tireless commitment, George's church tripled in size. It's only about a forty-minute drive from George's church to Rev. Smith's church, so they often attend each other's church.

Mary and God's Gang helped the rest of Clayton's Gang get jobs in different companies across the river near where they lived and encouraged them to return to school. Clayton's whole Gang was so excited about going back to school. They had never thought about going back to school. Mary suggested that they take only a few courses at first. That would make it easier for them to stay with it.

With Mary and Linda helping them and relying on God's help, the guys believe they can do anything they put their minds to with God's help. These ex-rival gangs of former drug dealers and their families are working tirelessly for God and others. Through God, they found strength and support in each other as well. Every month, they all meet to share a meal and praise God.

CHAPTER EIGHTEEN

Laura Faces Rejection At Work

THE SCHOOL WAS out for the summer. Kathy, Sue, and Anna worked at the mansion. Laura, however, found a summer position at the Seven's Building in the accounting department, an excellent opportunity to build experience for her future career. On her first day on the job, Laura reported being a few minutes early for work. She went first to Mrs. Rayburn, her supervisor, and wanted to make a good impression. Mrs. Rayburn greeted Laura.

"Hello, Laura. I'm glad you're a little early; it gives us time to settle things before you start working on your first day. Let me go over our general procedures with you. Then you need to finish your paperwork in Human Resources before you meet your supervisor on the second floor."

Mrs. Rayburn was the accounting department manager and a no-nonsense kind of woman. She quickly reviewed the general employee guidelines with Laura. Then Laura went to the first floor to complete her paperwork, returning about half an hour later. Mrs. Rayburn was speaking with another new employee, so Laura waited in the reception area for her to finish.

Mrs. Rayburn took Laura to Faith's office. As they walked down the hall, Laura was pleased to see several women who seemed to be her age. Thank goodness, she thought, I'll have someone to eat lunch with. But Laura soon learned the girls could have been more friendly. They were downright mean. As the morning progressed, Laura met dozens of people, including Pam, a young woman who worked in an office near hers. At lunch, Laura went over and reintroduced herself.

"Oh, right. You're the new girl," Pam smirked before returning to a project she was working on.

"I was wondering if we could have lunch together today." Laura asked.

"Oh, I couldn't have lunch with you. I'm behind and must catch up because I'm leaving early today."

"Well, maybe tomorrow we could . . ."

"Sure. Whatever," Pam replied before Laura could finish her sentence. Then she stuck her nose back in her work.

Laura went to the cafeteria alone. She bought a sandwich and a glass of milk and sat at a table near a window. There was no one Laura recognized. So she sat at a table, took out her Bible, and began to read as she ate her sandwich. A few minutes later, when she looked up, she saw Pam and two other girls from the same floor where she worked. Pam looked briefly in her direction and said something to the two girls, who laughed and went to a table on the other side of the cafeteria.

For the next two weeks, Laura tried to befriend Pam and the other girls on the floor they all worked on. She asked if she could join them at lunch and asked them questions about the office. She offered to help them when she finished her work. Still, they froze her out. But she was determined to make friends with them.

Sometimes, Pam and her friends pretended to be friendly, inviting her to lunch with them and then not showing up or leaving early without telling her. They took her up on her offers of help, though, dumping as much of their work on her as they could but always taking credit for it when Faith complimented the excellent jobs they had done.

There must be some way to reach them. Laura thought. Getting to know them outside the workplace might be better, so she invited them to church with her.

"You've got to be kidding," Pam replied when Laura asked, "Who goes to church? That's for weirdoes." Then she walked away, shaking her head in disgust.

Laura decided to keep trying. Persistence was the key.

One day, the three saw Laura reading her Bible in the cafeteria. Pam led the way to her table and stood there for a second, and then she snatched the Bible from Laura's hands.

"Why on earth are you reading this mythical junk?" Said, Pam.

"I believe it, and it's not mythical junk," Laura replied. "It's God's Word and one of the ways He speaks to us today."

"God speaks to you? Do you, like, hear voices?" The girls laughed as Pam dropped the Bible onto the table as if it burned her fingers.

"When will you realize you're wasting time with that religion junk? There's no one out there listening to us. No one is guiding our paths, as you Christians say. You are so stupid to believe in that nonsense. You need to realize that there is no life after death. When you die, you stay that way."

"Pam, I wish you would come to church with me. You would learn so much about how much God loves you." Laura tried to reason with Pam.

"Forget it. I wouldn't be caught dead in church. Let's go, girls."

And Pam swirled around and walked away. The other two girls were right behind her.

"I should have known that they wouldn't go to church with me," Laura thought, "But only if they would go; the church atmosphere might soften their hearts."

Still, Laura didn't give up on them, but she did stop asking them to come to church with her. She felt that they just weren't ready. But each day, she witnessed them through her actions. Laura continued to read her Bible at lunch, offer help whenever possible, and pray that Pam and her friends would understand the importance of the truth concerning God.

Sitting at lunch a few days later, the three young women watched

Laura read her Bible with a look of peace and serenity.

"She thinks she's so much better than us," Pam sneered.

"Doesn't she know we are better than her? We've been here longer. We wear the most fashionable clothes and make more money than she does!"

"Maybe she doesn't know that, Pam. The company doesn't allow employees to discuss their salaries with anyone. We know what she makes because you got Joyce to open her envelope with her check. I wondered how she managed to open her envelope and seal it back, and Laura didn't notice that it had been opened. Maybe Laura thinks we all get the same salary," said Jan.

"Jan, you finally said something brilliant. I know just how to let her find out how far beneath us she is," Pam said, slowly swirling the straw in her soft drink.

On Fridays, the floor receptionists usually receive paychecks from Human Resources and distribute them to the employees. The checks were placed in an envelope and sealed so no one could see anyone's salary. That Friday, Pam asked Joyce, the receptionist, to take their paychecks out of the envelopes and give the checks to Laura.

"But I'll lose my job if anyone finds out I did that, Pam," said Joyce.

"Joyce, you can be fired anyway if I let slip that you've been fudging your timesheet for the last month to spend an extra few minutes every lunch hour with that cute guy on the third floor."

"You wouldn't!" But Joyce knew that Pam would.

"Okay, Pam, but will you tell me why? This doesn't make sense to me."

"Leave that to me. Laura will distribute all of our checks when you give them to her." Pam was counting on Laura to see that their check showed a bigger salary than hers. That afternoon, about an hour before quitting time, Pam, Jan, and Helen appeared in Laura's office.

Almost everyone in this company had their own office. The company felt there would be no distractions and employees would be more productive if they worked alone in separate offices.

"Laura, we all have to be in a meeting that will last until after normal quitting time. Joyce doesn't have the checks yet, so we need you to get ours from her and keep them for us until we leave the meeting. We shouldn't be too long. We want to get our checks on Monday. If we don't get them on Monday, we won't be able to get them until the next day. And I have some bills that I have to pay today. You don't mind, do you?"

"Sure, Pam. Not a problem. I'll be happy to do it." Laura smiled as the girls walked toward the conference room.

"Wow, she thought, asking me to get their checks. Maybe the Holy Spirit is working on them!" Laura hopes the Holy Spirit is working on the girls.

Laura was trying so hard to reach these girls that she was not discerning their motives for asking for a favor. Being careful not to be seen by Laura, the three girls positioned themselves to see her reaction when she saw the amounts on their checks and realized they made nearly thirty percent more than she did. The girls didn't know that; even if Laura had noticed that they made more money, it would not have bothered her because Laura wouldn't have expected to make as much as they did, as Laura was new on the job. However, she was more capable, and her work was superior to theirs. Laura also worked in a field that eventually naturally paid more. So, she would soon be making quite a bit more than either of the girls.

Joyce walked over to Laura's office.

"Hi, Laura. Pam told me you would take the girls' checks to them. Is that right?"

"Yes, Joyce. I'll make sure they get them."

As Joyce started to hand her the checks, Laura noticed they were the only ones not in envelopes.

"Oh, sorry, Laura. I ran out of envelopes."

Joyce had put Laura's check on top so Laura didn't need to see the other checks. Evil people are often stupid, too.

"Joyce, do you know what room the meeting is in? I want to give the checks to them immediately since they're not in envelopes."

Before Joyce could lie and say she didn't know, Helen flew by Laura.

"Helen?" Laura called to her, waving the checks in the air.

"Later. I've got to get to the ladies' room." Laura looked at Joyce and followed Helen.

"Helen, I have your check." Helen thought Laura couldn't have had time to look at their checks.

"Well, give me mine, and then you can hold Pam's and Jan's until the meeting ends."

"But aren't you going back into the meeting?"

"Well, yes, but . . ."

"Then why can't you take them their checks? That way, I won't have to wait until the meeting ends."

"I just can't. That's all. You know how Pam gets when you don't do things her way; she specifically asked you to get our checks."

Laura realized the girls were trying to pull something over on her. But she wouldn't allow them to get away with this one.

It was one thing to make fun of her, but her having their checks could lead to a severe problem.

"Here, Helen, take the checks," said Laura

"No," Helen shouted and flounced angrily, leaving Laura still holding all the checks.

Laura immediately went to the receptionist's desk and handed the checks to Joyce. "I don't know what kind of games you people are playing, but you'd better leave me out of them," Laura said as she put the girls' checks on Joyce's desk and left.

Joyce looked at Pam and the girls hiding from Laura and shrugged. The girls were determined to find a way to upset Laura by flaunting their higher salaries. But they knew they couldn't try the same scheme. They all huddled in Pam's office, discussing options, when they heard someone clear their throat. All three froze.

"Is there a problem, ladies?" Faith asked. Although she was smiling at them, Pam knew Faith heard. Faith was promoted to the supervisor's position three months ago. She was fair but challenging and expected everyone she worked with to be respectful of one another.

"Ladies, I don't know what or why you're plotting, but if you carry out the plans I just overheard, know that you will lose your job. You should find better time-saving ways, such as doing company work. If you are not authorized to work on a project together, I suggest you return to your offices."

"Yes, Faith, right away," Pam said as they went to their office. Faith watches them walk toward their offices. They knew better than to cross Faith.

At noon, Laura bumped into a tall, good-looking young man. "Hi," he said.

"Hi. I'm sorry," said Laura, "I was going to the cafeteria the wrong way again."

"Are you lost?" asked the guy Laura ran into.

"No, I just got turned around. I guess I wasn't paying attention to where I was going."

"Come on, I'll walk with you if you don't mind since I'm on my way there too."

"Okay," said Laura.

"I'm Kevin."

"I'm Laura. I work in accounting, but I've only been here a few weeks."

"Well, welcome, Laura from accounting. Let me buy you lunch." Said, Kevin

In the cafeteria, Jan, Helen, and Pam saw Kevin and Laura walk in together. Pam swirled her straw in her soft drink, faster and faster, until some splashed over the side and onto her hand, "Oh, hand me a napkin!"

As she wiped her hand and the splotches on the table, she kept staring at Laura and Kevin, now seated just a few tables away. Jan and Helen kept quiet, trying not to upset Pam, knowing how she felt about Kevin. Pam had liked Kevin for a long time but couldn't get him to ask her out. Now, there he was with that Bible freak, Laura.

"This company isn't big enough for me and Laura, and I'm not going to be the one to leave," Pam said, her voice very angry and cold.

Kevin and Laura finished their lunches a few minutes later. "I have to get back. I lost a few minutes when I lost my way earlier," Laura said as she started to get up from the table.

"I'm glad you got turned around, Laura. I prefer to eat with others. I usually eat at this time. Most of my friends eat earlier in the cafeteria or leave the building for lunch. Would you like to join me for lunch regularly?" Asked Kevin.

"I don't like to eat alone either," said Laura, "I'd love to join you. I haven't been able to make friends with anyone here."

"What about Pam, Helen, and Jan? They work on your floor."

"Yes, and I've tried to befriend them," said Laura, "But some people get a little turned off when they discover you're a Christian."

"Hey, that's great." Laura looked at Kevin, a little puzzled. "Oh, I don't mean it's great that they are turned off because you are a Christian. It's great that you are a Christian. I'm Christian, too.

Later that day, Pam confronted Laura in her office. The janitor was emptying the trash when Pam walked in.

"I need to talk to you in private. There's no one in the hall right now. Let's go there," Pam said firmly and started walking in that direction.

Laura watched her a moment, put down her pen, and followed her out of the office.

Laura could tell Pan was angry, but she had no idea why.

"What's wrong, Pam?" Laura asked.

Pam stared at her for a moment, her eyes filled with anger. Then, she pointed her finger in Laura's face as she leaned in close.

"You're what's wrong; stay away from Kevin, and if you don't, I'll make it very hard for you to work here."

Laura shoved Pam's hand away from her face, which surprised Pam. She never expected Laura, who had always been so gentle and humble, to stand up to her. Pam realized she had grossly underestimated Laura.

"I'm not afraid of you, Pam. If you want Kevin for yourself, you need to know that he's a Christian and, unlike you and your friends, he likes Christians."

Laura walked away, angry but sad that reaching these girls for Jesus seemed impossible.

A few minutes later, Pam came to Helen's office.

"What's wrong with you? You look like you just lost your best friend." Pam covered her face with her hands and began to cry.

"Pam, what's wrong?" Helen asked again.

"That stupid Laura." Pam was distraught.

"What did she do?" asked Helen.

"I don't want to talk about it," Pam screamed.

"Don't worry, Pam, we'll get her back," Helen said as she put her hand on Pam's shoulder.

A couple of weeks passed, and Pam continued to stew. Whenever she saw Laura and Kevin together at lunch, she became distraught. Jan, their other friend, and Helen decided to get even with Laura for what they thought she had done to Pam. But they knew it wasn't going to be easy. Laura was not afraid of them.

That night, the girls planned to get back at Laura and stay in the building after closing time. Once the building was quiet and everyone had left, they met in Laura's office and started going through her desk, trying to find anything they could use to get her in trouble. They were so busy going through Laura's desk that they didn't hear footsteps coming down the hall toward them. Then they heard Laura's talking with one of the guys leaving the building.

"What are you doing with my things?" she yelled, "Why are you taking my things out of my desk?"

Jan babbled, "We heard that someone stole Joyce's watch, and we were checking everyone's desk to see if we could find it."

"I'm sure that's not true," said Laura, "So why don't you all get out of my office? I'll check with Faith in the morning to see if I can get to the bottom of these games you're playing."

"We're not playing any games, Laura," Helen said, replacing a secretary's manual she had in her hand.

"We're just trying to help a friend. There's no need to talk to Faith about this." Helen and the others were afraid of what Laura might do.

They were terrified because Faith had overheard them plotting earlier. She had told them that if they carried out their plan, they would be fired, so if Laura told Faith about this, they would all lose their jobs.

"I'm sure Joyce just misplaced it, and she'll find it tomorrow," said Helen.

Laura could hear the desperation in Helen's voice. None of them wanted to be reported to Faith. They couldn't manipulate her the way they could their former supervisor.

"We'll just put everything back," said Helen as they began putting things back into Laura's desk.

Before they could finish and leave Laura's office, they heard someone else enter. No one was supposed to be there at that time of night except for Laura, who had gotten permission to work late. The girls looked at each other, grabbed their purses, and started to leave when three men blocked their way. Helen and Jan screamed.

"Shut up, or I'll put a hole through your head," one of the men commanded, "Look at what we have here, boys. A little bonus for our efforts tonight."

With that, he grabbed Pam and kissed her as she tried to pull away. The man holding Helen threw her to the floor. Helen started crying. "Shut up before I quiet you permanently."

"Leave us alone," Laura shouted at the men.

"Look who's talking," said the most significant guy, holding Helen to the floor.

"And what do you think you can do about it?" The men laughed as the one holding Helen let go of her and headed toward Laura to grab her.

"Stop in the Name of Jesus," Laura shouted, "I command you to stop and move to the door in the Name of Jesus."

They all looked at her in disbelief. One of the men started to say something, but Laura held up her hand, "In the Name of Jesus, don't say anything. Sit on the floor."

Suddenly, the men fell to the floor and could not get up. Pam, Jan, and Helen stared at them in amazement and then looked at Laura.

"Jan, call the police," Laura commanded.

After the police handcuffed the men, one of them walked over to Laura, "What did you ladies do to those guys? They're shaking like leaves on a tree?"

"Jesus, let them know who was the Boss," Laura said as she smiled and walked toward Helen, who crying and apologized to Laura as the police handcuffed the men and then took them out of Laura's office.

"Can you ever forgive us, Laura? I don't know what we would have

done if you hadn't been here," said Pam.

Helen couldn't stop crying. Laura put her arms around her and attempted to comfort her.

"Those bad men are on their way to jail. They can't hurt you now, Helen. If or when they get out of jail, I don't think they'll ever try that again. I'm sure they will never come back here again." Said Laura.

"If it weren't for you, that man would have raped me, Laura. How can you forgive us for all the mean things we did to you?" Helen repeated several times.

"Easy," said Laura, "Jesus has forgiven me and given me eternal life. He loves you and wants to forgive and give you eternal life, too."

"How did you make those men obey you?" Pam asked, "I thought those men were going to kill us."

"God gives us power through Faith in Jesus Christ to protect us. I really didn't do it. Jesus did it." Laura became quiet, holding Helen, who had calmed down at last.

"What's wrong, Laura?" Jan asked, "Are you all right?"

"I forgot why I got permission to work late. I have to finish a particular project for Faith by tomorrow evening. With the police still investigating, I can't get any work done, so I'm going home now and coming in early in the morning."

Pam talked to Jan and Helen, and they all agreed, "We can help you tomorrow, Laura," said Pam, "Our work assignments are routine. We can even come in early tomorrow morning."

"Really? Thank you. I planned to arrive by seven, so I'll meet you then."

"We'll be here," said Pam, the other two girls nodding.

"One more thing, Laura," Helen smiled at her, "Could we go to church with you this Sunday?"

"Of course, I'd love for you to attend church with me. I'm just sorry it took three bad men to convince you." The girls looked at her, and then all started laughing.

"Wow, it's getting late. We all need to get home and sleep," said Laura.

This was a strange night, but something about it has been excellent. Will you be okay going home alone, or do you want to ask one of the policemen still here to take you home?" asked Laura

"I think we'll be fine," Pam said, "But to be safe, I'm asking one of them to wait until we hail a cab. No subway for us tonight."

"Forget the cab," the police chief said, "One of my men will take you home.

The following day, true to their promise, Pam, Jan, and Helen met Laura at seven to work on her project for Faith. By noon, they had completed the work.

"Wow!" said Laura, "I can't believe we have finished! Let's all go to lunch and celebrate together!"

For the first time since Laura had begun working there, Pam, Jan, and Helen were happy to have lunch with her.

Kevin saw them sitting at a table when he entered the cafeteria. Pam called to him as he started to go to a table across the room.

"Kevin, come join us."

He hesitated just a second until he saw Pam get a chair from another table and place it next to Laura.

"Thanks. It's so nice to have lunch with so many beautiful ladies," said Kevin.

A couple of minutes later, Joyce came into the cafeteria. As she got a sandwich, she heard laughter coming from Pam's table.

"What in the world is going on over there!" She thought. She shook her head and went back upstairs with her lunch.

When the group returned to their offices a bit later, Joyce went to Pam's office, "I saw you all laughing and talking with Laura and Kevin at lunch. What's going on?"

"It's a long story. I'll tell you after work," Pam smiled, then continued typing.

When it was almost time to go home, Joyce came to Pam's office.

"No, Joyce," said Pam, "We're not trying to get back at Laura anymore. We went to Laura's office last night to see if we could find something to get her in trouble. Laura showed up as we were taking things out of her desk. We didn't know she was going to be working late. Joyce, you won't believe the rest of this story."

"Try me," Joyce said, standing with her hand on her hip.

"Brace yourself," said Pam, "Because what really happened sounds unbelievable. Laura saved us from three gunmen. She just looked at them and commanded them to stop and sit down in the Name of Jesus. They all fell to the floor and couldn't get up until the police came. Can you believe it?"

"No. I don't believe that. Is Laura some kind of magician?" Joyce growled.

"No. Laura is nice, and we've decided to attend church with her on Sunday. You know, Christians really do have power that they get from God. We've changed our minds about Christians. And I truly believe God is real. Why don't you come to church with us Sunday, Joyce?"

"I don't think so, and I don't believe your little story. Why can't you just tell me what really happened? She must have put some kind of evil spell on all of you."

Joyce then stomped out of Pam's office and went home very angry. Why do people think there's power in an evil spell but not in God?

Sunday, Pam, Jan, and Helen met Laura at God's Gang so they could all go to church together. Laura introduced them to God's Gang family, and then Laura took them up to her room. "Wow," said Helen, I love your room."

"When I first moved here," Laura explained, "I shared a room with Kathy, Anna, and Sue for a while. I had been through so much that I didn't want to be in a room alone. I'll tell you all about it later. After a few weeks, I moved into a room with my mother, and later, I decided I wanted my own room. Six months ago, I got my own room. The three sisters still wanted to stay in a room together. I'm glad they kept the extra bed in their room because I still sleep in their room more than I do in my own room."

"Would you guys like to have a slumber party and celebrate our new friendship?" Laura asked, "We can have it in the sisters' room (Sue, Anna, and Kathy). They love meeting people and having slumber parties. Their room is huge. There's plenty of floor room for pillows, blankets, and sleeping bags, and I love slumber parties."

"We would love a slumber party, Laura," said Pam, "Wouldn't we, girls?" Jan and Helen ran over and hugged Laura, and both screamed, "Yes! Yes!"

Getting everyone to church required a small caravan. Mary took her daughters and the three sisters in her van. Linda took Laura, Pam, Jan, and Helen in her van. Clyde took Rob, Mike, Randall, and Tom in another truck. When they all entered the church, the choir was still rehearsing. Seeing them come in, the minister stopped the choir when he noticed new people with God's Gang.

Mary and God's Gang had come to church about thirty minutes early. "Looks like God's Gang is bringing more children to God's house," he announced from the front of the church and chuckled, "And we welcome you this morning."

Rev. Smith asked Mary to introduce them.

"I'm happy to introduce you to some of Laura's friends from her job: Pam, Jan, and Helen." Members of the church came over to welcome them

and invited them to lunch after church.

"Welcome, ladies," said Rev. Smith, "Mary, if you and God's Gang keep this up, we must add more rows to accommodate your whole family. We have bought 50 acres of land to build on our existing property because we will need it soon.

Others continued to arrive, filling the church almost to capacity. As usual, after the opening hymn, Rev. Smith welcomed everyone. When everyone was seated, Rev. Smith talked about how good it is to see so many young people coming to church and receiving Jesus. The church applauded for a long time. It made the young people happy to see how the church welcomed them.

After church, when everybody was at the church's lunch, Laura looked expectantly toward the girls, "Well, what did you think? Did you like the service?"

Pam smiled and answered, "Let's put it this way, Laura, may we come to church with you every Sunday?"

Mary, who had come up from behind the girls, placed her hand on Laura's shoulder as she sat at the table and said, "Yes." Then Laura said.

"Mon and I will pick you all up every Sunday."

"I'm so looking forward to going to church. I bought a new Bible, and I have already seen how Rev. Smith made what I was reading in the book of John clear," said Jan.

After months of being almost inseparable, the girls have all become excellent friends. Pam, Helen, and Jan worked with Laura and the sisters, Anna, Kathy, Sue, and Laura, and the Sue D that brought Laura food when she was locked in a room.

Laura wanted to show Sue D how much she appreciated what she did for her when she was at the Red Zone. Laura got with the God's Gang and planned a surprise party for Sue D. Laura told Sue D that her mom would be taking all of us from the Sevens Building.

"Who's giving the party?" Asked Sue D.

"I'm not sure," said Laura, "We'll find out when we get there.

When Sue D walked into the Gym, she looked at the big sign above the basketball hops that said We love you, Sue D. In the back was a pile of gifts with another sign that said Gifts of Love for Sue D.

Sue stood there in shock, covered her face with her hands, and began to cry when she realized the party was for her. Laura took Sue D's hand and led her to a table where they sat.

The band began playing as Randall walked out with a mike and stopped when he started talking.

"Good evening, everyone." Randall introduced himself and said, "You all know why we are here except Sue D. Well, Sue D., we want to honor you for the help and encouragement you gave the girls locked up at the Red Zone. Laura told us all the things you did for her. She said that she would not be alive if it was not for your care."

Other girls spoke about how you had talked with them when they walked the streets. She made them feel that they would be all right and often made them laugh about how stupid the men were. They all had fun as they ate delicious food and danced.

Mary sat with Linda, "They were all recused from the Red Zone. They all received Jesus after going to church for a few weeks. They were ready to receive Jesus when He showed courage and power through Laura. They were inspired by the mercy of Jesus that night. They have been working for God ever since.

CHAPTER NINETEEN

With God, Enemies Become Friends

Sunday after church a few months later, "Laura has no idea what a difference she has made in our lives. I will never forget that night in her office. Let's start a club to pray for the salvation of our neighborhood. We can start with the young people first. You know, parents usually go to whatever their kids are into, so that way, we can reach the adults too."

"Yes!" Exclaimed Helen, "That's a great idea, and you're right about the parents. My mom wants to attend church with me this Sunday to learn what I've been doing for the past few months. She had to see why I was getting up early on a day I used to sleep in, so I'll be riding to church with her Sunday."

"That's wonderful, Helen; boy, we're making a difference!" said Pam.

"Yeah, even if we miss our sleep-in mornings," Jan laughed.

The girls meet next week to plan their outreach.

"I hope it's okay that I asked Rev. Smith if he would help us," Kathy said, "We always check at our meetings with everyone before making a decision, but everybody had left when I thought of it. He loved the idea and will let us meet in one of the rooms at the church for our Bible study. He suggested we start with the New Testament because most people find it easier to relate.

He also said to pray before making any decisions and to let the Holy Spirit lead us."

"Great work, Kathy," Laura said. "Let's all pray about this and thank God for the progress He's helping us with. Helen, will you lead us in prayer?"

After Helen led them in prayer, "Hey, let's be a little different," she said, "and instead of calling our meetings Bible study, let's be professional and form a real Bible club and call it God's Bible Club."

Everybody cheered, and Laura said, "That's a wonderful idea, Sue D.; why didn't I think of that?" The girls' efforts were highly successful. Basing their club out of the church gave them instant credibility with the community. The people held Rev. Smith in high esteem.

Five months after starting their program and going door-to-door in their neighborhood, they had led thirty-three teenagers to the Lord, all of whom joined the girls every Thursday night for God's Bible Club. Over half of the new Christians had brought their parents to the Lord. The congregation had grown in number and stature in the community, and Rev. Smith was already planning to build a larger building.

The girls had found the perfect formula for God's Bible Club. Each meeting began with praise and worship. Then, they discussed the lessons the pastor and sometimes other church members had prepared and took turns teaching Bible lessons at their meetings, which meant they all had to study the Scriptures. After each session, they talked about the people they were praying for and the excitement of watching some of them receive Jesus as their Lord and Savior. They also shared with the group the names of individuals with specific needs for whom they prayed.

God's Bible Club members knew the power of prayer. One evening during prayer time, Helen asked for prayer, "I need everyone to pray for my father. He has a serious heart problem, and the doctors can't perform surgery because he's too weak. Please pray that God will heal him."

The group formed a circle and held hands as Laura led them in prayer.

"Dear God, thank You for giving us the right and power to come directly to You. We all agree that You will move on behalf of Helen's father, and we ask You to heal him of heart problems. You said that if we ask and believe (Mark 11:24), You will do what we ask. You **also** said that we were healed by Jesus' stripes (Isaiah 53:4-5). We believe in Your Word. You said that You sent Your Word, which healed them (Matthew 8:8). Thank You, Father, for keeping Your enduring Word and healing Helen, Father, in Jesus' Name. Amen.

Two days later, Helen rushed into work at the Seven's Building breathless. She ran down the hall to Laura's office, grabbing Pam and Jan. "What's the matter, Helen?" Laura asked.

"My father. My father." While trying to catch her breath, Helen barely managed to say, "He's going to be okay! The doctors are calling it a miracle." They hugged each other and praised God for Helen's father's healing.

"I can't thank you enough for helping me find Jesus, Laura, and helping us understand that He truly loves us. You are one special person, Laura, to love us after how we treated you. You have also taught us through Jesus how to love, which has made a wonderful difference in our lives."

Mary And Linda Met A New Friend

LINDA WENT WITH Mary to enroll Lisa and Lear at a summer camp near the mansion that summer. During their visit to the camp, they met Janet, a lovely lady who volunteered there. It was apparent she loved children. As Mary watched her work with one girl that afternoon, she noticed the sadness in Janet's eyes when the little girl returned to her teammates for the afternoon competitions.

Mary took Linda by the arm, and they walked over to Janet. "Hi, I'm Mary, and this is my friend Linda. We brought Lisa and Lear, my daughters, over today. I noticed you were working with that little girl. You love working here with children, don't you?"

Janet smiled at the two women. "Yes. Yes, I do. I'm Janet. Is this your first visit to the camp?"

Yes, we've been in New York for a few months. We're originally from St. Louis. When I learned of this Christian camp, I knew it was the right place for my girls."

"Let me show you around while the girls are busy with their activities." Janet was so happy to have an adult to talk with.

Months later, the three women had become good friends. After summer camp, Mary, Linda, and Janet often spent time at God's Gang. They learned quite a bit about Janet during those visits. Janet had married a wealthy man, Jack Davidson, who she later knew was part of the Mafia. They had no children, something Janet missed terribly. That's why she volunteered so much of her time helping at the camp and raising money for camp scholarships so children can come even if they can't afford it. Janet paid tuition for five of the children each year.

She was a good, kind woman, but she was very lonely. She seldom saw her husband. He is very busy with the Mafia and its connections to racketeering, narcotics, gambling, prostitution, and other illegal activities.

Mary and Linda were happy to bring some joy into Janet's life. They could see the sadness and loneliness in her demeanor diminish as they became friends.

One afternoon, the phone rang as Mary worked in her office at the mansion.

"Yes, this is Mary." What she heard was horrifying.

"Of course, I'll be right over." Mary replaced the receiver and ran out of her office to the kitchen.

"Linda, I've got to go to Janet's. That was the police. Someone's been shot. Pray for us." As Mary grabbed her purse and opened the door to leave, Linda began to pray. When Mary arrived at Janet's, she found lights flashing, police cars haphazardly pulled into the street's curb, and police walking around. She found a place to park and ran to the door, where she was met by one of the police officers.

"I'm Mary. Someone called me to be with Janet Davidson."

"Wait here while I check," the officer said, leaving Mary at the door. A few seconds later, he returned and escorted her into the living room.

When Janet saw her, she rose from the sofa and nearly collapsed in Mary's arms. "Oh, thank you for coming so soon, Mary."

Janet was shaking so much that Mary put her arm around her waist to make sure she could make it to the couch, where they both sat down.

"I can't believe what has happened," Janet said, looking lost and confused.

"Try to relax, Janet, while I get you some water."

Mary went to the kitchen and found cold water in the refrigerator. Then she returned to the living room and gave the washer to Janet.

"What happened, Janet?"

"I was in the kitchen this morning with Jane, a friend, when the doorbell rang. Jane looked at her watch and said she'd answer it since I was making coffee. I heard her open the door and a man's voice with a thick accent. I couldn't understand what he was saying and thought it was probably a salesman. Then Jane shouted, 'I'm not Jack's wife,' and I heard gunshots. What I heard was so upsetting that I dropped the pot of coffee and ran into the living room. I saw a man running from the house. My heart felt heavy as I looked at Jane with blood pooling around her. One of my neighbors heard the shots, ran in, and called the police when he saw Jane lying on the floor. Then he left, but he must have seen the man running away.

When the police arrived, they questioned me, and I told them everything except what Jane shouted. I'm not sure why I left it out, but I did. Then I started thinking about what she said. 'I'm not Jack's wife.' I must have fainted then because I remembered waking up with several police officers standing over me. As they were helping me, I asked them to call you. I can't believe she's dead, Mary," Janet said, still in shock.

"The killer meant to kill me. But why would Jack want me dead?"

A few minutes later, one of the detectives entered the living room and introduced himself as Detective Anderson.

The paramedic told Mary that Jane refused to go to the hospital. He said he checked her over and thinks she's okay physically, but he said she's suffered quite a shock, and she asked someone to call Mary.

"Thank you, Detective. I'll stay with her until her husband gets home. Has anyone tried to contact him?"

"So far, we haven't been able to reach him." Then the Detective left.

Mary put her arms around Janet. "You have to tell the police what you heard Jane say."

"I know, Mary, but I need time to think. I'm not sure what to do. I'm so afraid of Jack. What would he do if he knew what Jane said? Certainly, he'll know. I know he wants me dead."

Before Mary could respond, the phone rang. One of the police officers answered it and entered the living room. "Mrs. Davidson, it's your husband."

Janet looked at Mary, who squeezed her hand as she took the phone from the officer.

"Thank you, Officer."

"Jack," Janet explained as she tried to sound calm, "someone shot Jane." Jack was slow to answer. "Did you hear me, Jack? Someone shot Jane."

"I don't understand. Jane? Did someone shoot Jane? Is she all right?" Jack's voice was a mixture of disbelief and anger. Through the phone, Janet heard her husband pound something. The noise rumbling through the receiver was so loud that she had to hold it away from her ear.

"Is she all right?" Jack asked again, hoping he'd get a different answer.

"She's dead, Jack," said Janet.

"How can Jane be dead? But how? Why?" Jack has a problem accepting Jane's death. Jack was distraught. "Janet's alive, he thought, and Jane is dead. How can that be?"

Janet realized that he never even thought about asking how she was. He was too upset to pretend to care.

Jane's last words kept going through Janet's mind.

"I'm not Jack's wife."

Janet couldn't stop thinking about what happened to Jane and why Jack would want to kill her.

Jack was so upset that he mumbled as he walked through the house. Janet's grief and pain as she realized Jack had expected Jane to be alive and her to be dead.

"I have to go now, Jack," Janet said calmly, her voice now cold. "The police want to question me."

She calmly put down the phone and turned to look at Mary.

"What's wrong? Isn't Jack on his way home?" Mary asked.

"I'm sure my husband tried to have me killed, Mary. I thought Jane was my friend, but I think she and Jack were lovers, and he tried to kill me so they could be together, but something went wrong." Janet, unable to control her emotions, began to cry.

Mary was finding it difficult to comfort Janet as she became overwhelmed with grief and fear after reality set in.

"Janet, if you're right, you're not safe."

Janet looked at Mary, blinked back tears, and wiped her eyes with

a tissue Mary gave her.

"Jack's a powerful man, Mary. You have no idea how powerful. I can't even count on the police being able to protect me if he's trying to kill me. He's mad that Jane is dead and not me, so his evil brain must feel like killing me would be revenge for Jane's death."

"It doesn't matter how powerful Jack is; I know someone more powerful."

"Who? I'll hire him. Money is not an object."

"You don't have to pay for this person's protection, Janet. I'm talking about God. Do you know Jesus as your Savior?"

Janet stared at her blankly. "I don't know what you mean."

"Do you know anything about God?" Mary asked.

"I never really thought God was real. I know people at the camp think that He's real, and I've learned a lot about what they teach the children there, but I didn't believe any of the things they were teaching. They are so friendly and kind to me.

I like being around the adults and the children, and unlike some people who don't believe what they believe, I'm not turned off by what they believe."

"I have some excellent news for you, Janet. God is real and with us, and we can trust His promises. He promised to never leave us, even in times of trouble. So relax and believe his promises."

Janet was so distraught and miserable that she was ready to do anything to help her feel better.

"How do I accept Jesus?"

Mary explained the love of God and the plan of salvation to Janet to make sure she understood. She had to be sincere when she committed her life to Jesus. Mary could tell that Janet had understood and was genuine as she accepted Jesus as her Lord and Savior that afternoon; her countenance changed entirely, and she was at peace.

"Mary, I've never felt such peace. I feel full of warmth and light as a feather. I also felt a touch from God, and I felt Jesus accept me as I accepted Him. The love and power of God is exceptional."

"That's wonderful, Janet. Some people know they are saved because of a memorable encounter with God; others see it because they trust the Bible. God showed you something special. You needed God to show you His love and secure peace.

CHAPTER TWENTY

Kate And Kitty Reached Out To Troubled Friends

JERRY'S DAUGHTERS, ALSO members of God's Bible Club, contacted a group of girls they once ran with. They invited them to God's Bible Club."

Before we go through the Scriptures we have penned, said Anna, "I found some Scriptures for why reading the Bible is important, and I printed some of them." Then Anna gave copies to everyone. "These are a few of the scriptures:

There are vital reasons to read the Bible. Here is what God says:

All Scripture is breathed out by God and profitable for teaching, reproof, correction, and training in righteousness, so that the man of God may be complete and equipped for every good work. 2 Timothy 3:16-17.

If you study the Bible, you will learn that although the Bible does say some things you may not understand, you will still understand the things that are important for you to know. The Holy Spirit will reveal to you things in the Bible as you continue reading it.

For example, two Christians, Barbara and Kym, were talking." Barbara said, "I never vote. Both parties have problems."

"Yes," said Kym. "But the Bible indicates that we should vote."

"That's not in the Bible," said Barbara.

"Well, when the Bible says my people morn with a wicket leader, don't you think you should vote for a leader that is not wicket? We can always find out if a leader is wicket or not."

"Kym, you are smart; God's makes so much sense that I will vote in the next election. Let's study the Bible together."

"Here is one that is interesting. Did you know that several books in the Bible describe the earth as having a spherical shape? Job described a circle upon the face of the waters until the day and night end. Job 26:10. It also described a spherical earth in Isaiah 40:21-22. For many years, people who didn't know the Scriptures years ago thought you could walk of the earth like it was a flat surface."

"I don't like to talk about this topic because I don't want to make anyone feel bad. It should be clear that God loves everyone, and that includes gays. Some people say that God did not address gays because. Homosexuality is not in the Bible. Is that true? Doesn't that mean they are homosexuals? However, it is clear from the Bible that engaging in sexual activities between two men is a sin, and having sex with a man and woman who are not married is also a sin.

The word trinity is not in the Bible, but it means three: the Father, Son, and Holy Spirit.

No one extended their hand to take the papers, so Anna placed them on each girl's desk. The girls came but were uninterested in the Bible or God. They made fun of the Bible lessons that God's Bible Club members were teaching. Laura asked Rev. Smith to meet with them to help them deal with the girls.

"I want to talk directly to the girls, causing problems. We have all tried to show you love and acceptance. However, some of you have caused many problems. You have upset some of the girls and their parents by telling their parents that three of the girls were pregnant.

The girls told their parents that it was not true, but their parents had the girls tested anyway, only to find the tests negative. You have said other things that are not true and are causing problems. We want to solve your issues, so let's discuss it. There may have been a misunderstanding that we can clear up."

Sally, one of the eight girls causing problems, stood up and said, "I don't like this club. None of what you're talking about is true, and all the girls in the club are snobs and think we're stupid. They say they're the only people with the truth and that we're going to hell if we don't believe what they believe."

Then Anna stood up and said, "No one ever said anything like that. If you heard that somewhere else, that is not true. We didn't talk about anything; Brenda was the first to read the Bible verse on the lesson plan when we started our study. She seemed angry about the verses she read. Sally referred to verses she didn't understand, and no one understood what Brenda read but was angry about it: John 14:6."

> "I am the way, the truth, and the Life.
> No one can come to the Father except through Me."
> John 3:3 Jesus answered and said to him:
> "Most assuredly, I say to you, unless one is born again,
> he cannot see the Kingdom of God." John 3:15:
> "That whoever believes in Him should not perish
> but have eternal Life." John 3:16:
> "For God so loved the world that He gave
> His only begotten Son, that whoever believes in Him
> should not perish but have everlasting life."

"That particular night," Anna explained, "we only prayed, read the Bible, and sang three praise songs, and then Brenda read the selected verses. We didn't even have a chance to discuss the Bible verses that Brenda read the way we usually do because some of the members of our church surprised us with ice cream and cake.

Sally may be referring to those verses. We said nothing about the things she's accusing us of. Jesus is claiming in the verse that Brenda read that He is the only way to the Father, thus the only way to Heaven."

"I'm sorry, Sally," said Kate. "You were offended. We were so happy that you came. We would never have done anything to upset you. Remember, we used to be friends, and even though we did wrong things, we liked each other and had fun together."

"Does anyone else have anything to say?" Ask Rev. Smith. Then Tracy, one of the other girls that Kate and Kitty had invited to the Bible Study, sat in her chair defiantly and said, "We don't have to listen to you, people. Brenda, we can read our books someplace else. Let's go." They were reading books that dealt with the occult. Brenda, too, was reading an occult book, except when she read the Bible verses.

The eight girls left as they knocked over chairs and other things. One of them kicked over a floor plant as she walked out, laughing.

Brenda called Laura at work two months later, crying,

"Laura, I'm sorry for how I acted at God's Bible Club. Please forgive me. My mom kicked me out of the house because I told her I wanted to apologize to the God's Bible Club and ask them if I could come back."

"Oh, Brenda. I'm so sorry. Of course, you can come back," Laura assured, "Where are you? Give me the address where you are, and I'll have one of God's Gang pick you up."

Laura asked Faith if it would be possible for her to get off early from work so she could help someone in trouble.

"Faith, I'll make up my time on Saturday or work late one day."

"Oh no, you won't, Laura. You are an excellent employee and deserve some time off for your hard work. Take the day off. It won't affect your pay."

"Thank you so much, Faith."

Laura called the mansion, and Mary answered, "Hello, God's Gang. May I help you?"

"Mary, it's Laura," Laura explained Brenda's situation.

"Give me the address, and I'll have Clyde pick you up first, and then he can bring you and Brenda here."

Clyde picked up Laura, and then they went to the drugstore where Brenda was and found her crying at a table. Laura rushed over to Brenda and put her arms around her.

"It's all right, Brenda. Let's go to God's Gang. You can stay there as long as you need to."

That night, no one could comfort Brenda. She refused to go to God's Bible Club that evening. The girls had called a special meeting to welcome her.

"Why have you changed your mind?" I thought you wanted to return to God's Bible Club." Laura needed clarification.

Brenda still crying. "I'm afraid. I know the girls will hate me for the way I acted."

"You can see that I don't hate you? I care about you. Our other girls are just like me," said Laura.

"No, Laura, I'm sorry, but I just can't." Brenda was still crying.

"Then I'll stay with you until you feel better." Laura took Brenda to her room and held her while she cried, "Why don't you lie on my bed and relax for a while? I'll get you something to eat."

When Laura returned with a sandwich and a glass of milk, Brenda was fast asleep.

Laura called God's Bible Club members and told them about Brenda. About an hour later, all the girls left God's Bible Club and came over to God's Gang to comfort Brenda and welcome her back into God's Bible Club.

"We canceled our meeting at God's Bible Club to welcome you back. But since you refused to come, we came to you. "

"So. . .," said Pam, "You feel bad because you did a few mean things. We could tell you about some meaner things than what you did."

"Yeah," said Helen, "It was three of us: me, Pam, and Jan. We were so jealous of Laura, and we hated that she was a Christian. We did so many mean things to her that I don't want to think about them."

"Look what great friends we are now," Laura said as she put her arms around Pam."After a while, all the girls were laughing, including Brenda.

"You don't have to feel bad about anything. We want you to be happy, Brenda," Kate said as she pushed Brenda from a sitting position on the bed.

Mary called the girls' parents and asked if their daughters could spend the night, and all parents agreed except for Brenda's parents. When Mary called Brenda's house, her mother hung up on her. Mary wanted to call her mother, hoping she could connect with her and help restore the relationship between her and her daughter.

Mary got blankets and pillows, ordered pizza, and made lemonade. Linda made chocolate cookies and brought in milk. The girls had lots of fun as they laughed and played all night.

Mary and Linda were so happy to know that the girls were having so much fun as they watched television in the den.

CHAPTER TWENTY-ONE

Mary And Linda Met A New Friend

LINDA WENT WITH Mary to enroll Lisa and Lear at a summer camp near the mansion that summer. During their visit to the camp, they met Janet, a lovely lady who volunteered there. It was apparent she loved children. As Mary watched her work with one girl that afternoon, she noticed the sadness in Janet's eyes when the little girl returned to her teammates for the afternoon competitions.

Mary took Linda by the arm, and they walked over to Janet. "Hi, I'm Mary, and this is my friend Linda. We brought Lisa and Lear, my daughters, over today. I noticed you were working with that little girl. You love working here with children, don't you?"

Janet smiled at the two women. "Yes. Yes, I do. I'm Janet. Is this your first visit to the camp?"

Yes, we've been in New York for a few months. We're originally from St. Louis. When I learned of this Christian camp, I knew it was the right place for my girls."

"Let me show you around while the girls are busy with their activities." Janet was so happy to have an adult to talk with.

Months later, the three women had become good friends. After summer camp, Mary, Linda, and Janet often spent time at God's Gang. They learned quite a bit about Janet during those visits. Janet had married a wealthy man, Jack Davidson, who she later knew was part of the Mafia. They had no children, something Janet missed terribly. That's why she volunteered so much of her time helping at the camp and raising money for camp scholarships so children can come even if they can't afford it. Janet paid tuition for five of the children each year.

She was a good, kind woman, but she was very lonely. She seldom saw her husband. He is very busy with the Mafia and its connections to racketeering, narcotics, gambling, prostitution, and other illegal activities.

Mary and Linda were happy to bring some joy into Janet's life. They could see the sadness and loneliness in her demeanor diminish as they became friends.

One afternoon, the phone rang as Mary worked in her office at the mansion.

"Yes, this is Mary." What she heard was horrifying.

"Of course, I'll be right over." Mary replaced the receiver and ran out of her office to the kitchen.

"Linda, I've got to go to Janet's. That was the police. Someone's been shot. Pray for us." As Mary grabbed her purse and opened the door to leave, Linda began to pray. When Mary arrived at Janet's, she found lights flashing, police cars haphazardly pulled into the street's curb, and police walking around. She found a place to park and ran to the door, where she was met by one of the police officers.

"I'm Mary. Someone called me to be with Janet Davidson."

"Wait here while I check," the officer said, leaving Mary at the door. A few seconds later, he returned and escorted her into the living room.

When Janet saw her, she rose from the sofa and nearly collapsed in Mary's arms. "Oh, thank you for coming so soon, Mary."

Janet was shaking so much that Mary put her arm around her waist to make sure she could make it to the couch, where they both sat down.

"I can't believe what has happened," Janet said, looking lost and confused.

"Try to relax, Janet, while I get you some water."

Mary went to the kitchen and found cold water in the refrigerator. Then she returned to the living room and gave the washer to Janet.

"What happened, Janet?"

"I was in the kitchen this morning with Jane, a friend when the doorbell rang. Jane looked at her watch and said she'd answer it since I was making coffee. I heard her open the door and a man's voice with a thick accent. I couldn't understand what he was saying and thought it was probably a salesman. Then Jane shouted, 'I'm not Jack's wife,' and I heard gunshots. What I heard was so upsetting that I dropped the pot of coffee and ran into the living room. I saw a man running from the house. My heart felt heavy as I looked at Jane with blood pooling around her. One of my neighbors heard the shots, ran in, and called the police when he saw Jane lying on the floor. Then he left, but he must have seen the man running away.

When the police arrived, they questioned me, and I told them everything except what Jane shouted. I'm not sure why I left it out, but I did. Then I started thinking about what she said. 'I'm not Jack's wife.' I must have fainted then because I remembered waking up with several police officers standing over me. As they were helping me, I asked them to call you. I can't believe she's dead, Mary," Janet said, still in shock.

"The killer meant to kill me. But why would Jack want me dead?"

A few minutes later, one of the detectives entered the living room and introduced himself as Detective Anderson.

The paramedic told Mary that Jane refused to go to the hospital. He said he checked her over and thinks she's okay physically, but he said she's suffered quite a shock, and she asked someone to call Mary.

"Thank you, Detective. I'll stay with her until her husband gets home. Has anyone tried to contact him?"

"So far, we haven't been able to reach him." Then the Detective left.

Mary put her arms around Janet. "You have to tell the police what you heard Jane say."

"I know, Mary, but I need time to think. I'm not sure what to do. I'm so afraid of Jack. What would he do if he knew what Jane said? Certainly, he'll know. I know he wants me dead."

Before Mary could respond, the phone rang. One of the police officers answered it and entered the living room. "Mrs. Davidson, it's your husband."

Janet looked at Mary, who squeezed her hand as she took the phone from the officer.

"Thank you, Officer."

"Jack," Janet explained as she tried to sound calm, "Someone shot Jane." Jack was slow to answer. "Did you hear me, Jack? Someone shot Jane."

"I don't understand. Jane? Did someone shoot Jane? Is she all right?" Jack's voice was a mixture of disbelief and anger. Through the phone, Janet heard her husband pound something. The noise rumbling through the receiver was so loud that she had to hold it away from her ear.

"Is she all right?" Jack asked again, hoping he'd get a different answer.

"She's dead, Jack," said Janet.

"How can Jane be dead? But how? Why?" Jack has a problem accepting Jane's death. Jack was distraught. "Janet's alive, he thought, and Jane is dead. How can that be?"

Janet realized that he never even thought about asking how she was. He was too upset to pretend to care.

Jane's last words kept going through Janet's mind.

"I'm not Jack's wife."

Janet couldn't stop thinking about what happened to Jane and why Jack would want to kill her.

Jack was so upset that he mumbled as he walked through the house. Janet's grief and pain as she realized Jack had expected Jane to be alive and her to be dead.

"I have to go now, Jack," Janet said calmly, her voice now cold. "The police want to question me."

She calmly put down the phone and turned to look at Mary.

"What's wrong? Isn't Jack on his way home?" Mary asked.

"I'm sure my husband tried to have me killed, Mary. I thought Jane was my friend, but I think she and Jack were lovers, and he tried to kill me so they could be together, but something went wrong." Janet, unable to control her emotions, began to cry.

Mary was finding it difficult to comfort Janet as she became overwhelmed with grief and fear after reality set in.

"Janet, if you're right, you're not safe."

Janet looked at Mary, blinked back tears, and wiped her eyes with

a tissue Mary gave her.

"Jack's a powerful man, Mary. You have no idea how powerful. I can't even count on the police being able to protect me if he's trying to kill me. He's mad that Jane is dead and not me, so his evil brain must feel like killing me would be revenge for Jane's death."

"It doesn't matter how powerful Jack is; I know someone more powerful."

"Who? I'll hire him. Money is not an object."

"You don't have to pay for this person's protection, Janet. I'm talking about God. Do you know Jesus as your Savior?"

Janet stared at her blankly. "I don't know what you mean."

"Do you know anything about God?" Mary asked.

"I never really thought God was real. I know people at the camp think that He's real, and I've learned a lot about what they teach the children there, but I didn't believe any of the things they were teaching. They are so friendly and kind to me. I like being around the adults and the children, and unlike some people who don't believe what they believe, I'm not turned off by what they believe."

"I have some excellent news for you, Janet. God is real and with us, and we can trust His promises. He promised to never leave us, even in times of trouble. So relax and believe his promises."

Janet was so distraught and miserable that she was ready to do anything to help her feel better.

"How do I accept Jesus?"

Mary explained the love of God and the plan of salvation to Janet to make sure she understood. She had to be sincere when she committed her life to Jesus. Mary could tell that Janet had understood and was genuine as she accepted Jesus as her Lord and Savior that afternoon; her countenance changed entirely, and she was at peace.

"Mary, I've never felt such peace. I feel full of warmth and light as a feather. I also felt a touch from God, and I felt Jesus accept me as I accepted Him. The love and power of God is exceptional."

"That's wonderful, Janet. Some people know they are saved because of a memorable encounter with God; others see it because they trust the Bible. God showed you something special. You needed God to show you His love and secure peace.

Jane's last words kept going through Janet's mind.

"I'm not Jack's wife."

Janet couldn't stop thinking about what happened to Jane and why Jack would want to kill her.

Jack was so upset that he mumbled as he walked through the house. Janet's grief and pain as she realized Jack had expected Jane to be alive and her to be dead.

"I have to go now, Jack," Janet said calmly, her voice now cold. "The police want to question me."

She calmly put down the phone and turned to look at Mary.

"What's wrong? Isn't Jack on his way home?" Mary asked.

"I'm sure my husband tried to have me killed, Mary. I thought Jane was my friend, but I think she and Jack were lovers, and he tried to kill me so they could be together, but something went wrong." Janet, unable to control her emotions, began to cry.

Mary was finding it difficult to comfort Janet as she became overwhelmed with grief and fear after reality set in.

"Janet, if you're right, you're not safe."

Janet looked at Mary, blinked back tears, and wiped her eyes with

a tissue Mary gave her.

"Jack's a powerful man, Mary. You have no idea how powerful. I can't even count on the police being able to protect me if he's trying to kill me. He's mad that Jane is dead and not me, so his evil brain must feel like killing me would be revenge for Jane's death."

"It doesn't matter how powerful Jack is; I know someone more powerful."

"Who? I'll hire him. Money is not an object."

"You don't have to pay for this person's protection, Janet. I'm talking about God. Do you know Jesus as your Savior?"

Janet stared at her blankly. "I don't know what you mean."

"Do you know anything about God?" Mary asked.

"I never really thought God was real. I know people at the camp think that He's real, and I've learned a lot about what they teach the children there, but I didn't believe any of the things they were teaching. They are so friendly and kind to me. I like being around the adults and the children, and unlike some people who don't believe what they believe, I'm not turned off by what they believe."

"I have some excellent news for you, Janet. God is real and with us, and we can trust His promises. He promised to never leave us, even in times of trouble. So relax and believe his promises."

Janet was so distraught and miserable that she was ready to do anything to help her feel better.

"How do I accept Jesus?"

Mary explained the love of God and the plan of salvation to Janet to make sure she understood. She had to be sincere when she committed her life to Jesus. Mary could tell that Janet had understood and was genuine as she accepted Jesus as her Lord and Savior that afternoon; her countenance changed entirely, and she was at peace.

"Mary, I've never felt such peace. I feel full of warmth and light as a feather. I also felt a touch from God, and I felt Jesus accept me as I accepted Him. The love and power of God is exceptional."

"That's wonderful, Janet. Some people know they are saved because of a memorable encounter with God; others see it because they trust the Bible. God showed you something special. You needed God to show you His love and secure peace.

CHAPTER TWENTY-TWO

Jack Reacts To Jane's Death

JACK PACED THE floor in his office, trying to figure out his next move. He occasionally glanced at the hole in the wall he'd punched when he heard about Jane. What could have happened? He thought. More importantly, how do I go on without Jane? Later, after his call home, he grabbed his briefcase and headed out of his office.

"Have my driver meet me downstairs. I'll be at home for the rest of the day," he called to his secretary as he headed to the elevator. "My wife's best friend has just been killed."

Almost everyone who worked for Jack knew that Janet's best friend was Jack's lover, but no one talked about it.

In the elevator, he took several deep breaths to steady himself. He didn't want to see Janet. She was supposed to be dead. All he wanted was for this nightmare to be over. He needed to pretend to be a good husband for the police in case they got suspicious.

Thirty minutes later, the limo pulled onto his driveway. Yellow crime scene tape blocked off the entryway and front door, so he walked around to the back to get into his house.

"Janet?" he called as he entered through the French doors from the patio into the dining room.

"Janet, where are you?" Then he heard voices coming from the kitchen.

As he entered, he saw his wife and Mary, whom he had never met, standing at the counter talking. At the sound of the door opening, they turned toward it. Janet looked at Jack, her face void of emotion. Jack and Janet said nothing to each other and didn't make a move toward each other.

"You must be Jack," Mary said as she stepped toward him.

"I'm Mary, a friend of Janet's."

"Yeah," Jack didn't attempt to shake her hand or look at her, as his eyes were on Janet. "What happened?"

When Jack walked in, Mary and Janet were in the kitchen, and Janet was fighting hard to control her tears. She held onto the counter as she faced her husband. Blinking rapidly to keep the tears from falling, she began to tell him what had happened, trying not to let her fear show.

"I was making coffee when the doorbell rang. Jane went to the door and opened it. A few seconds later, I heard gunshots—three or four. Then I ran into the living room. A man was running from the house, and Jane was bleeding on the floor. I kneeled by her, but she was already dead. Our neighbor ran into the house, saw Jane lying there, and called the police."

"What time was it when the doorbell rang? And why did Jane go to the door?" Jack's face appeared crazy with rage, yet he managed to keep his voice even and controlled. Mary looked puzzled at the questions he was asking. Why should it matter what time it was? She thought, and why would it matter who went to the door?

"I don't know what time it was—sometime midmorning. Jane got here around nine-thirty. We'd talked a little while, and then she suggested we have coffee here instead of going out as planned, so we entered the kitchen. I was putting the coffee in the coffee maker when the doorbell rang. That's why she answered the door."

"I don't understand," Jack mumbled under his breath. He seemed lost in thought, forgetting that the women were there.

"What did you say, Jack?"

"Uh, nothing. I see you're okay." Jack tried to pretend he cared.

"Yes, I'm fine." She turned to Mary, and they went into the living room. Jack stood in the kitchen for a few more seconds, tensing and relaxing his grip on his briefcase. Then he left the kitchen and went upstairs to his office, his anger barely under control.

The next day, Jack returned to his office downtown and waited for the Russian. He walked in promptly at eight, early enough to avoid his secretary yet late enough to blend in with everyone coming into the building going to their offices, the restaurant, or the bar to start working.

Jack tells the Russian, "You killed the wrong woman, you idiot!" "No, understand," he managed in a thick Russian accent, "money."

"Sit down," Jack said in disgust and pointed for the Russian into one of the chairs in front of his desk. He picked up the phone and called the limo driver, "Edward, get up here now." Edward was the driver and also spoke Russian. He arrived in less than five minutes and knocked on the door before entering.

"What is it, boss?" Edward asked.

Not wanting to explain everything to Edward, who had no reason to know anything, Jack said, "Write these sentences in Russian."

The sentences Jack gave Edward read: Have someone you can trust read this to you in Russian.

"Sure, boss," Edward was used to being given orders he didn't necessarily understand. Edward knew better than to ask any questions. What he didn't know wouldn't hurt him. When

Edward left, Jack attached the note Edward had written to the one that Jack had written: You killed the wrong person. You will get your money once your job is complete. You reported to the wrong person. You must go to the same place and report to the right person. Make sure that there is no one else there.

The Russian looked at the notes and wrinkled his forehead as if it made no sense, "Nyet! (nyet means no in Russian) Money!" The Russian was becoming angry but not as sore as Jack over his assassin's stupidity.

Jack is just as stupid as telling him to take two notes to someone to translate when the Russian does not understand either message.

"Nyet! You got there too early. You were supposed to be there at 11:00; Jane was not supposed to be there," Jack yelled at the Russian. "Understand?"

He came around his desk and pulled the Russian coat sleeve up his arm. He put his finger on his watch and then pointed to the clock on his desk. See? Your watch needs to be corrected. You went to the house too early and killed the wrong woman."

Then Jack showed him the first note that Edward had written and said, "Read this; it's in Russian. Now get out of here."

The Russian could read Edward's note but didn't know what it meant. He never understood that he would take Edward's message and have someone read it, then translate the other message into Russian.

The Russian yelled something at him he couldn't understand, then stalked out of the office, slamming the door on his way out. Jack's secretary had just arrived and was putting her purse away when she heard the door, and the big man, all dressed in black, rushed past her.

Then she heard Jack yelling, "Stupid idiot!" She knew not to enter Jack's office unless he calmed down.

Later that day, the police questioned Jack about the murder. It was a routine part of the process. It's a day for staying as far under the radar as possible. His secretary thought.

The investigation: Jack was nowhere near the house when it happened, and they had found no connection between Jane and Jack, although Jane was Janet's friend. Still, the detective warned him, "Don't leave town."

"Jack could get away with murder if you don't tell the police what Jane said before the man shot her," Mary told Janet that afternoon when Mary came over to see how she was. Mary was highly disappointed that Janet hadn't talked with the police.

"I know, but I've got to tell them at the right time. As I told you before, if Jack finds out what Jane said before the man shot her, he will know that I know he sent the killer to me. What if the police don't believe me and think I'm just trying to get back at Jack? I believe that Jack and Jane were having an affair, but I certainly didn't know that until I heard what Jane said. The police may think that I learned about the affair. They may even blame me for her death. If I tell the police what Jane said and they don't believe me, I think I will be in greater danger. If Jack heard about it, you know he would want to kill me for no reason other than to protect himself.

"You may be right, Janet. We have to find more evidence that Jack

planned to have you killed."

"I know," said Janet, "But I just don't know what to do."

"Don't worry, Janet. God will help us with this."

The stress Janet was under, trying to maintain a cool façade whenever Jack was home, grieving for her friend yet angry with her and Jack for their betrayal, was evident in how she acted.

"I have a friend, Kirk Turner, a private detective. I'll ask him to help us with the investigation. We both know Jack hired someone to kill you who mistook Jane for you. I'm sure Kirk will be able to find proof that the police can use against Jack."

"Okay, call your friend Mary. Although this has been hard for me, I'm not as upset as I would normally be now that I have God and you are supporting me."

After Mary called Kirk, she arranged a meeting with Jack and Janet. Jack reviewed everything with Janet several times.

"Are you sure the man you saw running from the house shot Jane?"

"Well, I didn't see him do it, if that's what you mean. But he had a gun; he was running from the house, and Jane was lying on the floor bleeding. I believe he was the man who shot her. How could it have been anyone else?" Janet's voice revealed her impatience with repeatedly answering the same questions. She wanted this nightmare to end.

"I'm sorry. Going over all of this again is a bit upsetting. Still, sometimes, people start remembering more details after the shock of the event begins to wear off. Are you sure you don't remember anything else?"

"As I said, he had a thick Russian accent. I don't speak Russian but I love going to the Russian tea room. His accent was very similar to the servers there. He was big, probably about my husband's height, but heavier, although it was hard to tell because his clothes were loose."

Jack Davidson had his hand in numerous businesses, both illegal and legal, one of which was real estate. That gave Kirk the perfect opening to contact Davidson directly. Kirk had been buying and selling real estate to increase his income. He had done well until he purchased a piece of property for over a million dollars just before the economy plunged. He'd been trying to sell it for six months but had failed to succeed.

Always looking for prospects, Kirk hoped to accomplish two things at once: Find out about Davidson and sell his problem property. Getting in to see Davidson was going to take some skill. He only worked individually with real estate clients under unusual circumstances, doing just enough public work to cover his Mafia involvement. So, Kirk decided to use a less conventional approach.

Kirk went to the restaurant in Davidson's office building downtown that afternoon. He sat at a table near the back of the restaurant, where he could see who came and went, and lingered over a cup of coffee while seeming to read his paper. After he'd been there a few minutes, the waiter came over to refill his cup.

"Man, do you believe this economy?" Kirk told the waiter, "The real estate market still hasn't stabilized. If I've lost ten grand this week, I've lost a hundred."

"Yes, sir, I know what you mean. Tips this week have been lousy," the waiter responded as Kirk looked up.

"Well, I won't forget you, man. I need to find a good realtor. A realtor is experienced in selling problem property that has been on the market for some time. I must find someone to help me unload this property before it breaks me."

"I'm sorry, sir; we're not allowed to discuss our customers with anyone. I'll check on you again in a while."

The next day, Kirk returned to observing the room, his face shielded partially by the paper. The waiter came to his table with a pot of coffee and went straight to the bartender. Then the waiter returned to Kirk's table and told him that the bartender might be able to help him and suggested that he have a seat at the bar. The bartenders are the gatekeepers of information in any restaurant. They heard and saw everything. Kirk was pleased to have an opportunity to chat with the bartender, thinking that he might listen to some valuable news. Kirk nursed his coffee for another half hour before he knew he had to leave or end up drawing too much attention. Jack placed $10 under the sugar packet tray on the counter. Then, he folded his newspaper and prepared to leave.

"Sir. Sir." The bartender called to him as he was leaving. Kirk turned back to the bar.

"Yes?"

"I understand you're looking for a real estate agent?" said the bartender.

"Yes, do you know someone good?"

"The owner of this restaurant is a broker. Jack Davidson. He doesn't usually handle clients directly, but I'm sure his agency could help you."

"Thanks, man. But I work only with the top man. I've got too much cash tied up in this property to leave it to just any agent I'm assigned. At least, not unless I could talk with this Jack Davidson personally to know that he was assigned one of his best people to my property."

As Kirk finished, the bartender looked past him to a man who had just entered the restaurant, "As luck would have it, Sir, Mr. Davidson has just come in. Let me see if he'll meet with you. Wait here."

Kirk watched the bartender approach Davidson, bringing him his usual drink. When Davidson looked over at him, Kirk walked over to his table.

"So Danny here tells me you need a real estate agent?"

"That's right, but I need someone who handles high-end property. I've been sitting on this beautiful property for six months and need to sell it quickly. Much of my money is in this property, and I need to liquefy without losing my shirt."

"Turner. Kirk Turner." Usually, Kirk would not have given his real name, but the property was in his real name, so he had no choice. Kirt plans to get information on Davidon, before he finds out, Kirk is a private investigator his wife hires.

"If you can hold out for another week, I've got to go out of town for a few days but should be back by Monday. Come to my office around ten o'clock Monday morning, and we'll work something out. Here's my card."

"Thanks. I'll see you then." Kirk left the restaurant, whistling happily, as he walked down the block and across the street before hailing a cab back to his office.

While Kirk waited for Davidson to return to New York, he used his time to find as much information as possible. First, he wanted to know where Jack was going. A quick call to a friend who worked at one of the airports let him track Davidson's private plane to a field just outside New York. A little more digging gave him the flight information. He was going to Tucson. His source also confirmed that Davidson had often traveled in the company of a beautiful blonde.

Janet rarely, if ever, traveled with her husband, so this had to be Jane. Then it was on the Internet. Access to public records was pretty simple, thanks to the Internet. Janet had given him her husband's social security number, and he'd gotten his friend with the New York Police Department to provide him with the same information on Jane.

First, he located Davidson's residence in the foothills of Tucson. Next, he accessed Jane's financial records, noting large monthly deposits to her checking account. He also found that one of Davidson's businesses always paid one of her credit cards. Davidson's financial records showed matching withdrawals from one of his business accounts.

He specifically looked at the records for the business to which Jane's credit card bills. Again, the match was there. Her credit card bill account was paid in full each month from the proceeds of Davidson's business. Although Kirk had established a clear connection and probable affair between Davidson and Jane, he still had no concrete proof that the two had plotted to kill Janet. So he continued to dig.

Kirk entered Davidson's office promptly at ten on Monday morning.

"Hi," he said, smiling as he greeted the secretary. "I'm Kirk Turner. Jack asked me to drop by this morning around ten to discuss a real estate matter."

"Yes, Mr. Turner. I have noted it in his schedule. Have a seat, and I'll let him know you're here." She rose from her chair and walked toward Davidson's door. She knocked twice, waited for a second, opened the door, and entered. A few seconds later, she reappeared and said, "Mr. Davidson will see you now."

As Kirk entered his office, Davidson walked toward him, raising his hand as he walked to shake Kirk's hand. "What a nice office," Kirk remarked as he admired Jack's office. "How was your trip?"

"Oh, fine. I just went to close up my summer home there. I'm putting it on the market soon."

Kirk nodded in acknowledgment, deciding not to press Davidson on the reason.

"The property is a bit problematic, Jack. I bought it from a drug dealer just before he was convicted and sent to prison. He was trying to get a cash settlement before any conviction, resulting in his property being confiscated. I intended to do a quick sale and invest my profits. I was concerned about the cops' investigations, and I wanted to be sure that I legitimately owned the property and they couldn't take it. Our economic messes have left me holding this property for six months without any offers.

The investigation is finally over, and I have the title free and clear, but the economy is still a problem. Frankly, I have too much tied up in this property and need cash as soon as possible. Here are all the specifications."

Kirk handed him many papers detailing the five-acre plot's location, survey data, and zoning. He had even included photographs. Davidson skimmed the information.

"We can help you, Kirk. Let's see what the best approach might be."

By the end of the meeting, Davidson had agreed to sell the property himself and said he'd call when the contracts were ready for signing. A week later, Jack called Kirk and asked, "Do you play golf?"

"I play golf, but if you don't mind playing with someone who's not very good, I'm your guy."

Jack trusted Kirk and thought of him as a friend. Kirk felt slightly guilty because he knew Jack was sincere about his friendship. Kirk was only interested in getting information from Jack about the murder and other crimes. Kirk couldn't get emotional because Jack was very dangerous to the community. Kirk knew that he had to do what he could to protect Janet and the community from Jack.

"Great. My partner just bailed on me, and I need to talk with you about the property anyway, so meet me at the Westchester Country Club in an hour. We'll play nine holes and then have lunch," said Jack.

It had been only a few days since Kirk first met with Jack about the real estate deal, but he worked fast!

While waiting to tee off on the seventh hole, one of the foursomes in front of them approached Jack. "Buddy, this is Kirk Turner, a client and a new friend. Kirk, this is Buddy Roberts, one of my friends and business associates."

"Nice to meet you, Kirk. Jack, I just wanted to give you my condolences. I was out of town and just heard about Jane this morning. I'm so sorry. that she meant a lot to you."

"Thanks, Buddy. She was something special. I don't think I'll ever get over her."

Buddy left a few seconds later to rejoin his teammates.

"I'm sorry, Jack. I didn't know you'd lost someone recently. Was she a relative?"

"She was my girlfriend," Jack answered and paused, waiting for Kirk's reaction. But he just nodded his head and waited. "It's not exactly what you're thinking. I have never loved anyone the way I loved her."

"Not even your wife?" Kirt asked?

"Hmmm. I loved Janet once but realized we had nothing in common over the years. She seemed to be an intelligent person when I met her, but she's stupid. She doesn't know what I do for a living and believed I had to spend three months of the year in Tucson to conduct business. I hate her. She never knew that I was seeing anyone, and she never knew about my summer home in Tucson. That's where Jane and I spent every summer. When I returned to New York in the fall, I was with Jane most of the time. Did Janet suspect anything and ask me why I had to work late so many nights? No. She just volunteered at her camp, lunched with her friends, and cried." Jack hates Janet.

Over lunch, Kirt learned from their conversation that Jack was going out of town again for a few days. Perfect, thought Kirk, which should give me time to check his office computer.

Kirk returned to Davidson's office the next day, knowing Jack was out of town. His secretary smiled, "I'm sorry, Mr. Turner, but Mr. Davidson will be away for a few days. Can I set up an appointment with him?"

"I've lost my appointment book and have looked everywhere for it. This is the place I remembered taking it out to check on something. Is there any chance I can look around Jack's office to see if I left it there?"

"I'm sure it's not, Mr. Turner. Mr. Davidson would have given it to me, or I would have found it when I took things into his office. I'm sorry, but if it makes you feel better to look, go on in."

Kirk entered Jack's office and noticed a Solar Systems for Heating reference book. He asked the secretary if he could copy one of the chapters on purchasing equipment for installing Solar Systems For Heating. "Sure," she said, "The copier is over there. "Thank you." Davidson's secretary then gave him paper for coping. When she left Davidson's office, Kirk quickly pulled out a flash drive, inserted it into the computer, accessed the files, and began downloading them. The whole operation took only a few minutes. Then, he began to copy the chapter in the book. The secretary came in a few minutes later and asked him if everything was all right. "Yes. I can't wait to read this chapter on equipment for purchasing Solar Systems For Heating to know what I need to purchase. Then I'll get the rest of the information from the library."

"No. You can have the book. There's no way Jack is ever going to read it."

"Oh, thank you so much." Kirk was happy to get the book because he was interested in installing a solar system for heating his home and had been looking for a book on solar systems.

The downloading had finished, and Kirk had put the computer screen back as it was. The screen saver was on when the secretary came in, but he had not taken the flash drive out. As the secretary stood there talking to him, Kirk thought, how do I get the flash drive out of the computer? After what seemed like an eternity, the secretary's phone began ringing.

She left the room to answer it. Kirk dashed over to the computer, took out the flash drive, put it in his jacket pocket, picked up the book, and exited Jack's office. He walked over to the secretary's desk and thanked her again for the expensive solar system book.

Back at his office, Kirk scanned Davidson's files. In his email account, he located correspondence with someone who spoke Russian. Davidson used a translation program to read it and graciously left the translation attached to the original email: I will be at your house at 11 a.m. I will meet you at noon for my package. G. Jack had been able to help Gordon the Russian understand enough of what to do at the time, but he didn't understand anything else.

Most important, it was dated just two days before the murder. Kirk knew he was getting close. The man who ran from the scene was Russian. According to another email Kirk found, Davidson was dealing with a Russian, probably Gordon. Jack was having an affair with Jane, for whom he was grieving. He had also admitted that he hated his wife. Still, Kirk wanted more evidence to convince the police that Jack hired someone to kill his wife, but it seems that the Russians killed Jane instead. He had to find the Russian.

Kirk met with Janet and Mary that afternoon to bring them up to date, "I was able to get into Jack's office, and from the information on the flash drive, the police will have no problems convicting Jack of many crimes. I want to make sure he is put out of circulation forever. We need to convince the police that your husband hired someone to kill you. We have information on Jack and the Russian that will convict him of murder. but we still need to find the Russian. We've got to find the Russian. He has to be the one Jack hired."

Mary was concerned about Kirk's safety. "Kirk, you must be very careful. You know this man is a killer. If he finds out you are investigating him, you'll be in great danger."

"I know," said Kirk. "That's why we must stop him before he hurts someone else."

Danny was tending the bar when Kirk returned the next day.

"I just wanted to thank you for hooking me up with Jack." Then Kirk shoved a twenty-dollar bill toward Danny, who smiled and took the bill. "Thank you, Mr. Turner. I take it everything is working out for you?"

"Oh, yeah! He already has more prospects for that property than I had in six months! He knows what he's doing. I'll sit at a table; I haven't had lunch yet."

"I'll send a waiter over."

Kirk settled at a table in the back, the perfect place to watch the restaurant while he had lunch and read his paper. The same waiter he'd had before came to his table and took his order. Soon, a big burger with the works and crispy homemade potato chips in front of him.

As he ate, he watched the regular flow of customers and employees. Davidson was a real estate broker, and other legal businesses were all very successful. Kirk thought. Why all the unscrupulous, dangerous dealings? Greed can be the downfall of anyone. Kirk had almost finished his burger when a burly man dressed in black entered the restaurant and looked around. His facial expression was almost blank, but his eyes were like a fierce animal ready to attack. When the waiter tried to seat him, he stared at him and growled,

"Nyet." Then he walked to the bar.

Kirk picked up his newspaper, trying not to appear too interested in the conversation a few feet from him. "Davidson," the man commanded, his accent so thick Kirk almost didn't make out the name.

"He is not here, Gordon," Danny tried to explain. But Gordon wasn't convinced and strode back to the kitchen, returning in just a minute.

"Where Davidson?" Gordon demanded of Danny again.

"Gone. I don't know where," Danny shrugged and shook his head to make Gordon understand. Then Gordon frowned and started to leave.

Kirk looked at his watch and said loudly enough for Danny to hear, "I'm late." He then took a twenty-dollar bill out of his wallet, put it on the table, and headed toward the door. Knowing that Danny was watching, he turned toward him as he kept walking, "I lost track of time. That burger was so good. See you later."

"Sure thing, Mr. Turner."

Once outside, he spotted Gordon, still striding angrily up the street. He followed him as discreetly as he could for a couple of blocks until Gordon seemed to slow down, perhaps cooling off, and hailed a cab. Kirk could flag a cab just a second or two later to continue his chase. Gordon went to a warehouse near the docks. Kirk remained in his cab, knowing that dressed in a suit, he wouldn't blend in with the men loading and unloading merchandise. He couldn't just go into the warehouse Gordon had entered.

G was how the email Kirk found was signed. The same guy, the employees at the restaurant, called Gordon and the same name on another email Kirk had found on Jack's computer. About fifteen minutes later, Gordon walked back out around suspiciously. Gordon walked quickly to the main avenue to hail a cab, passing Kirk, who was still in his cab. Gordon went to a run-down area of town full of boarded-up buildings. "What's he doing?" Kirk asked himself. A few seconds later, Gordon's cab pulled to the curb, and Gordon got out. Kirk had his cab driver pass him and stop halfway up the next block.

"I know this seems a bit strange, but I'm working on a case for my client," Kirk told the cabdriver. Then he turned to see Gordon move a sheet of plywood out of the way and enter one of the boarded-up flats. Unfortunately, there was nowhere for

Kirk to go. He didn't have his car, and he needed to blend in the area, so he had the cab driver take him back to his office after mentally noting the exact address of Gordon's building.

At his office, Kirk changed into more appropriate clothing that he kept in his office for doing surveillance. He used an old, worn jacket that would blend in with the area and drove back to where Gordon was. Although he couldn't be sure, his instincts told him that Gordon was still there. Kirk approached the flat and knocked on the plywood covering the doorway. He could hear movement inside and consciously let out his breath to relax. A young woman peeked out of one grimy window. A few seconds later, Gordon stood threateningly in the doorway, holding a gun. "Da?" (da means yes in Russian). "Jack sent me." Gordon carefully looked him over from head to toe before motioning him inside and replacing the plywood. He motioned to the girl to leave. Kirk watched her leave the apartment before turning his attention back to Gordon.

"You do know you killed the wrong woman, don't you, Gordon?" Kirk used his voice to show a certain level of impatience and disgust. But Gordon looked at him, not understanding what he was saying.

"Here, let me show you," Kirk started to get something from under his jacket.

"Nyet, nyet!" Gordon growled and pointed the gun at Kirk's head, and Kirk raised his hands and smiled, "It's okay." Leaving one hand in the air, he used his left hand to lift his jacket open to show Gordon he had no weapon. Then he slowly lowered his other hand to pull out two pictures, one of Jane and one of Janet. "See," said Kirk.

"Da. Where money?" said Gorden

"That's the problem, my friend. This is Jack's wife." He held up Janet and Jane's pictures. Gordon looked puzzled and looked from one picture to the other several times.

Gordon was beginning to understand because he had seen both pictures in the news.

"Da, Gordon. You killed the wrong woman. No money until you kill Janet." Kirk pointed at Janet's picture like he was shooting it.

"Understand? Kill her, and you get your money."

Gordon seemed to understand. He snatched Janet's picture from Kirk's hand and motioned with the gun for Kirk to leave.

"Hold on. Janet is not at that address anymore. Here's her address."

Kirk took a slip of paper with God's Gang's address and gave it to Gordon. Gordon looked at it, recognizing it was an address, and nodded.

"Okay, Gordon. Jack is expecting you to take care of this tomorrow, da?"

"Kill the woman tomorrow. Get money." Kirk explained.

Although Gordon spoke little English, he had indeed mastered the essential phrases. Kirk left the building and drove back to the office. He had much to do before the next day.

The girls and guys were at school or work. Linda, Mary, and her daughters were at church. Inside the mansion, Kirk waited with the two detectives working on Jane's murder and an undercover policewoman. Kirk had gathered enough circumstantial evidence to convince the police that Gordon was the murderer and that Janet was the intended victim. Kirk thinks he can use Gordon to snitch on Davidson if he needs to.

Around ten o'clock, the doorbell rang. The undercover officer exhaled as she walked to the door. The others were hiding in the other rooms, waiting to apprehend Gordon.

"Yes?" The policewoman came to the front door, and the burly Russian stood. He tried to look calm, but anyone could tell he was unhappy. "Janet here?" he asked in broken English.

"Yes, she's in the kitchen. Come in, and I'll get her," she said, "Opening the door more." Gordon entered, grabbing her by the arm and holding her close.

"Where she is?" Gordon had to be stupid. Did he intend to kill Janet with this woman there, or was he planning to kill both of them? He had to be crazy. What made him think that they were alone in this big mansion? Did he understand when Jack said to ensure no one else was there? Did he really think there would be no one else in that building?

Gordon drew his gun but was not holding it directly at anyone.

"Go," Gordon whispered, pushing the policewoman toward the kitchen as he held her. Several officers and detectives came in from different rooms as they moved around Gordon.

"Stop. Put the gun down, Gordon. You're under arrest for assault with a deadly weapon, attempted murder, and murder." One of the detectives commanded. Gordon wasn't sure what was happening. He started to bring his gun down to the woman's head, but she was quick and knocked the gun from his hand. She elbowed him in the stomach, turned quickly, and kicked him in the groin area. She was then able to get out of his grasp as one of the policemen picked his gun off the floor. One of the policemen grabbed his arm, twisting it in the back of him, forcing him to his knees, where they handcuffed him.

"Is this the man, Turner?" asked the detective as he forced Gordon back into an upright position when Kirk walked into the room.

"Yeah, that's Gordon."

At the police station, Gordon pretended to understand no English. But a Russian-speaking officer joined the detectives in the interrogation room shortly after Gordon was booked. At first, he denied killing Jane and was attempting to kill Janet. The detectives found the picture of Janet on him when they searched for him at God's Gang. As they were questioning him, another officer brought the detective a sheet of paper.

"So you're here illegally as well. That makes this easy. We don't have to prosecute you. Can the Immigration and Naturalization Service send you back to Russia?"

Gordon seemed to understand that threat. He'd worked hard to get to America. The last thing he wanted was to return to Russia despite what he faced in the United States. He must have been facing something worse in Russia.

"Nyet! Nyet!" said Gordon, "Davidson pays for the job. Davidson no pay."

Kirk, watching the interrogation on television, said, "We got him at last. At last, we got him. We've got Jack for sure."

The district attorney issued a warrant for Jack Davidson's arrest on conspiracy to commit murder. When Jack's plane landed the following day, police surrounded the plane and arrested Jack. Before they could begin to interrogate him, his lawyers arrived. But the D.A. wasn't concerned. Because of Jack's involvement in Jane's murder, they also gained access to his business dealings.

Davidson's mob connections were unknown, but knowing about them and proving them differed. Now, they could access his records legally because he had used his business accounts to pay for his mistress. Gordon's payment for murder would have no doubt come from the same place, but Gordon never got a chance to receive his money. One thing is sure: They would imprison Davidson for life unless he received the death penalty. Gordon was also going to prison for a long time.

CHAPTER TWENTY-THREE

Janet Joins God's Gang

Kirk called the mansion, "Mary, I have great news for you and Janet. It's over. Both Jack and Gordon are under arrest. I'll meet you at God's Gang and tell you what happened."

"That's wonderful. We can't wait to hear all about it."

Kirk sat in the living room with Mary, Janet, and Linda. "They won't have any problem putting Jack away for life unless he's given the death sentence, Janet. The D.A. not only has enough evidence to convict him of conspiracy in Jane's murder, but they can also legally investigate his

businesses, which will soon expose Jack's connections with his illegal dealings and federal racketeering charges. He's not going to be a problem for you any longer. You're safe now.

"Thank you, Kirk," said Janet. "For everything, "I don't know how I would have survived without you guys supporting me. Mary introducing me to Jesus and having friends like all of you has made such a happy difference in my life. As tragic as Jane's death and her and Jack's betrayal were, some positives have come out of all this. I would not know Jesus today if all this hadn't happened, nor would I have found good friends like Mary and Linda. I've never had real friends like you and Linda, except for Rachel and Bill, and I'm so grateful."

"Praise God. He's the one who has brought us through all of this. He protected you and kept Kirk safe throughout the investigation.

God also keeps His promises." Janet hugged Mary, Linda, and Kirk as the three women wiped away tears.

"I have more good news, ladies." Kirk smiled as he handed Mary a check made out to God's Gang." Mary looked at the check and then at Kirk, obviously confused. Kirk was happy to explain the check.

"Remember that piece of property I used as a ploy to get to Jack? Well, he sold it before he had informed me about the delay in signing the papers, as the buyer required a few days to transfer the funds. It passed the D.A.'s investigation. Jack's secretary had one of the other agents take care of everything needed, except my signature on the contract, before Jack's arrest. So the deal stands.

Although Jack is many things, he excels as a real estate agent. He sold the property for $2.4 million, over twice what I paid. After commissions and fees, I cleared nearly 1.3 million. And I couldn't have done it without this case. So, it's only fitting that God's Gang also profits."

"But this is for nearly seven hundred thousand dollars, Kirk. You don't have to do this."

"Yes, I do, Mary. Because of you, my whole family has received Jesus as their Savior. That's worth more than any amount of money. With this, you can reach hundreds of others, and this is my way of helping to bring the lost to Jesus."

"Thank you so much, Kirk."

A couple of weeks later, Mary and Linda invited Janet for lunch.

"The last time I was here, I didn't pay much attention to how beautiful this place is, Mary."

"I can understand why décor wasn't at the top of your list the last time you were here with the things you were going through. Would you like a grand tour?"

Mary and Janet toured the mansion while Linda cleared the table and prepared lunch. As they left the living room to go upstairs, Laura, Kathy, Anna, Sue D, who brought Laura a box of food, Helen, and Brenda walked through the front door.

"Hi, Mary," the girls spoke to Mary. "Is Mom home?" Laura asked.

"She's in the kitchen, Laura."

"Great. We're starving."

"Don't rush off, ladies," said Mary. "Janet, I want you to meet our new girl," Mary introduced Janet to Brenda.

"Please, don't let us keep you from lunch. Your mother is a great
  cook, Laura," Janet said as the girls stood there, not knowing what to say or how to leave.

"I know!" Laura grinned as the girls ran to the Kitchen.

Mary and Janet stop their tour to start lunch for themselves and a bunch of hungry girls.

"Girls," said Linda. How would you all like to make your lunch? There are all kinds of lunch meat, tomatoes, lettuce, cookies, soda, milk, and other drinks."

Before Linda could finish telling them what there was for lunch, Laura interrupted, "Mom, that sounds great. We would love to have our lunch. Thank Mon."

The girls cheered, and Brinda said, "This is the best place in the world."

Mary pulled Linda and Janet into the next room and said, "Let's relax and order subways or whatever you ladies like, if that's okay. The girls will enjoy making their lunch."

"Oh, that sounds great, said Linda. "I had gotten everything ready for lunch but put it all back when the girls came in. They could make their lunch, and then we could relax and order food."

Linda brought a pot of coffee and a plate of freshly baked chocolate chip cookies from the Kitchen into the living room as they waited for their subways.

Mary told Janet more about her dream of opening a prominent place to help runaway teenagers, drug addicts, and others in trouble. "Kathy, Anna, Sue D, and Laura were our first successful missions when rescued from the Red Zone."

Then Linda told about Laura's running away and how Mary had found out that Laura was one of the girls that she and the guys were making plans to rescue. Mary said she had even talked to Laura on the phone but didn't know it was Linda's daughter.

"You can imagine how surprised I was when I saw Laura with Kathy," Mary explained.

Then Mary explained how Rob had come to join their group. She told Janet how they came to work with Clayton and his gang and George's church across the river. Mary talked about how proud they were of the girls for starting God's Bible Club, which meets at Rev. Smith's church.

"God's Bible Club is where we met Brenda. It's a long story; you'll learn more later as you work with us," said Mary.

After everyone had eaten, the girls cleaned the Kitchen. Mary asked them to join them in the living room. Brenda said as soon as they settled in the living room, "I'm so happy to be here. I want to say first that I love my parents, but I'm here because they put me out, and I had no place to go."

Everyone made Brenda feel at home and told her how happy they were to have; upon hearing from the sisters and Brenda, Janet expressed her admiration for the group. She believed the young girls would significantly contribute to the community."

"Yes," said Mary. "Our dream is coming true. I'm available for counseling and teaching classes. Linda joined our staff and helped educate and train our girls for independent living. Larry is one of the guys in Clayton's gang who has started to work part-time as a computer programmer. He is outstanding on the computer and has helped almost everyone with computers.

"Could you use another volunteer?" asked Janet.

I love working with children and young people. I only work a few weeks each summer at the camp, and I would love to have something to do the rest of the year."

"Oh, we would love to have you join us. Is there anything in particular that you would like to do?" Mary asked.

"Well, I have my bachelor's degree in home economics. I could teach sewing, cooking, family living, and similar things."

"Wonderful," Linda shouted. "I teach most of those things, too. With Larry's help, I could work more with computer programs with the girls. Sometimes, there needs to be more time to work with everyone daily.

When can you start?" The women laughed at Janet's eagerness.

CHAPTER TWENTY-FOUR

"Here, let me see them," Kevin opened the envelope and scanned the documents. Janet's Friends Need Help

Janet met with Mary and Linda to discuss a problem she hoped they could help her with.

"I met Bill and Rachel in Texas, where we lived, and became close friends. They are having problems, and I want us to pray that God will intervene in their lives and show them the way out of their problems."

"Of course, Janet, tell us what's going on so we can make our petitions to God specific to their needs."

"It's complicated. I'll try to give you the short version. We still keep in touch, even though I have left Texas. Bill became a Christian, and Ellen, his wife, became resentful. He could never get her to go to church with him. She became so aggravated with his attempts to 'save' her, as she put it, that she left him. He prayed that she would receive Jesus and return to their marriage. He told her that he would move out of their house, and she could move back into the house. He loved her and was still hoping they would get back together. Now, she's suing him for abandonment. He has given her the house and most of their belongings, and he's paying her alimony. He only makes a little money as a high school teacher.

Bill finally realized that Ellen was not coming back to him. Months later, he met a wonderful woman at their church, Rachel, and they fell in love. When I visit Bill and Rachel, I have so much fun with them. They want to get married but cannot because Bill is still married to Ellen. Ellen has no reason to claim abandonment. She's the one that left Bill.

He was being nice to her when he suggested that she move back into their house and he move out. The law is on her side because he's the one that moved out."

" turbing," said Linda, "I'll get us something to drink before you finish explaining everything."

"Janet, God will take care of this. We have to trust Him," Mary told her as they waited for Linda to return.

"I do trust God, Mary, and I know there's power in all of us praying for God's intervention. Bill said in a letter that he and Rachel have peace that God will take care of this very soon."

"My life has undoubtedly been blessed since meeting you guys. I want my friends to be blessed, too. Although I didn't know God then, I still couldn't see how Ellen could treat him that way," said Janet.

Bill and Rachel invited me to church with them often, and although I never went and didn't share their beliefs at that time, I was not turned off by what they believed. They loved me even though I didn't share their faith. One thing is going for them: they both love Jesus. They were so happy when I told them that I had received Jesus. Rachel wrote a letter telling me that they are planning to celebrate my acceptance into God's Kingdom as soon I come for a visit."

Linda returned from the Kitchen carrying a tray with glasses and a pitcher of lemonade. She filled the glasses, handed one to each woman, and took one for herself.

"Okay, Janet, make it clear what we need to pray for and let's trust God to answer our request."

Mary fills Linda in on what Janet has said so far.

"Well, a couple of months ago," Janet started again, "Rachel and Bill ran into a friend of theirs at lunch, Helen Parker. She told them about Ellen's marriage to a rich guy from New York, Kevin Black. Bill and Rachel were shocked. Bill is still sending Ellen money, thinking they are married."

Janet is happy to have friends to pray for her friends with her. She knows there is power in numbers.

"Is she living in Texas?" Linda asked.

"I wonder if she lives in Texas or New York. But Bill said he sends her checks to a Post Office Box in Texas. He never sees her, so he doesn't know if she lives in Texas. If Ellen divorced Bill, why has he never been served with the divorce papers? If she's divorced, there's no reason for her to sue him for abandonment. If she's married and not divorced, she's a bigamist and extorting money from Bill."

"I think, "Mary added, "Besides praying, we need to see if Kirk Turner can help us with this. Maybe he can find out if Ellen divorced Bill and whether she has married Kevin Black. That may be enough information for Kirk to take care of things in Texas," Mary looked at Janet and Linda and said, "Let's pray."

Kirk Turner was doing paperwork at his desk when his intercom buzzed. The Lord had blessed him through the years. He now had a staff of two other operatives and a secretary.

"Yes, Connie," he listened for a second, "Put her through. Hi, Mary," he said as he swiveled his chair to look out the window, "What can I do for you?"

Mary explained the situation, "Okay, Mary," said Kirk, "We need to find out if Ellen divorced Bill and if she's married to Kevin Black. That shouldn't be hard to discover. I'll get back to you in a day or two."

He then left his office and asked his two detectives to join him. After a brief meeting, both returned to their offices and computers, one looking for a divorce certificate in Texas or New York, the other for a marriage certificate in New York. Kirk had answers for Mary and called her office,

"It looks as if this Ellen is up to her eyeballs in criminal behavior. We can't find any evidence of a divorce granted in either state, just the current filing in Texas on grounds of abandonment. However, we did find a certificate of marriage issued by the state of New York for Ellen Philips and Kevin Black. We've sent for an official copy that our lawyer can use as evidence in Texas."

Thanks, Kirk. I owe you."

"Forget it, Mary. Working with you is another way of serving the Lord. Besides, this one was easy!"

Bill was ecstatic with Kirk's findings. The case was going to be easy. Using the information, he had Bill cross-filed for divorce on the grounds of adultery and abandonment (she was no longer living in Texas). He also sent copies of all the paperwork and information to the district attorney in New York to support charges of bigamy and extortion against Ellen.

A few days later, a process server rang the doorbell of Kevin Black's home in New York. Ellen answered.

"Ellen Philips Black?" The man asked.

"Yes?" Ellen answered. The person handed her a white envelope.

"What is this?" She yelled at the man, who had already started back down the driveway.

"What's wrong, Ellen?" Kevin called to her as he walked out of his library.

"Some guy just gave me these papers and left."

"Here, let me see them," Kevin opened the envelope and scanned the documents.

"This is a summons to appear in court for divorce proceedings from Bill Philips. It must be some mistake. You are divorced from him, right?"

"Of course. I don't know what is going on. But I'll handle it, sweetheart," Ellen said, taking the papers from Kevin's hand.

"Nonsense. That's what I pay my lawyers for," He kissed her forehead and went back into the library, not noticing the terrified look on her face as she turned white.

The next day, "What do you mean the charges are true?" asked Kevin as he yelled at his chief counsel.

"Just what I said, Mr. Black. Your wife was never legally divorced from Bill Philips, and he has been paying her alimony since she left him several years ago. Your marriage to her is not legal."

"Great. I can't believe this is happening to me?"

"Ellen needs to drop her abandonment charges against Mr. Philips," said Mr. Black's lawyer.

"She is to appear in court for divorce, which must mean that Bill Philips' attorneys have this information and are ready to sue her. She needs to divorce him as quickly as possible. Then, assuming you still wish to marry her, you will need to marry again once her divorce is final. We may be able to negotiate with Philips so that he does not pursue criminal charges against her for bigamy, but I can't guarantee that."

Ellen was waiting for Kevin when he returned home late that night, "Where have you been?" she demanded, "I've been sick with worry. You know how upset I am over this court thing. I needed you here with me."

Kevin placed his briefcase on the hall table.

"So you needed me. Really!" Kevin had been drinking but still seemed in control of himself.

"What's that supposed to mean?" asked Ellen.

"Well, Mrs. Philips, we're not married."

"How can you say that, Kevin? I told you this was all a big misunderstanding. Somehow, the paperwork has gotten mixed up or lost or something." She smiled and walked towards him, attempting to kiss him, but he pushed her away.

"Or something is right, my lying little 'wife.' You're still married to that poor sucker, and you've been lying to me since we met."

Ellen backed against the table, holding her breath for the next onslaught, trying to imagine how to escape this mess. Kevin could almost see her mind working as he continued.

"My lawyers are good, remember. It took them no time to discover you'd never really divorced Bill, and you were still collecting alimony from him. You married me under pretenses, and you're a bigamist. You charged him with abandonment when you lived in New York, and he's still in Texas. By the way, where is all that money he's been sending you?"

"I authorized a friend to cash the checks and put the money in a safe deposit box in a bank in Texas. I'll send it all back, Kevin. I didn't want his money; I was just angry with him."

"Stop, Ellen. I don't want to hear any more lies."

"What are we going to do, Kevin?" asked Ellen.

"We? We're going to do nothing. I'm not married to you. I'm not your husband. You have been lying and conniving, and I want you out of my house. Now!" Ellen stared at him, tears falling, "Kevin, I..."

"Now!" he yelled, "I don't ever want to see you again."

Two weeks later.

"Mary! Mary!" Janet shouted as she entered God's Gang late one afternoon.

"I'm in the office, Janet. What is it?"

Janet entered the office and grabbed Mary by the hands, nearly lifting her out of her seat, "I just talked to Bill. The court has granted his divorce from Ellen, and Bill and Rachel are getting married."

"That's wonderful news. God has answered our prayers again. But what about Ellen?" Mary has the heart of God. She was concerned for Ellen despite what she had done.

"Well, Kevin kicked her out," said Janet, "and she's looking to see what happens with the extortion. Bill is willing to drop the extortion charge, but the bigamy charge is up to the D.A. Kevin is sad about the whole thing. One of Kevin's friends said that Kevin still loves Ellen, although he's very angry with her."

"Remember, Janet. God is in charge. Things will work out for them if they let Him take control."

"Yes, I'm certainly a testament to that," said Janet, "and that's the other good news. You won't believe this. One of Kevin's friends invited him to our church, and he comes every Sunday. He joined the week you were out of town. Maybe he will be led by the Lord to help Ellen find her way. Ellen is an example of the destruction of hatred. She didn't take Bill's money because she wanted the money. She did things to hurt him because she hated him and his commitment to God. I ran into a friend of Ellens, and she said that Kiven was the only man she ever loved."

"We'll just keep praying."

"By the way, Ellen sent all that alimony money back and gave Bill the money from selling their old house. Rachel is on staff at the church now, but she still volunteers to work at the church whenever they need her. With the money for a significant down payment on a new house, the return of the alimony money, and both working, they have not only been able to purchase a beautiful home but were able to furnish their whole house and buy everything they need."

"Praise God," said Mary, "God has done more than we could ask or even think of. Let's have them visit us here soon."

"They would love that," said Janet, "Every time they write, they thank all of us for praying for them and hope to meet the rest of God Gang's family."

Janet met with Mary and Linda to discuss a problem she hoped they could help her with.

"I met Bill and Rachel in Texas, where we lived, and became close friends. They are having problems, and I want us to pray that God will intervene in their lives and show them the way out of their problems."

"Of course, Janet, tell us what's going on so we can make our petitions to God specific to their needs."

"It's complicated. I'll try to give you the short version. We still keep in touch, even though I have left Texas. Bill became a Christian, and Ellen, his wife, became resentful. He could never get her to go to church with him. She became so aggravated with his attempts to 'save' her, as she put it, that she left him. He prayed that she would receive Jesus and return to their marriage. He told her that he would move out of their house, and she could move back into the house. He loved her and was still hoping they would get back together. Now, she's suing him for abandonment. He has given her the house and most of their belongings, and he's paying her alimony. He only makes a little money as a high school teacher.

Bill finally realized that Ellen was not coming back to him. Months later, he met a wonderful woman at their church, Rachel, and they fell in love. When I visit Bill and Rachel, I have so much fun with them. They want to get married but cannot because Bill is still married to Ellen. Ellen has no reason to claim abandonment. She's the one that left Bill.

He was being nice to her when he suggested that she move back into their house and he move out. The law is on her side because he's the one that moved out."

"This is disturbing," said Linda, "I'll get us something to drink before you finish explaining everything."

"Janet, God will take care of this. We have to trust Him," Mary told her as they waited for Linda to return.

"I do trust God, Mary, and I know there's power in all of us praying for God's intervention. Bill said in a letter that he and Rachel have peace that God will take care of this very soon."

"Mary, I'm so happy I have found friends like you and Linda. My life has undoubtedly been blessed since meeting you guys. I want my friends to be blessed, too. Although I didn't know God then, I still couldn't see how Ellen could treat him that way," said Janet.

Bill and Rachel invited me to church with them often, and although I never went and didn't share their beliefs at that time, I was not turned off by what they believed. They loved me even though I didn't share their faith. One thing is going for them: they both love Jesus. They were so happy when I told them that I had received Jesus. Rachel wrote a letter telling me that they are planning to celebrate my acceptance into God's Kingdom as soon I come for a visit."

Linda returned from the Kitchen carrying a tray with glasses and a pitcher of lemonade. She filled the glasses, handed one to each woman, and took one for herself.

"Okay, Janet, make it clear what we need to pray for let's hear more so we know how to pray."

Mary fills Linda in on what Janet has said so far.

"Well, a couple of months ago," Janet started again, "Rachel and Bill ran into a friend of theirs at lunch, Helen Parker. She told them about Ellen's marriage to a rich guy from New York, Kevin Black. Bill and Rachel were shocked. Bill is still sending Ellen money, thinking they are married."

Janet is happy to have friends to pray for her friends with her. She knows there is power in numbers.

"Is she living in Texas?" Linda asked.

"I wonder if she lives in Texas or New York. But Bill said he sends her checks to a Post Office Box in Texas. He never sees her, so he doesn't know if she lives in Texas. If Ellen divorced Bill, why has he never been served with the divorce papers? If she's divorced, there's no reason for her to sue him for abandonment. If she's married and not divorced, she's a bigamist and extorting money from Bill."

"I think, "Mary added, "Besides praying, we need to see if Kirk Turner can help us with this. Maybe he can find out if Ellen divorced Bill and whether she has married Kevin Black. That may be enough information for Kirk to take care of things in Texas," Mary looked at Janet and Linda and said, "Let's pray."

Kirk Turner was doing paperwork at his desk when his intercom buzzed. The Lord had blessed him through the years. He now had a staff of two other operatives and a secretary, "Yes, Connie," he listened for a second, "Put her through. Hi, Mary," he said as he swiveled his chair to look out the window, "What can I do for you?"

Mary explained the situation, "Okay, Mary," said Kirk, "We need to find out if Ellen divorced Bill and if she's married to Kevin Black. That shouldn't be hard to discover. I'll get back to you in a day or two."

He then left his office and asked his two detectives to join him. After a brief meeting, both returned to their offices and computers, one looking for a divorce certificate in Texas or New York, the other for a marriage certificate in New York. By noon the next day, Kirk had answers for Mary and called her office,

"It looks as if this Ellen is up to her eyeballs in criminal behavior. We can't find any evidence of a divorce granted in either state, just the current filing in Texas on grounds of abandonment. However, we did find a certificate of marriage issued by the state of New York for Ellen Philips and Kevin Black. We've sent for an official copy that our lawyer can use as evidence in Texas."

"Thanks, Kirk. I owe you."

"Forget it, Mary. Working with you is another way of serving the Lord. Besides, this one was easy!"

Bill was ecstatic with Kirk's findings. The case was going to be easy. Using the information, he had Bill cross-filed for divorce on the grounds of adultery and abandonment (she was no longer living in Texas). He also sent copies of all the paperwork and information to the district attorney in New York to support charges of bigamy and extortion against Ellen.

A few days later, a process server rang the doorbell of Kevin Black's home in New York. Ellen answered.

"Ellen Philips Black?" The man asked.

"Yes?" Ellen answered. The person handed her a white envelope.

"What is this?" She yelled at the man, who had already started back down the driveway.

"What's wrong, Ellen?" Kevin called to her as he walked out of his library.

"Some guy just gave me these papers and left."

"Here, let me see them," Kevin opened the envelope and scanned the documents.

"This is a summons to appear in court for divorce proceedings from Bill Philips. It must be some mistake. You are divorced from him, right?"

"Of course. I don't know what is going on. But I'll handle it, sweetheart," Ellen said, taking the papers from Kevin's hand.

"Nonsense. That's what I pay my lawyers for," He kissed her forehead and went back into the library, not noticing the terrified look on her face as she turned white.

The next day, "What do you mean the charges are true?" asked Kevin as he yelled at his chief counsel.

"Just what I said, Mr. Black. Your wife was never legally divorced from Bill Philips, and he has been paying her alimony since she left him several years ago. Your marriage to her is not legal."

"Great. I can't believe this is happening to me?"

"Ellen needs to drop her abandonment charges against Mr. Philips," said Mr. Black's lawyer.

"She is to appear in court for divorce, which must mean that Bill Philips' attorneys have this information and are ready to sue her. She needs to divorce him as quickly as possible. Then, assuming you still wish to marry her, you will need to marry again once her divorce is final. We may be able to negotiate with Philips so that he does not pursue criminal charges against her for bigamy, but I can't guarantee that."

Ellen was waiting for Kevin when he returned home late that night, "Where have you been?" she demanded, "I've been sick with worry. You know how upset I am over this court thing. I needed you here with me."

Kevin placed his briefcase on the hall table.

"So you needed me. Really!" Kevin had been drinking but still seemed in control of himself.

"What's that supposed to mean?" asked Ellen.

"Well, Mrs. Philips, we're not married."

"How can you say that, Kevin? I told you this was all a big misunderstanding. Somehow, the paperwork has gotten mixed up or lost or something." She smiled and walked towards him, attempting to kiss him, but he pushed her away.

"Or something is right, my lying little 'wife.' You're still married to that poor sucker, and you've been lying to me since we met."

Ellen backed against the table, holding her breath for the next onslaught, trying to imagine how to escape this mess. Kevin could almost see her mind working as he continued.

"My lawyers are good, remember. It took them no time to discover you'd never really divorced Bill, and you were still collecting alimony from him. You married me under pretenses, and you're a bigamist. You charged him with abandonment when you lived in New York, and he's still in Texas. By the way, where is all that money he's been sending you?"

"I authorized a friend to cash the checks and put the money in a safe deposit box in a bank in Texas. I'll send it all back, Kevin. I didn't want his money; I was just angry with him."

"Stop, Ellen. I don't want to hear any more lies."

"What are we going to do, Kevin?" asked Ellen.

"We? We're going to do nothing. I'm not married to you. I'm not your husband. You have been lying and conniving, and I want you out of my house. Now!" Ellen stared at him, tears falling, "Kevin, I..."

"No!" he yelled, "I don't ever want to see you again."

Two weeks later.

"Mary! Mary!" Janet shouted as she entered God's Gang late one afternoon.

"I'm in the office, Janet. What is it?"

Janet entered the office and grabbed Mary by the hands, nearly lifting her out of her seat, "I just talked to Bill. The court has granted his divorce from Ellen, and Bill and Rachel are getting married."

"That's wonderful news. God has answered our prayers again. But what about Ellen?" Mary has the heart of God. She was concerned for Ellen despite what she had done.

"Well, Kevin kicked her out," said Janet, "and she's looking to see what happens with the extortion. Bill is willing to drop the extortion charge, but the bigamy charge is up to the D.A. Kevin is sad about the whole thing. One of Kevin's friends said that Kevin still loves Ellen, although he's very angry with her."

"Remember, Janet. God is in charge. Things will work out for them if they let Him take control."

"Yes, I'm certainly a testament to that," said Janet, "and that's the other good news. You won't believe this. One of Kevin's friends invited him to our church, and he comes every Sunday. He joined the week you were out of town. Maybe he will be led by the Lord to help Ellen find her way. Ellen is an example of the destruction of hatred. She didn't take Bill's money because she wanted the money. She did things to hurt him because she hated him and his commitment to God. I ran into a friend of Ellens, and she said that Kiven was the only man she ever loved."

"We'll just keep praying."

"By the way, Ellen sent all that alimony money back and gave Bill the money from selling their old house. Rachel is on staff at the church now, but she still volunteers to work at the church whenever they need her. With the money for a significant down payment on a new house, the return of the alimony money, and both working, they have not only been able to purchase a beautiful home but were able to furnish their whole house and buy everything they need."

"Praise God," said Mary, "God has done more than we could ask or even think of. Let's have them visit us here soon."

"They would love that," said Janet, "Every time they write, they thank all of us for praying for them and hope to meet the rest of God Gang's family."

CHAPTER TWENTY-FIVE

Ellen Seeks Mary's Help

MARY ANSWERED GOD'S Gang's office door one afternoon to find Ellen in tears. "Hello, are you Mary?"

"Yes? Come in." Mary invited Ellen into her office and offered her coffee or tea.

"No, thank you. I just wanted to talk with you."

Sitting in a chair opposite Mary's desk, Ellen seeks help from her.

"My name is Ellen," she said softly.

"How can I help you, Ellen?"

"You know who I am, don't you?"

"Yes, Bill's friend Janet told me about you in connection with Bill and Rachel. I know you have tried to make things right by canceling the abandonment charges, signing the divorce papers, and returning the money. Giving Bill the money from the sale of your house was very kind and generous, Ellen. God will surely bless you for blessing them."

"Bill and Rachel spoke so highly of you, Mary," Ellen said as she wiped tears from her eyes. "And your ability to help with my kind of problem. I've talked with Bill and Rachel, and they've forgiven me for what I did to them, and I'm so grateful. They said that I shouldn't feel bad anymore and that I had made things right with them, and they thanked me for everything. I feel so much better that they have forgiven me. But I can't seem to forgive myself. I feel guilty and depressed no matter what I do. Kevin still won't talk to me. I love him, but I don't want him to know it. I only want to ask him to forgive me. I know we won't get back together, and even though he may hate me, I still want to ask him to forgive me for what I've done. I want to tell him that I'm sorry for what I did. Even if he doesn't want to see me or be my friend, I'll understand. He might listen to a neutral third party. If I can tell him how sorry I am, and if he forgives me, then maybe I can find peace."

"I know of one person who can help you, Ellen, and that's Jesus. Have you received Him as your Lord and Savior?"

"Yes," said Ellen, "But I'm a new Christian, and I don't know much about being a Christian. I know enough to know how stupid I was when Bill used to try to get me to accept Jesus, and I refused to listen to him. There are times when I feel the joy of the Lord when I think about how much I resented God, and He lets me know that He loves me and has forgiven me. When I remember that I'm able to function.

I know that Kevin has also received Christ. Maybe he's just not ready to forgive me yet. But it hurts that I can't even see him long enough to tell him how sorry I am and to ask for his forgiveness."

"It sounds like you both could use counseling and in-depth study of God's Word. You must believe what God has promised in His Word and believe it's for you. When you asked God to forgive you, He did, Ellen."

Mary had a way of helping people understand God's liberating Words.

"It makes me feel good whenever I think about God forgiving me of my sins," said Mary, "He even forgets you sinned when you ask Him for forgiveness. I feel such peace. (God's Word says He does not remember the sins He has forgiven.) Ellen, don't think about the negative things. His Word also says, 'Think about whatever is lovely.' Fill your mind with good thoughts, Ellen. It doesn't matter how you feel. God is still there whether you feel like He is or not. Now, honey, you have to forgive yourself. Then, you will truly be at peace. Know that God has forgiven you, loves you, and wants the best for you. Then, turn Kevin over to God. We pray together on one accord and ask for what we need, and God will surely grant our request. I will ask Linda to join us in praying for your emotional healing."

Mary got Linda from the kitchen, and they joined hands and prayed.

"Thank you, God," Ellen said after they prayed.

"Thank you both for praying for me and spending time with me. Because or you guys I felt the presence and love of God a touch from God, and no matter what happens I know He's there for me."

"Stay in God's Word and keep praying, and then you'll know that God will always answer you," Mary promised.

CHAPTER TWENTY- SIX

Kevin And Ellen Get Together

KEVIN CAME TO Rev. Smith's church every Sunday. Mary invited Ellen to visit Rev. Smith's church. When Kevin saw Ellen, he spoke to her and kept going. She said hello as she fought back the tears. When Mary came over and asked if she was all right, Ellen began to cry and could not calm down.

"I believe God has forgiven me, but I still feel so sad that Kevin won't allow me to ask him to forgive me." Ellen is still in love with Kevin, and seeing him every Sunday at church is hard for her. She was thinking of changing churches, but Mary had asked her to join her every Sunday at church because it was a chance to counsel Ellen without her realizing it. Ellen didn't know how to tell Mary another church might help her forget Kevin, so there was no talk about it. Mary had told Ellen she would always be there when she needed someone to talk to.

After seeing Ellen at church every Sunday for three months, Kevin spoke to Ellen and asked her how she was doing.

"I'm fine," she answered. Even though Ellen Loves and wants to please God, she is sad and heartbroken over Kevin.

They talked for a few minutes. As Kevin looked at Ellen, he felt compassion for her. He could see that she was overwhelmed with sadness. The pain in her eyes made him very sad. He felt so sorry for her as he said, "Bye Ellen," and left.

After seeing each other and talking briefly every Sunday for seven months, Ellen stood outside the church on her cell phone calling for a cab when Kevin walked over and asked her if she needed a ride.

"I usually ride with Mary, but she had to leave early, and my car is in the shop."

"I'll take you home."

"Thank you, but I've called a cab."

A few minutes later, the cab arrived, and Kevin gave the cab driver the fair and waved him on.

"My car is parked over there," Kevin pointed to his car nearby.

"Okay," Ellen said as Kevin opened the car door for her to get in.

"Would you go to lunch first? I'm hungry."

Again, Ellen said okay without thinking. She was still so unhappy, going through the motions like someone just barely able to function. Kevin wanted to make her feel better while waiting for their food. Cheering her up was going to take a lot of work.

"Ellen, you have received Jesus as your Lord and Savior. You keep asking me to forgive you. I have forgiven you, and Jesus has forgiven you. Why can't you forgive yourself?"

"I don't know," Ellen covered her face with one hand but could not hide that she was crying. Kevin moved his chair closer to Ellen and put his arms around her.

"It's all right, Ellen." Kevin tries to comfort her.

She pushed him away. "I don't want your pity, Kevin. I'm fine."

"I'm not pitying you. Surely we can be friends, Ellen?" Ellen, still very sad, said, "I guess so." Kevin tried to make jokes and talked about funny things they used to laugh about. But nothing Kevin did or said cheered her up.

While they were eating, Ellen's phone was ringing, and Kevin asked,

"Aren't you going to answer your phone?"

Ellen looked at the phone as if she had just noticed it was ringing, "Hello. Oh, that's okay. I'll get a cab tomorrow. Thank you, Mary. Bye."

Ellen hung up her phone, stopped eating, and stared out the restaurant window. Kevin wanted to ease her pain and hold her and tell her he'd never stopped loving her, but he was afraid she wouldn't believe him.

"What are you getting a cab for tomorrow? Will your car still be in the shop?"

"Yes. The car dealer has to order a part. I have a doctor's appointment. Mary called and said she has to pick up some musical instruments tomorrow at the same time as my appointment."

"Will you let me take you to your doctor's appointment tomorrow?"

"You don't have to do that. I don't mind getting a cab."

"Ellen," Kevin was getting frustrated with her, "You said we could be friends. Why can't I take you to your appointment?"

"Well, all right if it's no trouble." Kevin was trying to say the right thing to make her feel comfortable. He was afraid if he pushed too hard, he wouldn't be able to see her at all. Depression was worrying him.

"I can tell that you are depressed and miserable. I know of an excellent doctor who specializes in depression. He's a Christian friend of mine. Will you let me take you to him?"

"No, Kevin. I told you I don't need your pity. I'll be just fine. Thanks anyway."

"Well, I'll pick you up for your doctor's appointment tomorrow. What time?" Kevin feared Ellen might change her mind about letting him take her to her doctor's appointment if he pressured her about anything.

"Nine o'clock," Ellen said as she stared into space.

Kevin looked at Ellen and thought, I want to gently hold her close and tell her how much I love her. She looks like a beautiful lost child that I desperately want to comfort.

After about two years, Kevin and Ellen became real friends. Ellen began to believe that Kevin just wanted to be her friend.

One Sunday after church, Kevin asked Ellen to come over to his house the following Sunday because he would cook dinner for his uncle and aunt and wanted her to help with dinner.

Kevin picked Ellen up early that next Sunday so they could start the dinner. Kevin's Uncle Dan and Aunt Esther came early because Aunt Esther's boss had invited them for dinner the same day.

"Will you please forgive us for being unable to stay," said Aunt Esther, "I remembered this morning that we had a dinner date with my boss on the same day. We want to make it up to you. Why don't you two come to dinner at our place next Sunday?"

"That sounds good to me. How about it, Ellen?" Kevin asked.

"I would love to come. Thanks for inviting us." Said Ellen.

After saying goodbye to his uncle and aunt, Kevin entered the kitchen, where Ellen made a salad. He approached her and asked if she wanted him to take her home since his uncle and aunt were gone. He said that to get her reaction.

"Why. Did I do something wrong?"

"No, Ellen. You didn't do anything wrong; I was kidding." Kevin approached, put his arms around Ellen, and held her close.

"Please don't try to push me away again, Ellen, because I won't let you this time. I've been miserable without you. I have never stopped loving you. Will you marry me again?"

Then he kissed her. She pulled back and said, "Are you sure, Kevin? I love you too, but . ."

He stopped her with a kiss, and she returned the kiss. They were married seven months later.

CHAPTER TWENTY- SIX

Tom Finds Love

THINGS HAD SETTLED into a more predictable routine at God's Gang. The girls, as did the guys, either went to school or to work. Linda, Janet, and Mary have become certified counselors and teach classes. Everybody helps at the church with Rev. Smith and still helps Clayton's guys with their church. God had blessed them wonderfully, which showed not only in their work but also in their loving relationships with one another. One evening, after everyone was around the dining room table, Mary and Linda stared at the five men, not saying a word. It only took them a few seconds, with the whispered exchanges of the girls, to get them to notice that Mary and Linda weren't happy about something.

Weeks before Tom came to the table that day, he had been depressed over girls who had rejected him when they found out what his life had been like before they met him.

"Hi," said Stacy as she watched Tom get in his car without putting the gas cap back on. "Are you going to leave without replacing your gas cap?

"Oh, 'said Tom, as he got the gas cap off the hood of his car and put it on.

"Thank you for saving my gas cap."

"You are welcome," said Stacy.

"May I buy you lunch since you saved my gas cap?" Tom asked.

"I don't have time for lunch," said Stacy. "I ate early and must be back at work."

"Well," said Tom, "Can I buy you lunch tomorrow?"

"Okay," said Stacy.

"I'll pick you up from work tomorrow." Tom offered.

"I don't work on Saturday. I'll be at home," said Stacy.

"Give me your address, and I'll pick you up at home if that's okay."

"That's fine. What time?" Ask Stacy.

"How about noon? Then we can go to the movies." Said Tom.

Stacy and Tom went to lunch and then to a movie. They dated for six months, and Tom had grown very fond of Stacy. When she found out he had been in a gang, she said, "Tom, you didn't tell me that you had been in a gang."

"I was afraid to tell you. I have become a Christian, and I'm not in a gang, and I'm serving God."

Tom could tell by the look on Stacy's face that it was over for them. The next day, Tom called Stacy and invited her to come with him to feed the birds in the park, something they used to enjoy doing, but Stacy was always busy, and they never saw each other again.

Tom met several other girls he liked, but they didn't see him again when they found out he had been in a gang.

Tom was depressed, and God's Gang prayed for him, and he became happy and was no longer depressed. Then he met Tina.

Everyone was ready to start eating when the guys noticed Mary and Linda were unhappy with them.

"What is it?" Tom asked.

"Didn't you guys forget something?" Linda asked.

But with wide-eyed looks of bewilderment, the guys were confused.

"Your hands? Did any of you remember to wash your hands? They're filthy. No one's eating with hands like those. You should really shower, but we're all hungry, so wash your hands so we can eat before everything gets cold."

The guys started laughing, left the table, and washed their hands. They came back a few minutes later and sat down at the table.

Kathy screamed, "What did you do?" Mary rolled her eyes in disbelief,

"Hilarious, guys."

The guys had come to the table with black hands as a joke.

"Let's bless the food so we can eat, then you can take care of your hands."

But when the guys returned to the table, they looked at Mary sheepishly and held up their hands. They were still black.

"Mary, we used hair color. We thought it would just wash off, but it won't come off. What can we do?" Tom asked.

Mary and Linda both covered their mouths as they started laughing. Then the girls started, and soon everyone was nearly hysterical.

"Let's eat, and then we'll see what we can find to remove the hair color," Mary finally said.

After dinner, nothing the guys did took the black hair color off their hands.

"I'm afraid it will just have to wear off, gentlemen. Didn't you notice the words' Permanent Hair Color' on the bottle?" Mary asked,

"Maybe think twice about pulling that kind of stunt again. The bleach has lightened the black color, but you can't use it too often, or it will damage your skin.

All the guys except Tom, who was too upset to eat dinner, seemed to resign themselves to having black hands for a few days until the dye slowly wore off.

"You don't understand," Tom screamed. "I have a date tonight." Then he stalked out of the room.

Mary followed him into the hallway. "Tom, I'm so sorry, but I'm sure she'll understand when you explain it."

"That's okay. I will call Tina and tell her I can't see her tonight. This girl is so special to me, Mary. She's a Christian who knows about my past and wants to go out with me. I don't want to embarrass her with my hand covered with black stain."

"Let me call her, Tom. Maybe I can smooth things over."

"Well, it can't get any worse. Call."

Mary dialed the number Tom gave her. When Tina answered, Mary explained who she was and what had happened.

"You know, the guys sometimes have a strange sense of humor. They also know little about permanent hair color or would never have done this." Tom watched from a chair in the office as Mary listened to his girlfriend.

"Sure, Tina." Mary covered the mouthpiece with her hand and looked at Tom. "She wants to talk with you." Mary handed him the phone and left the room.

"Tina, can you forgive me for having to break our date tonight?"

"Tom, you have a great sense of humor, but you guys went a bit far this time," Tina laughed.

"I know, I know."

"We don't have to go out to eat. Why don't you come over here? I'll make some sandwiches and lemonade, and we can watch a movie. You can take me to dinner again once your hands return to normal. Okay?"

"That sounds wonderful, Tina. I can be there in half an hour if that's okay."

"I'm looking forward to seeing you, Tom."

"Yahoo!" Tom was thrilled.

Mary, Linda, the girls, and the guys turned toward the hallway as Tom ran out of Mary's office.

"I'm going over to her house tonight," said Tom. "Thanks, Mary," Tom said as he lifted her off the floor in a bear hug. "You've helped me solve a problem again."

The next day, at dinner, Mary asked Tom, "How was your date with Tina?"

"She's a wonderful person," said Tom. "You'd like her. Last night, I got to meet her parents. They seemed to like me as much as I liked them. Tomorrow, Tina and I are going to church together. I have never been so happy in my life."

"Well, it sounds as if you're falling in love."

"I have fallen in love. God is truly blessing me, Mary. I never thought I'd ever meet a girl who would like me, especially when I told her about my past."

"That's because you are not the person you used to be. You are a child of God now. Jesus is the Lord of your life, and you are living for Him. And He lets you know that He's pleased with you and loves you."

Tom hugged Mary. "Thank you again, Mary. Without God leading you into my life, I wouldn't know Jesus, nor would I have a future to look forward to."

CHAPTER TWENTY-SEVEN

God Fulfilled His Promise To Mary

"Mary, I need your help. Yours too, Linda," Clyde called to the two women as he descended the stairs.

"I just talked with my mom, and she's visiting at the month's end. My room is in shambles. Can you help me make it presentable in time for her visit? She will want to see my room. I don't want her to know I don't keep my room nice and clean."

"Of course, we'll help you. Your mom can take the room just across the hall from your room. I know she will want to be near you to see your room, so we'll ensure she sees what a neat and clean guy you are."

"The guys and I will be off today, so you can call us if you need help," the guys assured Mary. "We'll be in the den."

After lunch, Mary and Linda went to Clyde's room. Mary could barely find a path to the bed. Clothes littered the floor, and every piece of furniture, including the bed, remained unmade and covered with clutter. Clyde had not cleaned his room in months, or maybe he had never cleaned his room.

"I can see why he asked us to straighten out this mess. We should call all the guys for help. If we did, he might keep his room more presentable in the future," Mary said as she surveyed the chaos.

Linda started picking up clothes from the floor and placing them in a laundry basket. Mary noted that the clothes on the chairs and dresser seemed clean. She started putting some in drawers and hanging some in his closet.

She picked up a briefcase from Clyde's closet to move it out of the way when she tried to step over the clutter and fell with the briefcase . It opened with a Bible and notebook falling out.

Mary looked at the bottom of the briefcase and noticed her name and aunt's address.

When Clyde and his gang members were looking for their money, they could have found it if they had noticed Mary's name and her aunt's address on the bottom of the briefcase.

God did not allow the gangs to notice the address of Mary's aunt on the bottom of the briefcase. He protected her from them.

When Mary opened the Bible, she recognized her name on the inside cover with a small dedication plaque bordered in gold trim.

TO MARY WITH LOVE FROM YOUR CHURCH FAMILY

Oh! This is strange. Mary thought. God took my Bible from my briefcase and filled it with lots of money. Thank you, Dear God, for the money that made my dream a reality. Mary thanked God silently. Thank You for returning my Bible. You said I would get it back, and I believed You, Lord. Whenever I read my other Bible, I wondered when You would return the big Bible the church gave me. I love You, Lord.

Mary showed the Bible and briefcase to Linda.

"Look what I found in Clyde's closet."

"What is it?" Questioned Linda.

"It's my briefcase that I left at my aunt's house," Mary answered. "The Bible wasn't in my briefcase when I left it there.

I know God must have used Clyde somehow, but where did he find my Bible?"

"How did it get in Clyde's closet? "Asked Linda.

"I don't know," said Mary. "I need to talk with Clyde. I'm glad the guys are off today." Mary and Linda went downstairs to the din, where the guys were watching a game on television.

"Clyde," Mary called out loud, "when did you get my briefcase from my aunt's house, and where did you find my Bible?"

Mary and Clyde need clarification about the whole thing.

Clyde looked confused. "Mary, what are you talking about? I've never been to your aunt's house."

Randall put two and two together and realized there had to be another briefcase on the train, and he began to laugh.

"What's so funny?" Clyde asked.

"Well," said Randall, "Do you remember when I told you that I left the briefcase for a minute to go to the restroom on the train? My briefcases must have fallen off the shelf and landed close to where Mary was sitting. Mary must have been the woman on the train that day, and she got our briefcase instead of hers. I only saw one briefcase, and I thought it was mine. What baffled us was that we didn't know that there was another briefcase just like ours. We thought it was strange that someone could take our money out of our briefcase and replace it with a Bible and notebook under my nose."

Mary was confused. "You mean this is not my briefcase? It has to be my briefcase. My name and my aunt's address are at the bottom, and my name is in the Bible in this briefcase."

"That is your briefcase," Randall explained. "The one at your aunt's is not yours. The one I was bringing to New York had our drug money, or so we thought. When we didn't have the money, John had instructions about the money that we needed. We went to many states to find out who might have taken our money.

"The note in the briefcase," Mary explained, "said it was from God and not to tell anybody about it. I thought all that money was from God." The guys begin to laugh.

Clyde, still laughing, said, "When Randall said that Mary was the woman on the train, I thought someone had taken the money and given Mary our briefcase. I would never have thought she had the money."

Then Mary said, "Why didn't you return my briefcase? My aunt's name and address were on the bottom of the briefcase." The guys all laughed so hard that they had problems talking.

"At that time," Clyde said, "We wouldn't have returned your briefcase, but we would have come to your aunt's house looking for our briefcase if we had noticed the address on the bottom."

Randall looked at Clyde, who was beginning to understand everything., said, "Can you believe Mary had our briefcase? Only God could make such a thing happen."

"Well, you remember we were a different gang before we met you," said Randall.

"Yes," Mary said, "That's why we call you guys the powerful God's Gang."

"What you don't know is that when I met you on the plane, I was going to Mississippi to find out if someone was suspiciously spending a large amount of money. The longer I spent with you, however," said Randall, "the more the money became unimportant, and I fell hopelessly in love with you."

"Start from when I went to the kitchen, guys," said Linda as she returned from the kitchen. "This is like an interesting movie."

"Okay," Clyde said. "Our gang was involved with buying and selling drugs. We had just dealt with the Cubans about delivering money to one of our guys. At first, John was to get the cash from St. Louis, have it laundered, and then return to New York. But I sent Randall instead because he knows all about the drug world. We also decided to take a chance and spend the money without having it laundered.

Randall came to New York with what we thought was our drug money from the Cubans. We know now that Randall, Mary, and her children were on the same train. Although neither realized nor knew they sat across from one another."

"I knew there was a woman and two children across from me," said Randall. "But you were all sleeping, and your heads turned away, and because you were all covered with blankets, I couldn't tell if your children were boys or girls. I couldn't describe anything about you or your children to Clyde; he was so mad."

Randall continued, "Clyde, at that time, was desperate to know who was across from me on the train. God was with you, Mary, protecting you from us. The train's computer crashed, and they lost all information for the week you and your children were on the train, and we had no way of finding you.

I slept briefly on the train and then went to the restroom. The train lurched while I was in the bathroom, sending a few things flying in the train. When I returned to my seat, I noticed things on the shelf above my seat were on the floor. I was upset when I saw my briefcase on the floor. That was stupid of me not to take the briefcase with me."

"Yes, I remember," Mary responded. "I had put my briefcase on the floor to get things for the girls and fell asleep before I got the briefcase off the floor of the train. I woke up to where things had fallen to the floor on the train. I saw that my briefcase had moved to the middle of the aisle. I picked it up and put it between the seats next to me. I had no idea that it wasn't mine."

Randall explained, "I had placed my briefcase overhead, and when I returned to my seat, I found it in the aisle about two rows back and assumed it was mine. Mary, you had grabbed mine, and because you had put it where I couldn't see it, I didn't realize there were two identical briefcases. We didn't discover that the money wasn't in the briefcase until I was back at the mansion in New York, and we opened the briefcase. It was a horrible shock when we found a Bible and notebook instead of our money in the briefcase."

"Well," said Mary, "I can certainly understand your surprise because I had a similar shock when I opened my briefcase. It wasn't a similar shock, but it was a shock. I couldn't believe it when I saw God's note, which I thought was God's note. I didn't know it was $7,000,000,000 until I saw the deposit slip and nearly fainted. God's note said, Oh dear! There I go again. I felt so strongly that the note was from God. I still believe God had a hand in writing that note. The note said not to tell anybody about this. That's why I still haven't said anything to you, honey, even though we were married."

Mary explained God's promise. "I heard God tell me that I would get my Bible back. Praise God! He always does whatever He says He's going to do."

God loves Mary and her love for Him and other people. He has blessed Mary by supplying her with whatever she needs to fulfill her dream. Through Mary, many people have become saved and successful, productive citizens.

"Remember when we thought the laundering instructions were no longer important?" said Randall. "But we thought John may have known something that might help us find the money. Now, they think of John differently. John is now with Jesus; I know he is happy to be with Him. Even though he got in with a bad crowd, he was gentle and kind even before being saved."

Clyde explained to Mary what he did with the briefcase she found in his closet.

"Speaking of the briefcase you found in my closet, I guess I'd just stuffed the Bible and notebook back in the briefcase and put it in my closet."

Clyde shook his head in disbelief, "Randall met you, and thus began the story of God's Gang. Through you, Mary, we have accepted Jesus as our Lord and Savior. Through His grace, we've all become happy as God-loving people."

Clyde grinned. "God protected you from us, particularly when He didn't allow us to notice the address on the bottom of your briefcase. He wanted you to share Jesus and His love with us."

"That's right, Mary," said Randall. "Because of that switch on the train, our lives have improved, and we are helping others not only gain salvation but also peace and joy."

Linda said, "I don't think I have ever heard a more interesting story."

"Mary, you have no idea how hard we looked for that money. I'm so glad you got it, even if it was a mistake and we didn't get the money," said Clyde.

"God doesn't make mistakes," said Mike. "He also works unpredictably and beautifully."

Randall was amazed at how things turned out. "I'm so fascinated with how God works in people's lives when they receive Him and obey His Word. Now we're all working hard to help drug addicts, runaway teenagers, and others in need."

Clyde picked up Mary's briefcase and looked at the other guys.

"I love God. Just look at how He has intervened in our lives. We are saved, happy, and helping others have the same blessings."

Clyde interrupted their storytelling. "I have to pick my mom up from the airport. " As Clyde was leaving, Linda turned to Mary and said, "It's going to be nice to see Mrs. Anderson; Clyde's Mother was good at explaining the Scripture. I love how she related the Bible to today's living. Let's ask her to talk to the young about the sin of the gay lifestyle. Schools and churches are trying to influence young people to accept that style as not a sin. They tell our kids that the world is changing and we must adjust.

God's gang has helped rehabilitate many girls who have returned to society and are now responsible, happy Christians. Some have good jobs and volunteer to work at God's Gang.

"I'm so proud of Clayton's x-gangs," said Mary. "They are making a big difference in their neighborhood, and their families are the happiest and most fun-loving people you'll ever meet."

We helped five other girls taken from their homes a few months ago because of abuse. They have been restored to health and are functioning normally now. They will be going to a university of their choice in the fall. Their parents received counseling and are now a happy and saved couple. They are all encouraged to keep in touch with God's Gang, and everyone looks forward to the yearly reunion.

Clyde comes in with his mother. They all greet her and make her feel welcome. Mary said that she had invited the kids' Bible study members to be here to listen to Randy's mother teach them about not letting the schools, churches, friends, or anyone draw them from God and His Word.

After dinner, they all gather around to listen to Mrs. Anderson.

After listening to Mrs. Anderson for ninety minutes and asking her questions, Mary came into the den where they were.

"Mrs. Anderson will be her for several weeks. You will get to visit with her another time, but Mrs. Anderson needs to rest from her trip, and I know she would like to visit with her son. Brinda asked Mrs. Anderson if she would come to their Bible study and explain the Bible's view on homosexuality.

"I have a friend who says that homosexuality is not in the Bible, and he does not think it's a sin," Brinda told Mrs. Anderson.

I would love to speak to your Bible study. How about tomorrow after lunch?" Said Mrs. Anderson.

The girl left and awaited Mrs. Anderson's teachings the next day.

That evening, Clyde took his mom on a tour of New York.

"I'm so proud of you, Mom," Clyde said, "As much as I loved you, I'll never understand why I never listened to you."

"That's okay, Honey; I knew someday you would listen to God." Clyde hugged his mom and then took her to dinner at a restaurant.

The next day, Clyde took his mom to church to meet with the girl's Bible study group and told her to call him when she was ready to leave.

Brinda informed the Pastor and other members of the church about Clyde's mother speaking at the Bible study on Homosexuality, and the Pastor and so many members came that they had to move to the auditorium.

When Mrs. Anderson stood up to speak, she greeted everyone and told them she was happy to be invited to talk to the young people.

"You are our future, and you must have a good foundation in moral living and the fundamental knowledge of right and wrong that can only come from God's word.

Some churches are teaching things that are contrary to Scripture. Some of you have friends who are in a church that teaches that homosexuality is not wrong and that word is not in the Bible. Do you need a word to be missing in the Bible, and it means that God didn't address Homosexuality? The Trinity is not in the Bible either, but it means three. These are reasons you have to think for ourself and rely on Scripture. for the truth. The Bible makes it clear when it says that man and man or woman and woman having sex with the same gender is a sin. Homosexuality means a man or woman having sex with the same gender.

Churches and other groups are succeeding in making people believe things contrary to the Bible. Some of what they are teaching is so strange. For example, they say science can change a man into a woman. Also, if a man feels like a woman, we must treat him like he is a woman.

I want to make sure that gays and lesbians know that God loves them and He wants them in his kingdom.

The students enjoyed Mrs. Anderon's talk and asked when she would return to revisit their Bible study.

"I would love to come back and visit your Bible study. Thank you for inviting me, and God Bless all of you."

Mary went to the door a month later, "Hello. My name is Sam, and I came to see Clyde."

Tom walked in from the den on his way out the front door.

"Tom, before you leave, will you tell Clyde that he had a visitor," Mary asked.

"Okay," Tom yelled, "Clyde, you have a visitor."

"Tom, I could have done that," said Mary.

Mary invites Sam into the living room. "Can I get you something to drink?"

"No, thank you. I was in the neighborhood and decided to visit Clyde. I saw him in the news and wanted to ask about some of the work he has been doing."

Clyde was surprised to see Sam standing there, "Hi. Were you here a while back to tell us about John?"

"Yes," said Sam. "You were getting ready to clean your gun."

"Well, Yeah, I don't have that gun anymore. I remember you invited me to come to church with you. I was not interested in God or church at that time. But I not only go to church, but I'm a born-again Christian."

Sam was happy to know that Clyde had become a Christian. His visit was to talk about the work he was doing. Sam and his wife want their children to participate in some of their children's programs.

Clyde introduced Sam to everyone. Sam and his wife became friends with God's Gang, and eventually, they became a permanent fixture of God's Gang, and they helped with many of their projects. With the growth of God's Gang, everyone was so happy to have other committed Christians who brought joy and much-needed help. God's gang has bought 100 acres of land next to their mansion, and they are building a new building that will be big enough for 300 additional girls.

This has become a huge, happy family, and they have fun with each other and are all grateful to God for His many blessings.

Milton Keynes UK
Ingram Content Group UK Ltd.
UKHW021626050624
443649UK00016BA/1006